SUCH A *Pretty Face*

What Reviewers Say About Bold Strokes Authors

Kim Baldwin

"*Force of Nature* is filled with nonstop, fast paced action. Tornadoes, raging fire blazes, heroic and daring rescues…Baldwin does a fine job of describing the fast-paced scenes and inspiring the reader to keep on turning the pages." – L-word.com Literature

Rose Beecham

"…her characters seem fully capable of walking away from the particulars of whodunit and engaging the reader in other aspects of their lives." – *Lambda Book Report*

Georgia Beers

"Beers weaves a tale of yearning, love, lust, and conflict resolution. She has constructed a believable plot, with strong characters in a charming setting." – *JustAboutWrite*

Ronica Black

"*Wild Abandon* tells how these two women come to realize that 'life was too precious to be ruled by…fears, by…demons.' While these two women struggle with their issues, there is some very, very hot sex. If you enjoy complex characters and passionate sex scenes, you'll love *Wild Abandon*." – *MegaScene*

Gun Brooke

"*Course of Action* is a romance…populated with a host of captivating and amiable characters. The glimpses into the lifestyles of the rich and beautiful people are rather like guilty pleasures…a most satisfying and entertaining reading experience." – *Midwest Book Review*

Cate Culpepper

"…an exceptional storyteller who has taken on a very difficult subject …and turned it into a spellbinding novel. As an author, she understands well that fiction can teach us our own history." – *JustAboutWrite*

Jane Fletcher

"*The Exile and the Sorcerer* is a mesmerizing read, a tour-de-force packed with adventure, ordeals, complex twists and turns, and the internal introspection of appealing characters." – *Midwest Book Review*

JD Glass

"*Punk Like Me*…is different. It is engaging. It is life-affirming. Frankly, it is genius. This is a rare book in that it has a soul; one that is laid bare for all to see." – *JustAboutWrite*

Grace Lennox

"*Chance* is refreshing…Every nuance is powerful and succinct. *Chance* is not a novel about the music industry; it is about a woman discovering herself as she muddles through all the trappings of fame." – *Midwest Book Review*

Lee Lynch

"Lynch, with a dozen novels to her credit dating back to the early days of Naiad Press, has earned her stripes as a writerly elder. She was contributing stories to the lesbian magazine *The Ladder* four decades ago. But this latest is sublimely in tune with the times." – *Q-Syndicate*

JLee Meyer

"*Forever Found*…neatly combines hot sex scenes, humor, engaging characters, and an exciting story." – *MegaScene*

Radclyffe

"…well-plotted…lovely romance…I couldn't turn the pages fast enough!" – Ann Bannon, author of *The Beebo Brinker Chronicles*

Susan Smith

"This disparate duo's lush rush of a romance - which incorporates reincarnation, a grounded transman and his peppy daughter, and the dark moods of a troubled witch - pays wonderful homage to Leslie Feinberg's classic gender-bending novel, *Stone Butch Blues*." – *Q-Syndicate*

Ali Vali

"Rich in character portrayal, *The Devil Inside* by Ali Vali is an unusual, unpredictable, and thought-provoking love story that will have the reader questioning the definition of right and wrong long after she finishes the book." – *JustAboutWrite*

Such a *Pretty Face*

by

Gabrielle Goldsby

BOLD STROKES BOOKS

2007

SUCH A PRETTY FACE

ISBN: 10-digit 1-933110-84-8
13-digit 978-1-933110-84-4

This Trade Paperback Original Is Published By
Bold Strokes Books, Inc.,
New York, USA

First Edition: July, 2007.

Credits
Editors: Jennifer Knight and Stacia Seaman
Production Design: Stacia Seaman
Cover Design By Sheri (GRAPHICARTIST2020@HOTMAIL.COM)

Acknowledgments

My stories start with the nucleus of an idea, often years before I approach a publisher. Those ideas are first shopped by my good friend and confidante Mecheal. I can't thank her enough for all the time she's given me over the years.

I have to thank Patty S. for her help with the early versions of this story and Linda for her willingness to put up with my last-minute beta requests.

Special thanks to Jennifer Knight and Stacia Seaman, my two editors. I have spent years requesting, begging, and plotting for an opportunity to work with the both of them. It was well worth the wait. Their willingness to share their wealth of information about the craft will always be appreciated.

This paragraph has been edited, changed, and deleted several times in an attempt to find the right words to thank my publisher. I drag myself out of bed every morning, pour a cup of coffee, and head down to my office. Inevitably, as I sit down before my computer, I am struck by fear. Only for a second, though, because then I remember that I am not alone anymore, and I won't be allowed to fail. I start to work. I start to do the very thing that I love doing. How do you even begin to thank someone for that?

Dedication

For Melissa, who *always* saw more than a pretty face

CHAPTER ONE

The moment she went down on me, I should have known that she was telling me good-bye. Spontaneity is not Brenda's strong suit, but for the last few weeks she's been acting like she can't keep her hands off me.

"Why am I complaining? I'm complaining because I was wearing baby blue sweats, a Mickey Mouse T-shirt, and Marvin the Martian slippers. I'm complaining because I was bent over a box with my big ass in the air when she slammed into the house. I'm complaining because she dropped her bag on the floor, and without so much as a, 'hey, hon, I'm home,' rolled me over and set about making it impossible for me to think, let alone worry about where all of her energy came from. Then, to top it all off, two minutes into the sex, the phone rang and she left me on the floor to answer it.

"She comes back twenty minutes later and tells me she's just accepted an assignment in the Fiji Islands to photograph fourteen swimsuit models for a new sports magazine. Oh, and she knew about the possibility of this assignment for at least a week before she decided to accept it."

I stopped speaking because my sales assistant, Matthew "Goody" Good, who was sitting on the edge of my desk, was now staring at me like I was a piece of three-layer, double chocolate cake.

"Mia, wait. Go back to the part where she was going down on you."

"Goody, is that all you heard me say?"

"I was listening. You were just getting into some good sex when fourteen skinny bitches interrupted your fun."

I nodded; he had been listening.

"So when's she leaving?" His voice held that tone that I hated; you know, the one that makes you want to cry.

"I take her—" I was interrupted by a commotion so loud that it made my ears itch and the walls of my office quake. From past experience, I knew that anything I said would be impossible for Goody to hear, so I stood up and walked to the window.

The whole office had been warned that when construction began, it would be loud. I would have liked to complain; "loud" didn't quite cover the ear-splitting, nerve-shattering, teeth-gnashing cacophony of sound coming from the room right next door. I would have liked to, but I couldn't because the construction was for my new, larger office space, so I kept my mouth shut.

Instead of just one window, I would have a wall of them to gaze out of once my new space was complete. I watched the ant-sized people milling below before my eye was drawn to Goody's reflection. He was studying his fingernails, his foot tapping in unison with the hammering that had begun after the drill quieted. Goody and I had been mistaken for brother and sister on more than one occasion. Our similar heritage meant we both had dark eyes and dark skin, but that's where the resemblance ended, in my opinion.

Goody was an exceptionally handsome guy. Everything about his slim but athletic frame, thick dark hair, olive skin, and sharp brown eyes screamed sexy. At least, that's what he wrote in his Yahoo Personals ad.

"I take her to the airport Sunday," I said during a lull in the noise.

"Sunday? As in, the day after tomorrow?"

That was my reaction too. "Yeah, *this* Sunday."

"And she's just now telling you? How long is she gonna be gone?" Goody was still looking at his nails, but his forehead was creased by a scowl. I would give him five seconds before he found a flaw and started in with the emery board he always kept in his front pocket.

I turned around and said, "Five months," just as he stood up and stuck his hand in his pocket. If he found the board, he didn't pull it out. Instead he stared at me, his perfectly chapsticked lips parted.

"What?"

"Five months. She's going to be in the fucking Fiji Islands, with a bushel of swimsuit models, for five goddamn months." I'm pretty sure I wailed the last few words.

"Damn. That's nearly half a year." Goody sat back down in his chair, the emery board temporarily forgotten. "And you're okay with that?"

"Hell no, I'm not okay with it. We just moved into that house. In another two months we might have all the boxes unpacked." I slumped back into my own chair. "We hardly see each other *now*, but—"

"At least you know where she sleeps at night, right?"

"Right."

Goody, as usual, had gotten right to the point. I was already worried about the stability of our relationship. The truth of the matter was, I had been for well over a year. So the thought of being apart from her for so long made me want to find a dark corner and curl up with something buttery, sugary, and warm.

"I got to be honest with you, *chica*…"

"You think there's more to it?" I was careful not to let the fear creep into my voice, but I could tell by the look in Goody's eyes that my face gave me away.

"Yeah, I do. And so do you. That's why you called me in here, isn't it? You want me to confirm that you're not overreacting?"

"No, I called you in here to tell me I *am* overreacting."

"Have you tried talking to her? Maybe ask her not to go?"

I shook my head. I had tried many times over the last few days to talk to her, but how could I when I was afraid of where the conversation might lead?

"Why not? Begging her not to leave is the first thing I would have done." Goody was smiling, but the pain and embarrassment in that smile had nothing to do with my situation.

"Does begging work?" The question was, I hoped, a deterrent—an opportunity for Goody to segue into his own problems instead of mine. The sad thing is, even if I were able to force myself to grovel I knew it wouldn't do any good. Brenda had made up her mind to leave even before she told me she was.

"Didn't work with Emil," Goody said, with forced nonchalance. "He left me two days after he proposed. He had the most gorgeous blond hair."

I frowned, struggling to differentiate Emil from the other half dozen boyfriends Goody had fallen in lust with over the last two years.

"He was a librarian? Remember?"

"Oh yeah, Emil." I barely kept myself from adding, "How could

I forget *him*?" Emil, the long-haired librarian, would always stand out in my mind for all the wrong reasons. I knew within two seconds of meeting the guy that he was a player, a bisexual one. The first time I had caught him staring at my chest I figured it was envy. When he invited me to dinner *sans* Goody I could no longer turn a blind eye. Goody claimed he was just trying to earn my approval, but the truth was in the ogling. I had learned to recognize that creepy feeling of being used as some guy's sexual fantasy at far too young an age. "You swore off men after him, didn't you?"

"Yeah, but then I met Paul about nine days later. He was a waste of time, great in bed though." He paused. "Why are we talking about me? What are you going to do?"

"It's her career. I can't ask her to give up an opportunity like that." Based on the exasperated look on Goody's face, he didn't agree. "So let's say I tell her I don't want her to go and she goes anyway?"

Realization followed by sympathy crossed Goody's face. "You're scared it's already too late, aren't you?" I shrugged my answer, but he went on as if I had agreed. "Then you have to find a way to start over."

"Goody, Brenda isn't just some chick I met online or picked up in a bar. She's my wife. I don't give a shit—" I cut myself off because I could see that he was taking what I said personally. I reached for his hand. "I'm sorry. I didn't mean anything by that."

"I know," he said, but when he didn't take my hand, I dropped it back in my lap.

See, that was Goody's problem. He wore his heart on his sleeve, and every pretty boy in Portland had used that sleeve to wipe their asses—twice. *He* was a sucker for a pretty face; I wasn't. I was in a committed relationship, the "until death do us part" kind of relationship, and five months in the Fiji Islands with swimsuit models just didn't fit into that picture.

The wall behind my bookshelf shuddered as someone methodically hammered away with apparent disregard for anyone working within a two-mile radius.

"Damn it, I'm done dealing with this bullshit." I pushed my chair back and stood up. As I walked around my desk I knocked my hip on a sharp corner and hissed in pain.

Goody winced in sympathy. "Ouch, I hate when that happens."

I rubbed at the sore spot and kept walking. For once I was grateful for the extra padding on my hips, but the pain wasn't going away easily and it stoked my annoyance into full-blown pissed-off mode. It took me two angry seconds to stalk next door and yell, "Hey, I'm trying to get some work done over there!"

The hammering had stopped almost as soon as I walked in, so the words came out far louder than I'd intended. A muscular blond woman wearing goggles, blue jeans, and a white T-shirt turned to face me. "Sorry?" She straightened to her full height and pulled a piece of yellow foam from her ear.

I allowed myself a moment to take her in. Boots, long legs, slender hips, a small waist. She had obviously found that one elusive pair of jeans that fit its owner like a second skin. She wore no belt, and her white T-shirt had managed to avoid being spattered with plaster. The floor surrounding her hadn't fared as well. I forced myself to meet her eyes. They were just blue, nothing special, so why was I having such a hard time looking away? "Uh, no…no, I'm sorry. I was just…"

"Was I being too loud?" Her "I" sounded like "ah."

"No, you're fine." I heard Goody come up behind me. "I mean, if you don't mind holding off on the power tools for a few minutes, we'll be heading out to lunch soon."

She gave me a small, closed-lipped smile, but said nothing. It was the kind of gesture I had seen the folks in the cage give *other* brokers. I, on the other hand, got everything from affectionate teasing to Christmas ornaments and invites to parties and housewarmings. It mattered to me that this woman hadn't gotten the memo that I was one of the "cool ones."

She had started to look uncomfortable before I realized that I had been staring much longer than appropriate. Heat crept up around my ears as I fumbled for something useful to say. "I should probably… uh…"

"Mia, we should get back to that account we were discussing," Goody said quietly from behind me.

I turned and gave him a grateful smile. "I'll be right there." With a quick parting glance at her, I said, "I'm sorry for interrupting you."

"I'll try to be quieter," she said, the closed-lip smile looking a little less forced.

I walked away thinking I should have said something smart and sassy, maybe left an opening for further conversation. I was back in my office staring owl-eyed at Goody when I realized that I should be grateful

I'd made it back without tripping over my own feet. "I had nightmares all last night about supermodels, and now there's one building my new office. Where the hell did she come from, anyway?"

"I don't know, but did you hear that accent? Did you see those arms?" Goody was back to studying his nails.

"Yeah, I heard it. I was thinking Texas."

"She's gorgeous," Goody said. "I wonder how she got that scar."

"What scar?"

"You didn't see the scar on her cheek? Hell, the way you were staring, I thought you knew her. Maybe had a tryst or something in the past."

"I've never seen her before in my life. And I wasn't staring that hard." Goody raised his eyebrow and I winced. "I hope she didn't think I was being rude."

"Nah, I doubt she noticed."

I tugged the lapels of my suit jacket together and wondered if they had been gaping apart when I talked to her. "What were we talking about before?"

"Brenda moving to Fiji."

"She isn't moving. She's working there for a while."

Goody shrugged. "Might as well be moving."

I hated that he was right. I hated the fact that my clients trusted me with a little over two hundred million dollars in assets, yet I was afraid to tell my partner that I didn't want her to leave me for five months. I hated that she didn't appear concerned about being away from me. And worst of all, I hated feeling like my life was teetering on the point of a pin and one false move could easily send it toppling into the unknown.

I sighed and stood up. "You up for an early lunch? I could use a panini and fries with an ice-cream chaser."

❖

Sunday morning came faster than Brenda did after our good-bye sex. You would think good-bye sex would be the best ever, right? The thing is, the good-bye sex that morning was really no different than a lot of the sex Brenda and I had been having over the last few weeks, fast and vaguely unsatisfying.

I was still lying in bed trying to figure out what was bothering me besides the obvious, when Brenda got up, murmured something about a shower, and walked into the bathroom. I watched each languid step with detached admiration. Although she had purchased all of the exercise equipment currently gathering dust in our basement, she was genetically blessed with a slender yet feminine physique. Because I worried about hurting her, I always made sure that she ended up on top when we had sex.

My mind slipped to the construction worker and the lean muscular arms flexing beneath her T-shirt. I wouldn't have to worry about hurting her at all. I felt an immediate tightening between my legs.

Nice, Mia. I pulled the blankets up to my chin. Brenda was leaving and I was lying here thinking about a stranger. I should have been worrying about the fact that my partner was going to be on a tropical island working closely with supermodels for five months. *Maybe I'll put all that exercise equipment in the basement to good use. Who knows, she could come back to a slim and trim Mia.* I turned over, wondering if I should go pick up bagels or just cook something for breakfast.

The pipes squealed, groaned, and finally released a gush of water. The house stopped protesting and the sound of running water lulled me into a half-sleep until a soft whine and a thumping noise wrenched me back to wakefulness.

I leaned over and lifted the bed skirt. "Pepito, what are you doing down there?"

I knew exactly what he was doing. Listening to the bed squeak while plotting revenge on my best high heels. Brenda had been given the Chihuahua mix six months ago, and since then, the dog and I had come to a kind of mutual understanding.

We hated each other.

I glanced at the clock. Ten past ten, which meant that we had just enough time to have breakfast and drive to the airport. The water stopped and the house moaned again. I was used to Brenda's short showers, but this one had to be a record. *She's in a rush to get to her models.* I dragged myself out of bed, quickly reached for my robe, and covered myself with it just as Brenda entered the room, naked except for the towel draped over her short, graying hair.

"God, the water pressure sucks," she said, for the umpteenth time since we had moved into the house.

"I'll try to get someone in to see about fixing it while you're gone." Of course I wouldn't. Things like water pressure just didn't concern me. My father was fond of saying that Brenda was the perfect woman for me. She had practical sense. The implication being that I had none.

Brenda shrugged and disappeared into the closet. She had been acting odd since Friday night. One moment she couldn't keep her hands off me, the next she couldn't string two words together. I went into the bathroom and was about to shut the door behind me when I heard her muffled voice from inside the closet.

"I'm going to put some eggs on. You want something?"

"Yeah, I'll just have a croissant and some coffee."

"That's not healthy," was her standard automated response, but the racks of clothing made her sound farther away than she actually was.

"Okay, I'll have a croissant, some coffee, and two cigarettes." The old joke dropped like a stone and I shut the door to the bathroom without hearing any response. I had smoked until about the second week of our relationship, when Brenda let me know, in no uncertain terms, that she had no interest in being with a smoker. So I quit. Brenda liked to say she was responsible for saving me from lung cancer.

I took longer than I should have with my shower, but by the time I got out I had come to a decision. As much as our relationship felt off kilter, I didn't want Brenda to know how upset I was. If being apart for five months didn't bother her, I would try not to let it bother me. She was gone when I came out of the bathroom, so I walked downstairs in my robe. I found her sitting at the kitchen table, slumped forward, staring into her mug.

"I haven't told my parents that you're leaving." I walked over to the cabinet and pulled down a mug for myself. "I figure I'll just tell them when I go over there this afternoon. That way they don't have time to come up with a bunch of questions." I poured my coffee. Brenda was still looking down into her cup.

"Mia, I need to tell you something."

Pepito's claws clicked across the floor as he took his position beneath the table where Brenda, much to my annoyance, would feed him scraps.

"What is it?" I bit into my croissant and sat down across from her.

"I don't think I'm in love with you anymore."

Her words hung in the air between us before reaching in, grabbing my throat, and closing off my esophagus. I swallowed hard. The bread hung for a few moments longer than was comfortable before making its way down my throat. I had been pushing her since Friday, poking for answers because I had already had a premonition that there would be no "us" in five months.

I searched Brenda's face. She met my eyes with the candor she always had. I wanted to believe I had misheard. Except that her ring, the one I had bought her when we got married at the Multnomah County Courthouse, was sitting on the table beside her coffee. She twirled it on the table as if it were a penny.

"What are you saying?" My words came out cool, unemotional. I would have been proud of how composed I sounded if I hadn't been in shock.

"I don't know what I'm trying to say. It's…this has been on my mind for a while." I heard a little whine followed by a sneeze from beneath the table. Brenda stopped spinning the ring long enough to pinch off a piece of her croissant. Her hand disappeared beneath the table. I pictured Pepito taking the bread from her fingers and spearing her with one of his deformed front canines.

"So is that why you took this assignment? Because you don't…" I was unable to finish the sentence. *Is it possible to just stop loving someone?*

"I've been thinking about this for a while. Last weekend I realized that it was time to do something about it."

"Last weekend?" I repeated and she looked away from me. I heard the ring spin two more times before it fell flat on the table. Getting married had been Brenda's idea. She'd said we should take advantage of the loophole that allowed gays to marry in the Multnomah County Courthouse.

I still remember how the light had glinted off the ring when I first put it on her finger. I remember how she smiled at me, her eyes large and bewildered. How the kiss that pronounced us partners for life had been so chaste because we were both shocked by what we had done. The letter revoking our marital status was buried in a dresser drawer, but I still considered myself married. I thought we both did. Thirteen months ago that ring had stood for so much, but now it looked like how I felt. As if someone had leached all of the life out of it.

"Mia, are you listening to me?"

"No. Sorry."

"I was saying that the trip will do us both good. Give us both some space."

"I don't need any space."

"I think you do. We've been together constantly for four years."

"We live together. You're my partner. We're *supposed* to be together constantly." Tears prickled at the back of my eyes and I stood up, grabbed her plate along with mine, and set them on the counter. I flipped on the water and squeezed my eyes shut. *Please, dear Lord, tell me this isn't happening.*

"Mia, that can wait." Brenda had to raise her voice over the rush of water from the faucet. I wiped my eyes, shut off the water, and returned to the kitchen table. Small claws scuttled on tile as Pepito tried to avoid my feet. Normally, he would have growled at being disturbed. This time he didn't. Even the house was hushed. There were none of the usual groans and moans that accompanied turning off the water.

"Say something," she said. Frustration was evident in her voice.

"What do you want me to say? I don't think you should go anywhere before we fix this. If there's a problem we should be able to work it out. It's not like you have someone else, right?" Even as the words left my lips, I could see the answer in her eyes. She looked apologetic. Guilty. My heart sank.

"Let's not start accusing each other, Mia. I'm talking about our relationship. Things haven't been good."

"Since when? Since when haven't they been good? We've had sex more in the last few weeks than we've had—" I stopped because I had given myself the answer. It had been right there all along and I hadn't noticed it. Although Brenda's hours had been crazy over the last few weeks, we had found time to have sex at least three times in the past two weeks. A record for us. How had I missed it? The new clothes, the attention to grooming, the impromptu sex. Brenda had been cheating on me and I hadn't had a clue.

"Who is it?" I demanded.

Brenda stood up and went to the counter to refill her coffee cup. She took so long to answer that I contemplated repeating my question. Her answer was not unexpected, but it was painful. "I'm not cheating on you."

"You're lying to me now?"

She went on as if she hadn't heard me. "But even if I were, wouldn't that tell you something? Don't you always say that if a person cheats it means the relationship wasn't strong to begin with?"

"That's not the point. If you've been cheating on me, I deserve to know who I've been sharing you with." I hated the bitterness in my voice. I wanted to sound like she did, calm and sure of myself. But I couldn't because my life was falling down around my ears and I was sitting in my kitchen wearing a terry cloth robe that had seen better days five years ago. I pulled the robe tight across my breasts. "I deserve more than 'we need our space.'"

Brenda's mouth tightened. Finally, something more than that absent look of boredom. "I'm sorry you feel like this has come out of nowhere, but I've been trying to change things around here for a long time. You don't want to go out. You don't like doing any of the things I like to do. We don't even have the same friends."

"I didn't know it meant that much to you. We could have gone out more. I could have called—"

"Who, Mia? There's no one. Amy and Dominique can barely pull themselves away from playing mommy to play poker. All of our friends have either moved away or moved on with their lives. This is it." Her voice was bitter, cutting. "Don't you get it? I want more than just this." She gestured at our surroundings.

I looked around—at the brightly colored walls, the marble countertops, the Spanish tile that didn't really fit the kitchen motif—and tried to determine what in it could have made her so unhappy. A cold moist nose tapped at my shin twice.

"I've watched you avoid looking at yourself in the mirror for almost a year now," Brenda said in an impatient tone. "Do you really believe you're happy? How much weight have you gained this year?"

"What does my weight have to do with anything?"

"Everything. You eat when you're not happy, and lately you've been eating twice what you used to. I asked you to run the marathon with me, but you refused. Hell, if you would just go downstairs once a week it would do you a world of good. You refuse. It's like you're scared to get yourself into shape because then…"

"Because then what?" I was shaking my head. "Brenda, where the hell is all of this coming from? You just told me you didn't know if you were in love with me anymore. You're going to Fiji for five months in less than an hour. Why are you telling me this now? Why couldn't this wait until you got back?"

"Because I don't know if I'm coming back." The words were

softly spoken but I could hear the pain in them. If she hadn't sounded like she understood what she was doing to me, it might not have hurt so much.

I stood up without looking at her. "I better get dressed."

"I called a cab while you were in the shower. It'll be here soon." I turned her words over in my head. I studied her facial expression, her eyes. I was looking for a crack, some show of weakness or emotion. I found none.

"I'm sorry I have to leave like this," she said. "I'm sorry that I hurt you. I just didn't want to drag this out until I got back, and I didn't want to run the risk of telling you over the phone."

"So this is it, then? It's over?" I don't know why, but a small laugh left my mouth.

Brenda's eyes grew large as if she too had just begun to understand the ramifications of what she was saying. "I don't know that we can end four years in five minutes of conversation, but I thought you had a right to know how I felt."

Anger warmed the chill in the pit of my stomach. "I had a right to know before you cheated on me!"

"I never said I cheated on you, Mia."

"You didn't have to. You forget that I know you. Now you're just trying to make yourself feel better about the fact that you're going to do it a lot more times. You know what's sad? I would have never guessed in a million years that you would be this chicken shit."

Brenda didn't answer me and I followed her out into the hall just as a car honked outside and she turned the knob. "I'll call you, okay?"

"I'm not going to wait for you to come back, Brenda."

She acted like she didn't hear me. "Try to take better care of yourself."

She picked up her three bags and walked out the door, closing it firmly behind her. I pulled my robe tight across my chest and stared at the door waiting for the pain to hit. There was a soft whine from behind me and the sound of tiny claws clicking across hardwood floors.

Pepito sniffed at the front door, looked at me, whimpered, and settled down to wait for Brenda's return.

CHAPTER TWO

Once a month I'm forced to suffer a special kind of hell that no woman should have to willingly deal with. No, not my period—Sunday brunch at my parents' house.

You would think my being a lesbian would have caused some strife for my family, but it didn't. At least, not enough for them to disown me. If anything, it gave them more reason to feel they had a right to run my life, since I obviously didn't know what to do with it.

Brenda had left and the pinging sound of the taxi's engine had faded to nothing by the time I shook myself from my stupor and climbed the stairs to get dressed. While looking for something to wear that wouldn't garner unwanted attention from my mother, I tried not to notice how empty the closet was. Brenda, normally a light packer no matter how long she planned to be gone, had shipped almost every piece of clothing she owned.

I told myself that she would be gone for a long time. So what if Fiji was a tropical climate? It was possible that she might need long sleeves, sweaters, and jackets, wasn't it? I grabbed the outfit I was going to wear and shut the door, my bottom lip caught firmly between my teeth to keep it from trembling.

I got ready for brunch just as I normally would: makeup, hair spray, and conservative clothing. Brenda's last few words, though spoken twenty minutes before, had set off a painful resonance in the back of my mind. I didn't want to go *anywhere*, least of all my parents'. I was tempted to make up an excuse about being sick. It wasn't exactly a lie, but even the dull, empty feeling in my chest was not worth the month of short telephone conversations and hints about the importance of family that I would endure from my mother.

The woman did guilt as if she had written the manual. After a week of such treatment, not only would I have begged forgiveness for my transgression, I would no doubt have offered to drive ten stakes into my eye as I walked over hot coals, butt naked, while being filmed for *SportsCenter* as penance.

My parents' place is four thousand square feet of house sitting on a half acre of the greenest grass you'd ever want to see. As I turned into the circular driveway, the owner of the landscaping company that took care of the massive lawn waved a greeting.

"*Hola*, Hector. *Cómo está*?" I called as I stepped out of my Explorer, careful not to hike my leg up too high. I had decided to wear a dress that my sister, Christina, had helped pick out a few weeks earlier. Now I worried that the size fourteen should have been more like a sixteen.

"*Hola*, Mia, I'm fine, thank you. *Mi* Helena said that you should give her a call."

"I will," I said, though I wouldn't. His Helena had broken my heart at sixteen. Once I'm hurt, phone calls and lunch dates are out the window. Besides, she was married to a lawyer named Rudy who had less hair than Pepito. I couldn't imagine what we would have to talk about.

With another wave to Hector, I walked into my parents' home. The three-bedroom house that Christina and I grew up in was smaller than the master bedroom of this house. My father had had the dumb luck to buy land in the Pearl District before it was trendy.

I found my dad and, to my disappointment, Christina's husband Ned, sitting in matching recliners in the family room. Shoes off, black-stockinged feet up on dual footrests, both men clutched cans of beer, and in each of their laps was a large bowl filled with peanuts. Shells littered the floor around a small trash can. The room smelled of floral deodorizer, peanuts, flatulence, and feet. The same woman who could not stand the scent of cheap laundry detergent would eventually step into this room and, with nary a blink, announce that dinner was ready. I, on the other hand, was about ready to gag.

"Hi, Daddy. Ned." Peanut shells crunched beneath my feet as I bent to kiss my father's temple. Bending over was never a good move around Ned, I remembered, and straightened quickly, but not before his eyes had zeroed in on what little cleavage the dress didn't hide. "Where're Mom and Christina?"

"We're in the kitchen, Mia," Christina called out.

Of course you're in the kitchen. Where else would you be? The thought was both petty and the truth.

My father still hadn't bothered to remove his eyes from the TV screen and Ned was alternating between popping peanuts into his mouth, shell and all, and staring at my chest. If I were brave, I would have asked him what he was doing looking at his sister-in-law's chest. I contented myself with glaring at him. He grunted and turned back to the TV as if I were a commercial that, although interesting at first, had already lost its appeal.

I had never acknowledged Ned's ogling before, but Brenda's exit this morning had me on edge. I was angry and I had no place to direct it. I crunched over the peanut shells toward the kitchen, grateful that he wasn't an ass man.

Both my sister and mother were wearing aprons over their dresses and pearl necklaces. It looked as if I had just walked into an episode of *Leave it to Beaver*—the stuck-up Mexican American version. "What's for lunch? It smelled like Frito pie when I walked through the living room, but I'm pretty sure that was one of your husband's feet."

My mother's lips tightened into tight little buds of disproval. "Don't talk like that, Mia. As long as they are out of our hair, we should be grateful." She held out her hands, which was her signal for me to walk toward her so that she could look at what I was wearing. "Looks like you've put on more weight since I saw you last."

It wouldn't have been so bad if she wasn't about five pounds heavier and two inches shorter than I, but I had learned a long time ago that arguing with her only made the conversation last longer, so I just shrugged. "It's probably the dress."

"No." She studied me carefully. "The dress I like. You pick that out, Christina?"

My younger sister, Christina, looked up from her mixing bowl and squinted at my outfit. If the house was my mother's dream house, Christina was her dream daughter. Always dressed to the nines, she managed to weigh less than me when she was nine months pregnant with her son, Justin. She'd lost all of her baby weight within a few months of giving birth.

"I helped pick it out," she said demurely. The truth was she *had* picked it out while telling me that the top would help de-emphasize my breasts. Apparently she didn't notice that her balding lump of a husband salivated over them like a dog waiting for a dropped morsel.

"I thought so." My mother gave Christina an approving smile. "It's a wonderful dress, but, darling, you know it's never a good idea to call attention to Mia's bust."

Christina picked up a towel and walked toward me, her eyes riveted to my chest. She stopped and had the nerve to duck her head and crease her brow as she took a closer look. "It's a little tighter than I remember," she said and walked away. *The bitch.*

My mother tweaked the second button on the dress and I looked down to see that the seam was gaping. "Are you sure you haven't gained some weight? Did it fit like this when you bought it?"

"No, I'm probably bloated. I need to cut back on the salt."

"Try cutting back on the food. Look at Christina. She lost all that weight after she had Justin."

"Speaking of, is Justin taking a nap?" I was hopeful that I could escape my mother's eye under the guise of spending quality time with my favorite family member.

Christina scowled as if slicing cucumber required all of her attention. "He had a play date with Bryan Kemp's son."

"Who's Bryan Kemp?" I picked up a knife and looked for something to cut.

My mother took the knife from my hand and answered before Christina could. "You know who Bryan Kemp is, Mia. He ran for mayor a few years back."

"Oh, that Bryan Kemp." A headache throbbed right between my eyes.

"I'm sure Christina would be happy to tell you her weight-loss tricks, wouldn't you, Christina?" We had had this same conversation off and on for years, but each time it came up I felt like a dozen new little daggers were being shoved into my back.

"Oh, sweetheart, don't look so sad." My mother put the knife down and cupped my face between her hands. "You have such a pretty face. I just hate to see you at such an unhealthy weight."

"I am not so large that my health is in danger, Mom. When I'm ready to lose weight, I will."

I could tell by the look on her face that she didn't believe me. She released my cheeks. "Well, you're an adult. You'll do as you want. I won't say another word about it." This was a lie. I'd be lucky if we got through dinner without the subject of my weight coming up again.

"What's Hector doing here, and on a Sunday?" I asked in order to change the subject.

"We had some of those ratty weed things coming up in the lawn. That high school boy he hired must have missed them. Your father called him this morning and he hurried right over."

"I'm surprised he would do that himself. He must have something like forty people working for him now," I said.

"I hear he's doing really well for himself. Have you tried getting his accounts, Mia?" Christina asked.

I shrugged and didn't answer. I liked Hector a lot, and Christina was right, it was obvious that his business was flourishing, probably because he still did things like go to his customers' homes on Sunday afternoon. But the fact that he was the father of the first girl I ever kissed would always ensure that I kept my distance.

"Where's Brenda?" my mother asked. "I wanted to show her this gorgeous photo I saw in a magazine to see if she took it."

"She doesn't take every photo in every magazine, Mom."

"I know that, Mia. You don't have to take that tone with me. But I think I recognize Brenda's style after all these years."

"Then you know her better than I do," I muttered.

"So, is she coming later? Should we hold dinner?" Holding dinner was something my mother only offered to do for the menfolk and apparently Brenda. Any other female who'd ever had the audacity to be late got a cold shoulder and an even colder dinner.

"She's not coming. She took a last-minute assignment in Fiji. She left earlier today. She told me to apologize to you." The lie came too easily.

"Oh, really?" My mother looked at me with wide eyes. I realized too late that I had made a mistake by mentioning Fiji.

Brenda had a theory that my mother secretly wanted to be a model when she was younger. I found the notion hard to believe, despite the fact that my mother was still a beautiful woman, but her incessant interest in Brenda's work forced me to concede that she was right.

I had been given the honor of sitting in on one of Brenda's photo shoots. The first few hours had been mildly interesting; I was shocked and pleased to find out that the shoots were catered. But what I didn't like was the fact that Brenda turned into a raving bitch around hour number three. I felt protective of the emaciated models that she bullied into poses. I kept expecting her to walk up and pop one of their little heads off. None of them acted as if they minded, but I had had enough and never asked to be invited again. In retrospect, that was probably a mistake.

"The salad's done, Mama," Christina said. Had I imagined an "I helped and you didn't" tone in her voice? I tried to scowl at her, but she wasn't looking my way.

"Good. Why don't you take it on out to the table. Since Brenda and Justin aren't here, you can sit next to your father and Ned will sit next to you. Mia, you can sit across from Ned, and since you didn't get here early enough to make anything, why don't you take this pitcher of water out with you."

I followed my sister into the dining room. The table had been handed down from my grandparents. It was one of the few pieces of furniture that made the transition from our last little house to this huge monstrosity. A leaf had to be added to comfortably seat my parents, Christina, Ned, two-year-old Justin, Brenda, and me.

"Mama, is this where you want this?" Christina asked as she placed the salad in the center of the table.

"Mama, is this where you want this?" I mimicked and set the water pitcher down with more force than was necessary.

My mother glanced at it, pronounced it fine, and began cooing over my sister's lasagna. I have to admit here that I did the same. Lasagna, bread, salad, and pie; in any other household such a heavy meal would have been dinner, but in mine it was lunch. *And they wonder how my ass got this big.*

For as long as I can remember, my dad has sat at the head of the table, although my mom ruled over our meals. Ned, Christina, and Justin would sit on one side, while my mother would sit closest to my father, which left me next to her and Brenda next to me. Today was a little different in that Justin and Brenda were missing, which meant that Ned was sitting directly across from me, giving him the bird's-eye view of my breasts.

I served myself a large square of lasagna and tried to ignore my mom's quick, furtive glances at my plate. It made me angry, but I still found myself dishing up more salad than I was likely to eat in a month. To my relief, Mom busied herself with filling a plate for my father. I waited patiently, even though my mouth watered and my stomach was growling, until we all bowed our heads for the quick prayer before our meal.

"Mia, would you lead the prayer?" It's hard to describe how my mother's voice changes at family gatherings. She pronounces her words carefully and gives more orders than necessary. It's as if she doesn't realize it's just brunch and nobody else gives a shit.

It may sound sacrilegious, but I really hate this part of Sunday brunch. It isn't that I particularly mind saying grace, or even being the one who leads it sometimes. It's the fact that I feel like such a fake because I haven't set foot in a church since my grandfather died. I bowed my head and said grace, and based on my mother's pleased expression, I must have done so with the right amount of piety in my voice. She inclined her head as she thanked me, then picked up her fork, signaling that we were all allowed to eat.

A fork full of cheese and meat was on its way to my mouth when my father asked, "So, where's Brenda? She too busy for a meal?"

"She had to go out of town," I said and shoved the fork into my mouth so that I wouldn't be expected to go into detail. For once the food tasted bland and uninteresting.

"She went to Fiji for a photo shoot," my mother supplied, and I tried to ignore the pang in my chest.

"Oh? How long will she be gone?" I could tell by the way he didn't look up from his plate that he was asking out of politeness and had no real interest.

Speaking with your mouth full at Ardis Sanchez's table was grounds for banishment, so I was given a brief reprieve. The problem was, we had all been trained well. They would wait until I had finished chewing.

"Five months," I finally announced.

Christina stopped chewing. My parents glanced at each other, my father's knife and fork suspended in midair. I made the mistake of looking at Ned. He had totally ignored the conversation and his eyes were planted firmly on my chest, just as I had expected. He chewed slowly, his eyes fixated on my breasts. The dress seemed to constrict my stomach. I felt like a tube of toothpaste being squeezed in the middle. The silence around the table was excruciating.

I hadn't told them about the argument, or the fact that I'd accused Brenda of cheating on me, but it felt like they all knew. Hell, even before the argument I had known, right? I concentrated on my plate, grateful that I was being left alone. My lasagna disappeared too fast and I actually considered eating my salad to keep from having to talk.

"Here, dear, why don't you have another piece," my mother said and passed me the pan of lasagna.

I accepted gratefully, and without looking at anyone for too long, I cut off another smaller piece and began to eat. My mother can be quite nurturing when she wants to. I remember when I came home crying because I didn't make cheerleading; she put me and Christina in the car and took us to an ice cream parlor, where we all ate sundaes until we were too sick to sit up straight. I remember when I was seventeen and my first real girlfriend dumped me. Mom and I sat in the kitchen late at night while she made chocolate chip cookies. I came out to her then, and though she was shocked, it wasn't as hard as I thought it would be. It got hard twenty-four hours later, when she'd had time to think on it, but on that night she was a mother. She even polished off half of the dozen or so cookies and drank some of the milk. She hadn't been able to resist mentioning she would have to diet it off the following day, but I had appreciated her sacrifice on my behalf.

"I've been to Fiji once," Dad intoned.

"Really? I didn't know that." Mom sounded very interested, which was amazing, since I'm sure she knew he was about to tell a whopper.

My father had been everywhere. Europe, Asia, South America, the Bahamas, and now, of course, Fiji. If a country was bombed, elected a new female president, legalized gay marriage, or was mentioned in the news for whatever reason, my dad had spent time there while in the Army. Now, as far as I could tell, the Army part was true, but his world-traveler status was not supported by pictures or any other form of proof. I'm not calling him a liar; he just likes to tell stories, and he has a captive audience in my mother.

"Do you believe anything Daddy says?" my sister once asked me when we were young and still forced to share a bedroom.

"No, but I think Mama does."

"You think we should ask her?"

"Ask her what?"

"If Daddy is telling the truth."

I thought about it for a long time before I answered. "No, because what if she asks him and he has to tell the truth? She might get upset and they might get a divorce like Mary's parents."

"Mia, would you like some pie, sweetheart?" My mother's voice, and the fact that I was "sweetheart" for the time being, yanked me back to the present. Although my stomach protested, I said yes, because the pie she held out looked good. Plus as long as I kept my mouth full, I wouldn't have to talk about Brenda and the fact that I would have to sleep in that big house alone, or the fact that she had not kissed me good-bye.

The conversation moved to other things, and I felt like an outsider in my parents' home. My heart ached when I thought about how Brenda and I had left things that morning, and my stomach hurt from the effort of holding it in when I thought someone might be looking. All I wanted to do was go home, climb into bed, and have a good cry. Instead, I would have to sit for at least another hour, listen to my father tell his umpteenth fucking lie about something no one cared about, and be ogled by my sister's husband.

I put another bite of pie in my mouth. I had been wrong. It tasted like sawdust. I looked around to see if anyone would notice if I spat the pie into my napkin. The only one paying me any attention was Ned. He had given up all pretence of chewing and was blatantly staring at my chest, his face flushed. He was still holding his fork, and I had this vision of him reaching across the table to prod my chest with it. Heat rose up my neck and settled around my ears.

Mom's head was bobbing parrotlike in response to a story my father was telling about the native Fijians, while Christina was concentrating on pushing her lettuce leaves around on her plate rather than eating them. Anger caused me to sit straighter. Ned gave one automatic chew before stopping once more to feast his eyes. That was it; the minute he broke from his tit-induced trance I was going to mouth a warning to him, let him know I didn't appreciate being stared at like a piece of meat.

"The women in Fiji are all very slim and exotic," my father said. "It's so hot there that everyone walks around naked."

I don't remember eating all of my pie, but I must have because my fork landed on my empty plate with a loud clatter. I took a deep breath so that I could keep my words calm. My plan was to quietly ask him to stop looking at my chest, but what came out was, "Stop looking at my tits, you balding little bitchhead bastard."

My nonsensical words cracked like thunder in the silent room. My breath caught. I gasped and inhaled hard. Another panicked breath forced air down my windpipe. Finally I heard a sound, like dry fingers snapping, and an object bulleted across the table and into Ned's right eye. My chest stopped feeling like I was going to have a heart attack. A button was missing from the front of my dress. My bra and consequently my breasts had tumbled out like two escaped convicts during a prison break.

Ned screamed, "Oh, my God, my God. My eye. She shot me in the eye." No one moved as he pushed away from the table and stood, both hands trying to cover his right eye.

My sister and mother reacted at the same moment, rushing toward him, trying to get him to let them inspect his injury. But Ned was swinging his elbows from side to side and they had to step back in order to avoid being hit.

"Emanuel, we need to get him to a hospital," my mother said imperiously.

My father stood and calmly walked toward the front door. My sister led her husband down the hall by the arm. I could hear her telling him that he would fine.

"Mia, lock up before you leave," Dad said just before he shut the door behind them.

Hot tears streamed down my cheeks and hit the center of my empty plate.

CHAPTER THREE

Goody walked into my office, shut the door, and sat down, his hands steepled in front of his face. "Okay, I know you don't want to talk about this, but I think we should. Have you heard from the skank yet?"

"I wish you wouldn't call her that. I probably just jumped to conclusions. I don't have any proof that she cheated on me." My voice sounded more nonchalant than I felt. I hadn't heard from Brenda. The only reason I knew she had made it to Fiji at all was because after days of not hearing anything, I had called her room and quickly hung up the phone when she answered. That was five days ago.

"I think most people would have jumped to that conclusion."

"Most people would have noticed what was going on with their partner before it got this bad."

"Maybe." He stood up and moved closer to my bookcase. I knew what he was going to do even before he picked up the framed picture of Brenda and me sitting with two of our friends enjoying one of Portland's few really hot summer days. Goody did this often. I figured it was a nervous habit, similar to his preoccupation with his fingernails. I didn't mind, since the only time the photo got dusted was when he got contemplative. The picture had been taken before Brenda and I had moved in together and it wasn't a particularly good shot of any of us. We had lost touch with Saundra and Nora well over a year ago.

"What's your fascination with that picture?"

Goody frowned at it and instead of putting it back down on the shelf, took it back to his seat and sat down with it. "You, I guess." He looked up. "In all the time I've known you, I don't think I've ever seen you in jeans and a T-shirt, or with your hair down like that."

"Here, let me see." I held out my hand for the picture and glared at it as if I'd never seen it before. According to Christina, my lips and hair were two of my best features. Both were full and thick, and I had to admit, both looked good in this picture. Maybe that's why I had yet to replace the photo despite the fact that Brenda and I had probably taken better over the years.

"I can't even remember the last time I tried to get into a pair of jeans," I confessed before I could stop myself.

"Damn, girl, you act like you're huge."

"Brenda thinks I'm well on my way." I handed the photo back to him. "I have gained a few pounds since that was taken."

"Hmm, maybe a little. But I bet ten or fifteen of that is from all that makeup and those heavy-ass suits you wear."

I wanted to be mad, I really did, but it was hard to get mad at Goody when he was being honest. Besides, it's not as if he knew I weighed myself every damn morning, butt naked and after a pee. Nor could he know that the scale hadn't moved but one way in the last six months, and it wasn't the good way.

"So, have you heard from her?" he asked again as he slouched back into his chair.

"No, I haven't. I think she's giving me time to think over what she said."

"And have you thought it over?"

"Yeah, a little." I stomped down my annoyance at receiving the third degree. I had been on the other side of the desk questioning Goody about his relationship choices too many times to count. Now that I was the one under the microscope, I didn't like it one bit. "And part of me knows she's right. I mean, she had no right to cheat on me—if she did—but…I guess I just don't get it. Our relationship was never bad…"

"Was it ever good? I mean *really* good? Did your heart leap into your throat the first time you saw her? Did you ache for her at inopportune moments?"

I chuckled, "Are you serious? I haven't felt that way about anyone since high school."

Goody's expression was somber. "I am serious. Don't get me

wrong, Brenda is a beautiful woman, but I always got the feeling that you two led completely separate lives. She's been gone almost two weeks, right? Has your life changed that much?"

His words shocked me. Of course my life had changed since Brenda had left. How could it not? I searched my brain for specific instances where Brenda's absence was the most acute, but aside from sleeping alone and the monthly brunch at my parents', I drew a blank.

"Having a hard time coming up with stuff, huh?"

I was saved from answering by a flash of white just outside my line of sight. My office has two floor-to-ceiling windows on either side of a glass door, so when the blond construction worker stopped in front of my door, I could see how startled she was when she realized I was looking at her. Before I could gesture for her to come in, she had already walked away. I was on my feet so fast you would have thought someone had just yelled *Fire!*

Those long legs had already taken her halfway down the hall. I called after her. "Hi, we aren't busy. Do you need something?"

As she turned around, I put on what I thought was a warm and encouraging smile. The natural reaction to that would have been to smile back. She didn't. Instead, she cleared her throat and held up a piece of white shiny plastic, a stencil. "I need to put this on your door."

"You do that too?"

She did smile then and I felt myself wanting to move closer to her. The smile, though genuine enough, seemed tired, tentative, and, well, uncomfortable. Who in the hell has a hard time smiling? Especially someone as beautiful as this woman?

"May I ask you something?" I had already begun to ask before I noticed that her body had become rigid and she was looking off to my right as if preparing to be reprimanded. "How did you learn to do all this stuff?"

Confusion transformed her face once again and she murmured something I didn't hear.

Apparently my clitoris didn't need to hear the exact words to give an answering throb. I felt my face heat. Because she seemed awkward, I said, "Sorry if I made you uncomfortable."

"You didn't." She spoke so quietly that I had to lean forward to hear her. I found myself wondering what her voice would sound like after a night of making love. *Where the hell did that come from?*

"My grandfather," she was saying. Her voice changed the same way that mine did when I talked about my grandfather. "He was a carpenter and a fix-it man. He taught me most of what I know."

I was going to ask her another question, anything to keep her speaking, when the smell of expensive cologne interrupted my train of thought. I tensed even before I heard Brad Jackson's affected voice. "Things seem to be moving along quite quickly on your new wing," he said as he came down the hall toward us.

The statement might have sounded like friendly commentary to a complete moron, but I had been dealing with Jackson's barely hidden condescension toward me since I had inherited Henry's book. "It's not a wing. My new office*s are* coming along nicely, thank you for noticing."

"Good, glad to hear it. You do realize you have caused some strife amongst the other assistants because you're giving Matthew Good an office?"

"I'm sure they'll feel less upset when they realize that they could have an office if they helped their brokers get the assets needed to go Business Formula. Of course, that would require some of the brokers to give up that round of golf or that extra-long lunch so that they could talk to clients about their assets."

"Well, most of us didn't have the opportunity to inherit a book."

I could see the construction worker's eyes going from Jackson to me and back again. I liked the fact that she hadn't walked away. I liked the way her eyes had taken in Jackson's impeccably tailored clothes and hundred-dollar haircut with no more interest than if he were a mannequin in a store window.

"I'm pretty sure if you ever do inherit a book you'll be able to add the extra million and a half needed to go Business Formula." I raised my eyebrows. "But let me know if you want some pointers. I'd be happy to help in any way I can."

Jackson had this little writhing vein thingy on the side of his forehead that signaled that he was about to get pissed. Goody once said he thought it was sexy. I thought it was gross as hell.

"Thanks for the offer," he said, but the turn of his lips informed me that he felt there was really nothing I had to offer him. "I actually came down to speak to you." He turned to the construction worker and I could tell by the way her body tensed, she didn't like the shift in attention. But where I got the cold shoulder, he was all charm and friendliness with her. It was like watching a bug skate on an oil slick. "I have a few shelves in my office that need to be reinforced. I was hoping you could help me out with that, in between your building of Ms. Sanchez's new wing, of course."

"It may be a few days before I can get the time." I loved the fact that Jackson didn't get the smile that I did. In fact, with the exception of the flaring of her nostrils, it looked to me like the woman had gone out of her way to show no expression at all.

I waited, as did Jackson, for a clearer timeline as to when she thought she would be able to get to his office. When none came, he looked annoyed, said a curt, "Thank you. No rush," and without so much as a glance in my direction, walked away.

Relief didn't set in until after he was out of sight. "Sorry you had to be a part of that."

"What was that?" she asked.

"Jackson's got a problem with me. He's had one since my senior partner ended up taking early retirement and I inherited his book. He felt the book should have been split amongst the more senior brokers, but," I shrugged, "that's not how it works. I had been working closely with Henry Ballard for a little over two years. The clients knew me."

"So, is that why you'll have a bigger office than anyone else in this place?"

I must have inadvertently moved closer to her because I could clearly see that her eyes were no longer as distant, and she acted as if she was genuinely interested in what I had to say. "You cut right to it, don't you? That's the consensus around here, but the truth is, the accounts I inherited constitute less than half of the assets I manage. I just plain bring in more money than he does. Twice as much, actually. It means I get to take home a higher percentage of the income."

I'll admit to a little bragging here, but my ego was quickly downsized when she didn't look anymore impressed than she had for Jackson.

"Does Mr. Jackson know that?" she asked.

"He knows it. He needs something to accuse me of because he's unhappy. Even before I reached Business Formula status, he always had something to complain about."

There was something disconcerting about the way she was

watching me. For a brief moment her eyes came to rest on my hair, and as if in reaction to her gaze, the clips that I used to pull it away from my face felt as though they were digging into my scalp.

"I'm sorry, I'm probably boring the hell out of you." I gestured to her hand and she held up the plastic material as if she had forgotten about it. "You needed to do something with that?"

"Since we're going to reuse the door, I figured I would go ahead and put these on now."

"Oh, okay. Sure, go ahead."

What in the world made me think she was looking at my hair? She was probably looking past me to my door. All the poor woman wanted to do was add the stencil, and instead, she'd been forced to listen to my life story. I muttered something about getting back to my office, where Goody would still be waiting to finish our conversation. I was acutely conscious of the fact that she was walking behind me. I felt like my clothes were shrinking. Who was I kidding? I should have moved up to the next size months ago, but I hadn't because I didn't want to have to tell my sister when she picked out my clothes.

"You didn't bore me," I heard her say in a soft, caressing voice. Or had I imagined that?

I glanced back at her and smiled. She looked surprised and then slowly smiled in response. A dash of red at her cheek caught my eye and I remembered Goody's comments about the scar. I wasn't sure how I could have missed it before. It was certainly vivid enough. Her smile faded and we continued to my office.

Goody was still sitting where I had left him. I could tell by the expression on his face that he had heard everything. "I don't know why Jackson is so horrible to you," he said. "He treats me like a queen, and I mean that in a good way."

I shrugged, acutely aware of the construction worker standing just inside my office while she worked. Goody was perfectly comfortable talking with her there, but I felt tongue-tied. I realized that I hadn't asked her name. Her back was to me, and once again I marveled at how well her jeans fit. I wondered how she got away with wearing jeans that tight without having a panty line. *Maybe she doesn't wear panties.*

The thought sent heat right to my face and I hoped she hadn't picked up on the fact that I was imagining her jeans hitting her in just the right spot as she bent down to pick something up off the floor.

"So anyway, back to that ex-girlfriend of yours. You know what I say, the best way to get over them is to get even."

The background noise that was Goody's voice stopped. I ripped my eyes from the construction worker's ass long enough to notice that he was grinning at me like he had just been given a large raise. It dawned on me that he had outed me in front of a complete stranger, but my surprise was eclipsed by the realization that I wasn't at all angry about it.

"You're not listening to me, so I'm going to go."

"Goody, don't go. I was just about to—" Actually, I was about to lie, but I was saved from having to do so because my telephone rang. Goody rolled his eyes, stood up, and walked out of the office as if I had wounded his ego.

The caller was a client, Beth Margolis. I greeted her warmly, and she said, "I hope you got my card thanking you for the wonderful flowers you sent for Tony's funeral. Everyone commented on how lovely they were."

"I did get your card. And you're very welcome." Tony and Beth Margolis were two of my inherited accounts. Although I had never met Beth, Tony had come to the office once to have lunch with Henry. I had found him delightfully funny and full of life. Henry had called and told me about Tony's death, and although I hadn't felt it appropriate to attend the small funeral, I had enlisted my college roommate, Fiona, in finding a funeral arrangement. Thinking about Tony Margolis's death made me think of my own grandfather, causing the dull void that I always felt when I thought of him to reappear.

"I won't keep you long, but one of the things Tony and I discussed before he…passed away was a college fund for my grandson, Hugo. I don't know that he ever got around to it. I don't remember signing anything."

"If you wouldn't mind holding for a few moments, Mrs. Margolis, I would be happy to check the accounts for you."

"Of course, and it's Beth. Take your time."

Ordinarily I would have just put my call on hold and yelled to Goody, but since the construction worker was still working on the door, I used the intercom instead. "How about lunch on me?"

"Is that code for, 'Will you go get me lunch because I'm hungry and I have to take this call?'"

"I'll let you pick the place this time."

"Then I want sandwiches from the deli." Goody's voice took on a pitch similar to my nephew Justin's when he was tired or hungry. I hated when he did that. I also didn't particularly care for the deli. They always managed to put too much mayo or too much mustard on my sandwich. But I agreed and quickly brought up the Margolis accounts with a few keystrokes.

"Thanks for holding, Beth. It doesn't look like Tony opened an account for your grandson. Is this something you'd like me to handle?"

I looked up from my computer screen just in time to see the construction worker turn away from my door in order to stifle a sneeze. Without thinking I reached for a tissue and held it out to her. She hesitated, stepped into my office, and took the Kleenex. I don't know what possessed me, maybe it was because of a small frown I thought I saw, but I held on to the tissue longer than I should have and when her eyes met mine, I felt the heat of attraction burn throughout my body again. She gave me a curious smile, and I flushed and released the tissue. As she returned to her work, she swung a covert look my way, as if trying to figure out what I was playing at. Since I could not answer that question for myself, let alone her, I forced my attention back to my client.

Beth Margolis was talking about transferring some Disney stock for the college fund. "What's the likelihood that I'm going to live another twenty years anyway?" she said, and I was pretty sure I didn't imagine the sadness in her voice. Goody's question about feeling tingly when I thought of Brenda came to mind and I knew, without being told, that Beth Margolis would understand exactly what he meant.

"The account you shared with Tony requires both your signatures," I said gently. "We would need to switch you to a new single account before we can make any changes."

The first time I had been forced to speak with a client about making the necessary changes after his wife's death, he had dissolved into tears and hung up on me. His wife had passed away three years before.

"Oh, I see." Beth Margolis sounded shocked at first, but then resigned.

As I explained how it would work, and which forms she would need to fill out, I let my eyes wander to the construction worker again. She was carefully running something along the sign that she had just placed on the door, and this time I got a clear view of her cheek. The scar went from her ear to within a half inch of the corner of her mouth. On a less remarkable face, the scar might have been, well, less remarkable. But on hers it seemed cruel, as if it had been done with the specific intention of marring her beauty.

As I stared, Goody walked in carrying my lunch bag. I smiled a thank-you and my stomach squirmed as I realized that even if I put the phone on mute long enough to steal a bite, there was no way I was going to scarf down my lunch with the construction worker standing only a few feet away. Goody said something to her on his way back out and they both looked at me. Instead of smiling back or, God forbid, giving the woman a flirtatious little wink, I shyly lowered my eyes.

"I know Tony kept some old stock certificates in his desk too. But there's so much in there. I hate going through his things."

The tears in her voice caused me to straighten. I had been so busy watching the show, I had missed how upset Beth Margolis was becoming. She and her husband had been married for fifty-two years. Of course she felt bad going through his things. And I had just calmly requested a death certificate. The requirement was intended to prevent a client's removing access to shared accounts by lying about their spouse's death. I still hated asking for it.

"Beth, please don't cry. I understand completely. If you want, we can do this some other time. Or…would you feel better if I came by? The phone is so impersonal. We could take care of the new account documentation."

Her voice changed perceptibly at my suggestion. "I'd like that, but I don't want you to make the trip for nothing. What if we can't find the stocks?"

"I know what they look like, so maybe I could help you, if you don't mind a stranger going through Tony's things?"

"You're not a stranger. What time do you get off work? I can have coffee ready."

I was going to tell her that I had taken the MAX train in, but her voice had lightened twofold and I tried to remember the few things I knew about Mrs. Margolis. Her closest relative was a daughter living in California. Her other daughter, who was the youngest, lived in Chicago. I doubted she got to see either them or her grandchildren often.

Even though I had never met the woman, her loneliness reached through the phone and pulled at my heart. I cared about the fact that she would be able to live out her life in relative comfort. I minimized my accounts page and pulled up my schedule. "I don't meet with any clients tonight, so how about I plan to leave here no later than five thirty. Does that work for you?"

"Yes, that would be fine. Mia, thank you for everything." Once again I could hear the tears in her voice and I wondered, do you ever stop missing someone who has shared your life for fifty-two years? It had been four for Brenda and me. Shouldn't I be missing her more? Shouldn't I be worried about the fact that she might call me tonight while I was at Mrs. Margolis's? Shouldn't I feel something more than irritation that I would have to rush home to Brenda's little snaggletoothed dog because I hadn't left him extra food?

Beth Margolis sounded a lot happier when she hung up the phone, and I spent a few minutes eating my lunch and going through her investments. Henry had done a phenomenal job. When the whole world was going nuts on tech stock he had placed Tony and Beth Margolis in them, but he had also been smart enough to get them out right before things got bad.

I stood up in order to knock the melancholy from my system. At some point, I had forgotten the construction worker was working on my new door and I murmured, "Excuse me," as I approached. Instead of moving out of the way she stepped closer to the door. She was smiling. At least I think she was. It wasn't so much that her lips turned up, but her eyes lingered on mine as I passed and they looked warmer than they had before. More friendly.

A giggle threatened from the back of my throat and I cut it off right before it could come out and make me feel like a giant fool. *Oh boy, what the hell was that?*

"Do you *need* something?" Goody asked, and his emphasis on the word "need" made me want to reach out and pop him one. Thankfully, he would no longer be sitting right outside of my office once construction was done. He saw entirely too much.

"Yeah, I *need* a ride to Mrs. Margolis's. I took MAX in."

Goody bit his bottom lip and rifled several sheets of paper. "Ah, sorry, *chica*, I rode in with Robin today. You want me to call her and ask—"

"Nah, that's okay. I'll take the bus." Robin was Brad Jackson's admin assistant. She was nice enough, but I could never get over feeling that she disliked me because Henry and I had not considered her for the job when Henry's assistant retired. "Besides, if you and Robin start talking about how great Jackson's ass is again, I might go nuts on both of you and I'd end up on the bus anyway."

"You need a ride somewhere? I can take you." I didn't turn around and I suspected that my eyes might be as big as Goody's looked. He inclined his head as if to say "answer her, damn it," and I turned around too quickly. She was still standing in the entryway of my office, but the words *Mia Sanchez Investment Group* were now on my door in neat white lettering.

"Oh no, I don't want to take you out of your way."

She shrugged. "I don't mind taking you, if you don't mind riding with a stranger."

"Well, what's your name?" Goody asked from behind me and I whipped around to glare at him before I realized that he was probably being smart by asking her name.

"Ryan Benson."

"Where do you live?" Goody asked as if checking off questions in his head.

"I live right off Hawthorne. The building has all my information on file."

She looked like she was trying to figure out if she should be offended or not when Goody sniffed and said, "Since you're cute, I guess it's okay. Murderers and rapists have those prominent foreheads, you know. I saw it on Discovery." He looked at me and said in all seriousness, "You'll be just fine with her."

He stood up with his sheaf of papers. I could see that the top one at least was a blank wire transaction form. "I need to run these down to the cage before close of market." He walked off, leaving me and the construction worker alone. I knew, without looking, that it was barely noon, a full hour before close of market. *Thanks a lot, Goody.*

"Sorry about the third degree. He really doesn't mean any harm."

"He's just looking out for you. I get off at five. Do you want me to wait for you somewhere?"

"No. I mean, I can leave any time I want."

"Then how 'bout I meet you in the lobby a little after five?" she asked.

I agreed and watched as she bent to pick up some minuscule thing from the floor in my office and walked toward me. I know for a fact that my eyes got wide when she leaned really close to me. I breathed in deeply and wondered how she could smell so good after spending half the day working, like soap and plastic.

"No problem. Thanks for the tissue, earlier," she said.

I felt odd and off kilter as I watched her walk away. It didn't surprise me that I might be attracted to her; she was gorgeous. But not my type. The women that usually caught my eye were always dark and typically curvy, like Brenda. This woman was tall, obviously in great shape, and blond. Even if she was a lesbian, she wouldn't be the least bit interested in me.

I stared at the glass door with my name on it in perfect white letters and thought about the way Goody had outed me earlier. Had the construction worker—she said her name was Ryan—picked up on that?

Maybe she was warming toward me because she figured that I might be a lesbian, which would imply that she was a lesbian. The idea made my heart beat double time for exactly ten seconds before I made myself stop. Even if she was a lesbian, and even if she was, for some odd reason, interested, I wasn't available to explore whatever it was that zipped between us whenever our eyes met.

But I would be lying if I said I didn't want to.

CHAPTER FOUR

I was waiting for Ryan in the lobby at five. My grandfather liked to say that people who were consistently late for events were either attention seekers or had no respect for other people's time. I couldn't remember when I had ever left work this early, and I was amazed at the number of people from Goldsmith who came laughing out of the elevator as I stood there, waiting for my ride. The minute they saw me they stopped, guilt on their faces. It annoyed the shit out of me and I couldn't quite figure out why.

The moment she appeared, carrying a worn leather jacket and a brown paper bag, I knew I had made a mistake. See, here's the thing: Goody was right. Brenda had never made me feel tingly just by thinking about her. We'd met at a fund-raiser. I thought she was charming and yes, beautiful. But this woman—Ryan—well, she made me think about sex. Call me crazy or even mentally challenged, but I have never ever looked at a woman and thought, *Good Lord, I must do a face plant into that one*. But at that moment, as she walked toward me, her hair pulled back, her white T-shirt tucked into those wonderful jeans, that's exactly what crossed my mind.

"Hi, am I late?" Her voice surprised me again. She looked like she would have a deep voice, not shy and sweet.

"No, I think I'm a little early." My eyes focused on the bag in her hand and I wondered if she hadn't finished her lunch. The idea was foreign to me. I always ate everything I was served, even when I was the one preparing it. It seemed rude, somehow, not to.

"I rode the bus in too. Steve is letting me borrow the work truck for the night." She held up a set of keys.

"Oh no, you didn't need to do that. I could have taken the bus."

Ryan smiled, and this time her smile appeared to come easy. "I wanted to take you. Truck's parked downstairs."

I followed her to the bank of elevators that went to the underground garage. I could see our reflections in the shiny faux gold doors. Like Mutt and Jeff, I thought.

"Thanks again for doing this," I said as the door slid open and she gestured for me to step on.

"You're welcome. Where are we headed?"

"Sellwood. The house is right across the street from Sellwood Park, actually."

"No problem, I know where that is."

"Hold the elevator." The voice was annoyed, familiar, and made the hairs lie down that had been at attention since I had seen Ryan. Before I could stop her, Ryan reached out and pushed the Open button. Jackson stepped heavily onto the elevator. As the doors shut behind him, he glanced at me and turned around so that he was standing next to Ryan and I was standing like an outsider, behind them both.

"Thank you," he said pleasantly to her.

"You're welcome."

"I'm curious, do you do work outside the building? I have a few projects in my home that I keep putting off because I'm so busy here." I rolled my eyes at his back.

I hated that I could not see Ryan's expression or somehow signal her not to trust Jackson. But who was I to give advice? For all I knew, he could be on the up-and-up. But something about him had always caused me to keep my distance. His blatant jealousy was one thing, but I sensed an element of dishonesty that I could never see past.

"I do take on some outside work. But I couldn't do that with you since we met here in the building. My company has a strict no-moonlighting clause." Ryan's voice was smooth, unemotional. I could have hugged her. I leaned back against the elevator rail wishing I could get a better look at her. She stared straight ahead even though Jackson was looking at the side of her face. The line of the scar seemed a lot more evident, as if his gaze had made it angry. The elevator door slid open and emitted a soft ding.

"I believe this is your floor," I said.

Jackson started and stepped off the elevator. "If you should change your mind."

The doors slid shut and Ryan said, "He gives me the creeps."

For some reason the comment caught me off guard. Ryan had never really said anything to me that wasn't to the point. Her reaction to Jackson was so unexpected that I answered her without censoring myself. "He thinks he's God's gift, so there's something wrong with any woman that isn't interested in him sexually."

Her eyebrows shot up and I felt the prickling at my armpits that usually signaled I had just put my foot in my mouth about something. "He's definitely barking up the wrong tree with me."

Okay, what does that mean? Is she or isn't she? We reached our floor, and Ryan stepped to the side as the door opened. "After you."

I felt awkward being let off the elevator first. For one thing, I didn't know where the hell I was going; for another, I didn't want her seeing my ass jiggling when I walked.

"Truck's over here." She walked up to a white Ford pickup with the words *B and R Contractors, Inc.* written on the side.

"I'm surprised your boss let you take the work truck."

Ryan unlocked the passenger door and held it open while I got in. She was in the seat with her seat belt in hand when she finally answered, "He figures he owes me for helping him move into his new place."

She started the engine and I realized that I didn't know this person and I had nothing to say to her. My heart beat a staccato on my eardrums and I took a deep breath in order to calm myself. "So, it looks like the office is coming along nicely. I can't believe you can do all that work so fast."

"Yeah, we're right on schedule. Should be finished in no time."

The silence grew and would have become awkward if I hadn't forced myself to break it. "So, how long have you been in Portland?"

Ryan turned toward me and I caught the scent of spearmint gum and a perfume that I had never smelled before. "All my life."

I can only imagine how I must have looked with my mouth hanging open, but I couldn't help it. Her "my" came out like "mah," and it made me think of *Gone with the Wind*, and how I had wanted Scarlett to be my best friend and come over to sleep in my room when I was just six years old.

"Nu-uh?" was the only thing I could articulate. Don't get me wrong; I love Portland, but Ryan's accent was like warm peaches with a hint of cinnamon. It had the slightest hint of huskiness, a warning that things weren't always going to be pretty, or soft, or even nice. There was no way Portland spawned that accent.

Ryan was looking away while she made a left turn, so it took me a minute to realize that she was smiling. But boy, was she—and not that tentative *I'm not sure if I like you* smile, either. This was a full-on, toothy white thing that made me catch my breath. Good Lord, the woman had a beautiful mouth, a beautiful smile, and if her hair wasn't pulled back in a rubber band, I'm sure that would be beautiful too. What the hell was I doing sitting next to her in a pickup truck thinking about doing the pajama-party hump with Scarlett from *Gone with the Wind*?

"I've been here about fourteen months," she admitted.

"Whew, you had me going there. Let me guess, a lot of people ask you that, huh?"

"Pretty much everyone I talk to. I'm from Texas."

"Texas is a long ways from Portland. What made you move here?" The warmth inside the truck dropped a few degrees. I could tell that I had stepped into off-limitsville, but I didn't understand why.

"My little brother Brady got a baseball scholarship to Portland State," she replied. "I moved down here to keep an eye on him. How 'bout you?"

"Born and raised."

"Really?"

"Why so surprised?"

"I don't know. I haven't met many people who were born and raised here. Mostly Californians."

"Tell me about it. The influx of Californians is one of my dad's favorite topics to rant about." I mimicked his accent. "'Pretty soon good working folk won't even be able to buy a house anymore.'"

"You can still find good homes if you're willing to put some sweat into it." Her voice got quiet, contemplative, and wishful.

"Do you own a home here?"

"Not yet. I've always wanted my own place, though. My mother's rented for years. She could have paid off a mortgage by now."

"I know what you mean. I just bought a new home right off Northwest Twenty-third."

"I don't know much about that area. Do you like it?"

I hesitated before answering. It was a great area, an expensive area. But did I like it? I couldn't really say. I hadn't spent all that much time outside of my home other than to catch the public transportation to work. "Yeah, I haven't lived there long, but I like it fine."

The truck slowed and I realized with some disappointment that we were in front of Mrs. Margolis's home. The front porch light had been left on despite the fact that at five thirty in early August there would be sufficient daylight until well after eight.

"Ryan." I held out my hand and she took it. "Thank you very much for the ride. If I can ever return the favor…"

She kept hold of my hand. Her expression held an odd intensity. "How are you getting home?"

How had I thought her eyes unremarkable? I couldn't imagine not telling the truth under the onslaught of those eyes. "I thought I could just take the bus."

Ryan finally released my hand and I nearly closed my eyes in relief. She peered up and down the street. "I don't see a bus stop. I'll wait for you."

"Oh no, that's not necessary, and I could be a while. I'll take a cab if the bus stop is too far." A flicker of movement from Mrs. Margolis's window drew my eye. "I better get going."

"Take your time. I don't have anyplace I need to be." Ryan unbuckled her seat belt and pulled off her jacket.

"Look, I appreciate you staying, but I don't want you waiting out here too long. Promise me you'll leave if I'm in there longer than an hour?"

"Nope."

"Nope?"

"I don't make promises I won't keep."

I felt strangely giddy. For some reason the fact that she was going to wait for me felt, well, intimate. It was the kind of thing people in relationships did for each other, or at least, the romantic in me thought they did.

"You better get going before she calls the police about the strange truck outside her house," Ryan said.

I scurried out of the pickup and took a deep breath. I couldn't believe she was waiting. I couldn't believe I was happy that she was. As I walked up Mrs. Margolis's steps, my back felt hot. I felt like each of my imperfections was being reviewed under a microscope. I rang the doorbell and refused to glance behind me to see if she was watching. Five percent of me hoped that she would be gone when I came back out, but the vast majority of me wanted to see those eyes and that wonderful mouth one more time before I went to sleep.

Whoa, girl. Before you go to sleep in a bed that until recently you shared with Brenda. How can you be thinking of another woman in that fashion so soon after Brenda left? Mrs. Margolis opened her door at that moment and saved me from having to answer my own question and possibly breaking my own heart in the process.

❖

"Would you like coffee, or is it too late for that? My husband always drank coffee at the oddest hours, and I guess I just picked up on the habit." Mrs. Margolis looked nothing like what I had expected. Her husband had been quick on his feet; the only evidence of his age were the color of his hair and smile lines permanently etched at the sides of his eyes.

Beth Margolis walked slowly, but her posture was perfect and the slacks and cardigan that she wore were impeccably pressed. Her hair, skin, and eyes had dulled with age. Whereas her husband had been bright and alive when I had met him, Mrs. Margolis seemed like a shadow. I wondered if she had always been that way. A shadow living in her husband's sun, or had that happened after he passed away? Either scenario left me feeling sad and even more determined to make things as easy for her as possible.

"Coffee would be great. Thanks." I looked around as I pulled my jacket off. "You have a lovely home," I said automatically. Those words were on page one of my mother's guidebook for entering a complete stranger's home. But in this case, I meant it. Mrs. Margolis's walls were chock full of family photos.

"May I?"

"You go right ahead. That's what they're there for."

At a glance, I would have guessed that Mrs. Margolis had lined her walls with at least fifty or sixty pictures of family members, spanning at least three decades. All of them were in black and white and seemed so similar, they could have been taken by the same person.

"Here you are, dear."

I tore my eyes away from a photo of five men with nothing but sailor hats on posing behind a fallen tree trunk.

"That was my Tony, always looking for reasons to take his pants off."

I tried to reconcile this photo of a mischievous, barely twenty-year-old boy with the seventy-eight-year-old I had met in my office. "I'm sorry I only met him in passing. I bet he was an interesting person to talk to."

"He was." Mrs. Margolis took a sip of her coffee. "I still can't figure out why the Lord was so cruel."

I kept my attention on the picture because I had no clue how to comfort her. I didn't even know how to comfort myself.

"I suppose I'm being a fool. God gave us fifty-two years. That's longer than even your mother has been on this earth, I'd guess."

"Not quite, but she'd love you for saying so, I'm sure."

Mrs. Margolis laughed and I realized that she was the beautiful young woman in the photos. *You're turning into your mom and Christina, judging people when you shouldn't.* I shivered.

"Are you cold? I suppose I could turn on the heat. I never get cold because Tony never turned on the heat or the air. He said he would never pay Portland General Electric one red cent more than he had to."

"Oh no, I'm fine. The coffee's already warming me up." I had this vision of Ryan sitting out in the truck without the engine running. She was probably freezing out there. "Mrs. Margolis, I had a friend bring me over and it's gotten cold outside."

"Oh, go and get your friend. I was going to suggest you invite him. I saw the truck pull up."

"Thank you. It's a she, and I'll be right back."

As I approached the truck, I could see that Ryan was leaning back, her arms folded in front of her, probably trying to keep warm. I felt guilty that I hadn't thought to ask if she could come inside before this. Despite the chill, the driver-side window was half opened. I leaned closer, meaning to say her name softly, but my breath caught in my throat because her nostrils flared and her lips parted. I found myself both wanting her to wake up, so that I could see her eyes, and wanting her to continue to sleep so that I could watch her. A large invisible foot planted itself firmly on my chest, and I grabbed the truck door in an effort to keep myself stable.

She awakened. No flicker of the lashes or gasps. She was just awake and staring at me. "Mia?" My name on her lips sent a thrill to the back of my neck.

I think I was the one who blinked, maybe even gasped. At some point I had leaned into the truck because I was close, too close. "Yes?" I said like an idiot.

"Something wrong?" She didn't seem alarmed. I had to wonder how often she woke up with a strange woman hovering over her. I flushed at the visual and moved back a few inches.

"Mrs. Margolis made coffee, and it's cold out here."

Ryan smiled and did this squirming thing that for some reason made me want to look down at her crotch. I didn't, but I damn sure wanted to.

"I don't mind waiting for you out here, it's not too cold."

"I think it makes her nervous having a stranger sitting in a truck outside her house."

Ryan glanced at the house and sat up. Her hand went to her head and pushed the strands of hair back that never wanted to stay bound. *When did I notice that about her?*

"I won't be long, I promise. And she has some great pictures in there." Ryan's hand went to the door handle and hesitated. It took me a few seconds to realize that Ryan was waiting for me to step out of the way. I did so hurriedly.

When Ryan got out of the truck I couldn't stop myself looking from her boots to her denim-clad legs again. I imagined they would be just the right combo of muscle and smooth femininity. I traveled up her pant legs to her waist—*I can't ever remember having a T-shirt tuck that neatly into the waistband of my jeans*—then finally, to her face.

She stomped her boots twice. "I'm a little dusty. You sure she wants me in her house?" Her forehead was creased by a frown.

"I think you look great," I said too quickly.

"Thanks."

Her face darkened a little and I realized that I had probably embarrassed her, which in turn embarrassed me. What the hell was I doing? This woman was helping me out of kindness, and here I was ogling her and forcing her into a situation that she was obviously uncomfortable with. "If you don't want to come in, I'll make an excuse. I just thought…"

"No, I would love to come in. I bet the house is beautiful inside."

Her voice sounded wistful and soft. Once again I felt an attraction, a curiosity that made me want to know more about her.

"She's got pictures all over the walls spanning at least three generations." I walked back toward Mrs. Margolis's house and Ryan followed. It was disconcerting to realize that not only was Ryan paying attention to me, she seemed to hang on my words.

"Do you think she'd let me look around?"

"I don't see why not."

Beth Margolis appeared in the doorway. The smile I'd noticed in the pictures was on her face. I made the mistake of glancing at Ryan and almost stumbled. My God, she was so gorgeous. The wind blew a few strands of hair away from her face, displaying the scar clearly. Call me crazy, but it didn't detract from her features. If anything, it kept her from being too perfect. Her long fingers engulfed Mrs. Margolis's hand as they introduced themselves.

"Ryan? Unusual name for a girl."

"My mother was a *Ryan's Hope* fan."

"Ah," Mrs. Margolis said as if that explained everything. I wished someone would explain it to me, because I hadn't the slightest idea what the hell *Ryan's Hope* was.

"I was almost Hope."

"Now that would have been a travesty," my client noted.

Ryan gave her another one of those smiles that she was giving away freely now that we weren't alone.

Mrs. Margolis offered coffee and gestured toward a credenza that held small, delicate pastries. My mouth watered, despite the fact that I had finished my mayo-laden sandwich about an hour before I had left work.

"Nothing for me. Tha—" Ryan stopped speaking, her lips slightly parted and glistening in the soft light of the living room. She took in the pictures just as I had, then I followed her eyes upward and noticed for the first time that the home had white tin ceiling tiles that I had previously seen only in photographs. Ryan then walked over to the fireplace, her hand outstretched, to touch the mantel. She stopped just short of it and turned toward Mrs. Margolis.

My own fireplace mantel was plain and unassuming. The only thing placed on it was a pair of ornate candlesticks that my grandparents had carried with them from Mexico. Mrs. Margolis's mantel was obviously the focal point of the room. Someone had taken great care to make it. I understood Ryan's reaction completely.

"It won't break. Go ahead and touch it," Mrs. Margolis said with amused pleasure in her voice.

I watched Ryan's fingers glide along the mantel's surface as if caressing a woman's body. I couldn't see her face, but I imagined her eyes were closed. Muscles flexed in the back of her arms as she leaned close to the mantel as if to smell the wood. She straightened and then faced me. Our eyes tangled and I felt the same jolt that had shaken me the first time I saw her.

"Beautiful," she said. Her voice sounded reverent and inexplicably sexual.

Mrs. Margolis's face flushed. Good Lord, surely she hadn't picked up on it too?

"Tony had his uncle carve that for me as a wedding present," Mrs. Margolis said. "When I walked into this room on my wedding night, I cried so hard that he thought I didn't like it."

"I think I've seen his work before." Ryan's voice was still quiet. "I rent an apartment in one of the old colonials off of Harrison. The house has similar woodwork throughout."

"It's probably one of Ted's. That was my Tony's uncle. He did a lot of work in this area. Most of it was destroyed by the flood, or by fire, but you can still find some of it. And there's this house. If you want to take a look upstairs, the crown molding is exquisite, especially in the children's rooms."

Emotions played across Ryan's face. Like a child offered freedom in a toy store, she asked, "May I?"

"Of course you may. It'll keep you from being bored while Mia and I go through Tony's desk. But before you go, I have something else you might be interested in." Mrs. Margolis sat down on her couch and lifted the lid on the trunk that also served as her coffee table. She pulled out a large coffee-colored photo album.

"Here, let me help you with that," Ryan said as Mrs. Margolis's arms quaked with the weight.

"My Tony loved taking pictures. His whole family did." She indicated the photos on the walls. "I never had much of a family myself, so I liked putting those up to remind me what a real family life should be like. I tried creating that for my girls." She sighed. "There are pictures of Ted's work throughout this album, if you're interested."

"Yes, ma'am." The enthusiasm in Ryan's voice left no doubt that she was indeed interested. She sat down next to Mrs. Margolis and they studied the photos for a while. I was content to watch them until Mrs. Margolis said something so low to Ryan that I couldn't hear it. Ryan chuckled and I felt a ping of something close to jealousy, which made me feel really odd.

Mrs. Margolis patted Ryan's thigh and stood up. "You head upstairs any time you want." With a smile, she said, "Tony's desk is right through here, Mia," and I perked up at finally being remembered.

Ryan was so engrossed in the pictures that she didn't look up when we left the room. As we entered Tony's office, Mrs. Margolis said, "What a gorgeous girl."

"Yes," I agreed and hoped she was content to leave it at that.

Tony's desk wasn't the mess I had expected. Everything was neatly stacked in several cubbies, and I found myself wanting to call out to Ryan so she could see it too, but I didn't. Each document had been left in its original envelope. I pulled one out and deciphered the postmark; it had been sent twenty-five years earlier from Tunica, New York.

"I'm afraid he didn't throw anything away," Mrs. Margolis said.

"Don't apologize, that's a good thing. At least we know the documents are here somewhere."

"That's what I thought too. I think I have his system figured out: correspondence on one side, and finance on the other."

"See, you already have it narrowed down. Why don't we take a stack each and go back into the living room so we can have our coffee while we look for those stock certificates?"

I was a little disappointed to find Ryan gone when we returned to the living room. For the next hour, as we located the documents I needed, I could hear her slow footsteps above us. At one point she stopped walking for so long that I feared she had fallen asleep up there. Mrs. Margolis sipped her coffee, seemingly unconcerned that a stranger was wandering around her home unescorted.

When Ryan reappeared, she said, "Your home is amazing. The craftsmanship is just unique."

Mrs. Margolis beamed. "Thank you, I'm glad I'm not the only one that thinks so."

I made a mental note to add craftsmanship compliments to my mother's list of things to say when entering someone's home for the first time.

"Did you have a leak near the window in the attic bedroom?" Ryan asked.

"Yes, Tony had the roof repaired but I never got around to having the seal replaced."

"I could do it for you."

"Oh, Mia didn't tell me you were so handy."

I blushed. I wanted to assure Ryan that Mrs. Margolis and I had not been talking about her in her absence, but she didn't seem concerned, so I let it go.

"Why don't you work up a quote for me and I'll see if I can swing it this month."

"I can do that, but it'll just be the cost of parts. The labor will be my pleasure."

Mrs. Margolis started to protest, but Ryan held firm and as we all walked to the front door they arranged a date for Ryan to return and do the repair. Mrs. Margolis stood in the doorway waving as we pulled away from the curb.

"I'm sorry I didn't talk to you before I offered to help," Ryan said.

"Oh, don't apologize. I think it's fantastic."

"Really, then why were you so quiet in there?"

"I liked watching you with her."

She glanced sideways at me, her eyes large. "What do you mean?"

"I was proud that you were offering to help her."

I didn't feel at all embarrassed when the side of her face darkened in a blush. The scar moved back and I caught a flash of white that meant she was grinning. My heart shouldn't have warmed, my body shouldn't have tingled, but there was nothing I could do to stop either of those things. I wasn't even sure why I should want to.

CHAPTER FIVE

The inside of the truck cocooned us in a comfortable intimacy that I was afraid to breach with my voice. She seemed equally reticent, because she only nodded when I gave her my address. She was gripping the steering wheel tightly and I couldn't help but notice the muscles in her forearms. The dashboard clock glowed white to the right of her hands and I gasped.

"What is it?" Ryan slowed the truck immediately. "Did you forget something? Want me to turn around?"

"No, I just noticed it's nearly eight o'clock. I had no idea it was so late."

Ryan glanced at the clock as well. "It still looks like five. Gotta love summer."

"I'm a winter girl myself," I said. "All this sunshine kind of makes me depressed."

"Spoken like a true Portlander."

"Hey, what can I say? Sunshine is overrated."

"Ah, so I guess that means I won't ever catch you slathering your body down with oil and laying out in a skimpy bathing suit, huh?"

"Are you kidding? They'd probably call out the whale patrol." The words slipped out of my mouth before I could stop them.

Ryan was silent so long that I thought the comment had slipped by unnoticed. A frown creased her forehead in several places. "That's kind of harsh, don't you think?"

I think it's been established that I don't think. "I meant I haven't been in a bathing suit in a few years."

"Me either," Ryan said.

"Hey, have you had dinner yet?" Again my words had somehow escaped my lips without me thinking about them. *Of course she hasn't had dinner yet, you idiot. She's been with you.* "What I mean is, I would love to thank you for your time. There's a great little restaurant not too far from my house and they have the best pasta sauce I've ever tasted."

"You don't need to do that," she said with no trace of a smile on her lips.

"I know."

The ensuing silence in the cab of the truck was almost more than I could bear. I couldn't tell her that I didn't want to go home to that house, to that little horror of a dog, to that empty, hard bed, without talking about Brenda. I wasn't even sure she was gay. I snuck a look at her profile.

"I have an idea," she said and pulled the truck over before I could even think to question her. She got out and jogged around the corner, leaving me sitting alone.

The engine ticked and I kept pace with it by drumming my fingers on my kneecap. I was somewhat familiar with the area because Brenda and I would take leisurely strolls to a wonderful little market around the corner that specialized in wine and cheese. At least I knew how to get home if she decided to leave my ass here. I jumped as a figure appeared in the driver's window. Rather, a torso. And then Ryan's face appeared in the window. Her smile melted any embarrassment I had been feeling.

"Can you open the door?" I saw, rather than heard, her say. I jumped to do so and noticed that she was holding something wrapped in paper in both of her hands. "Here, can you hang on to these for a minute?"

I reached out and took the warm bowls. The aroma told me what they were before I peeked into the wrappers. "Oh," I said as the scent of hot clam chowder and fresh baked bread filled the air. "These smell wonderful."

"Yeah, they do. There's a little park with a pond around the corner. Ever been there?"

"I don't think so."

"I found it by accident when I was riding my bike over here." She pulled the truck into a turnout. She opened her door and held out her hand in a silent gesture for me to hand her the soup. The idea of having dinner, even of the quick takeout variety, made me feel shy, but by the time I got out of the truck, Ryan was walking across the grass toward a mass of trees. I could hear the sound of splashing and the soft honk of ducks, but I was still left speechless when I rounded a corner and came to the small pond. Two ducks, along with several ducklings, floated on the surface.

Smiling like a parent at Christmas, Ryan said, "We got lucky. It's kind of late for ducklings."

My expression must have pleased her, because her smile widened and she indicated a bench. I stepped onto it and we both sat on the backrest. I imagined the displeasure on my mother's face if she ever found out I had done something so unladylike. The idea increased my enjoyment of the moment even more. I could feel the soup through the bread shell Ryan passed me and I pretended to bend my head closer to smell it in the hopes that she wouldn't notice how red my face had gotten. I picked up the long spoon and stirred my soup.

"Why so quiet? Not into clam chowder?" Her voice was so soft and so near to my ear.

"No, it's one of my favorites. Thank you for this. It was very sweet of you." I was having a hard time meeting her eyes. I forced myself to taste the soup. I must have moaned as it hit my palate because she said, "Good, huh?" evidently watching me.

The sound of the water, even the gentle sound of the mother duck quacking made the moment almost surreal. We sat for a few minutes, both enjoying the soup, before I felt obligated to speak.

"May I ask you a question?" The air probably didn't shift but it felt as though it did. "You did that last time. You stiffen when I ask if I can ask you a question."

"Do I?" She shrugged. "I think it might be because it's one of those things my father used to say right before he said something shitty."

"Did he do that a lot? Say shitty stuff to you?"

Ryan studied me as if trying to figure out whether she could trust me. I forced myself not to look away. "He did it enough. My mother and brother got the worst of it." She shook her head as if pulling herself from a bad memory. "Anyway, what were you going to say?"

It took me a moment to remember that I had wanted to ask her a question. "I was just wondering why you changed your mind about dinner."

"You want the truth?"

"Always."

"You looked lonely."

I blinked at her twice before turning away to look at the pond. I looked lonely? What kind of shit was that? Was this a pity meal? Did she think I didn't have friends or something? Hell, I had friends. I had Christina, Goody, Amy, and Dominique. Hell, Naomi counted as half a friend. I took another bite of my soup to hide the fact that I was probably about to cry. I really didn't have that many friends and I *was* lonely. The waistband of my skirt bit into my belly button. "So is that why you did this? Because you felt sorry for me?"

"Hey, look at me. Please?" To my surprise she reached out and gently turned my face toward hers. I doubt she meant for me to see so much, but in the instant before she spoke I knew she had been hurt by so many people she trusted that she protected herself by not getting too close. I knew all that in just a split second, and by the next second, I knew that she wanted to kiss me. "You don't need to be embarrassed, I'm lonely too. I like being around you, okay?"

"Okay," I said, but there was no doubt in my mind what I saw in her eyes. For the first time in my life, I had stared into the eyes of someone who lusted after me. Goody was right; it wasn't a fantasy. It was real, and if I wasn't careful, I was going to leave a telling wet spot on the top of the bench.

Aside from giving Ryan my address again, the ride to my house was quiet. It was evident something was bothering her, but I didn't know her well enough to ask her what was wrong. She pulled the truck to a stop in front of my house and I found myself studying it with her, trying to see what she was seeing.

"Shit," I muttered.

"What is it?"

"I forgot to leave the light on this morning. I thought I would be home long before dark."

"Here, let me walk you to the door."

I reached out to stop her from getting out the truck. I was going to tell her that I would be fine, but when my hand covered the back of hers, I forgot how to speak. Neither of us moved. The engine ticked. If it had been faster, louder, I could have mistaken it for my heart.

The dome light cast a cruel white light on us as Ryan opened her door and I had a fleeting glimpse of my darker hand covering her pale one before it slipped away. The door shut and I was left in darkness for a brief moment. Then the light came on again and Ryan was at my window, her forehead creased in concern as she bent down.

"Sorry, guess I was woolgathering." I got out of the truck and shivered. The house looked unwelcoming. Not only had I forgotten to leave the outside light on, I'd forgotten to leave lights on inside too. The line of the roof seemed drawn in against the silver of the darkened sky and it smelled like rain outside. I found myself walking slowly toward the front steps. I thought I heard a small yip and I imagined Pepito staring up at the door, waiting for Brenda to walk in carrying her gadget bags and a treat for him.

"Nice house," Ryan murmured at my side.

"Thanks. I've only lived here for two months."

"The neighborhood seems quiet. Mine is full of college students. Someone's probably blaring music out their window right now." She was actually making small talk—trying to, anyway. But she was no better at it than I was, because she hadn't left me with anything else to say to that.

"Would you like to come in?" I offered. "Maybe have some coffee?"

"No, I better not."

"Oh yeah, I forgot you need to get the truck back." I fumbled to get my key in the doorknob. There was an inexplicable heaviness in my heart. "I…thank you for taking me to Mrs. Margolis's, and for dinner."

I could barely see her outline in the dim light. It unnerved me that the shadows were hiding her scar. It was as if, in the few minutes I had taken my eyes away from her, something of her had already disappeared. The night had grown so silent that I heard her breathing when it increased. I don't know why I did it, but I reached out to touch her face, to bring her closer to me. I told myself that I would give her a friendly peck on the cheek, but she took a deep breath and her arms went around me. I was enveloped by leather and a fainter paint smell and all conscious thought slowed as warm, moist lips captured mine in a kiss so insistent, so engrossing, that I almost forgot to breathe.

Someone made a noise and then all I heard was the sound of her jacket and my own heart in my ears. My hands found their way under her shirt and she inhaled sharply. Her back muscles rippled beneath my hands. She shivered and tightened her embrace. Every part of me was aroused. Her hands were in my hair holding the back of my neck. I could feel the door pressing into my back. I felt her lifting me, and then my skirt was up around my hips and her thigh was between my legs. I knew for a fact that it was me that whimpered now. She was strong, using gravity and my own body weight to drive me insane. I couldn't catch my breath or stop my speeding pulse and then her hands were at my hips, helping me to grind roughly against her. Warm fingers touched my bare sides.

I froze and wrenched my mouth away. "No. We have to stop."

"Open the door, please," she said against my temple.

I wanted to give in, wanted to continue to feel this good. Her strength and her need were almost too overwhelming. The idea of her touching me, of her feeling my love handles, touching them, made me shudder.

"I can't. I have a partner."

"A partner…what? Why would you…"

"I, that's not what I meant to say, She isn't here…I'm sorry. I didn't think this was going to happen."

"Your assistant was talking about your ex?"

"Yeah, but we haven't really finalized things. She's—out of the country."

The viselike grip Ryan had on my hips eased. I almost cried out when we were no longer in contact. She took a step back and I felt cold.

"You should get inside." Her voice was impersonal, much like the day we had first met. Standing there, feeling the cool air whip through my hair, I tried to figure out why I had said what I did. Yes, I did have a partner, one who had left me for five months. One who had broken my heart and claimed not to love me. And I had an attractive woman practically shaking with desire…for me. Hell, maybe it wasn't for me, but I was there and I'd had her in my arms, and I had fucked it all up.

"Ryan."

"Just go inside, Mia."

"I want to explain. Brenda—left me. We were together for four years. I haven't…I haven't been with anyone else in a long time. I didn't mean to lead you on."

"You don't have to explain. And you didn't lead me on. I misunderstood. It won't happen again."

"You're angry." I tried to reach up to touch her face again, only this time she stopped me. Her grasp was firm around my wrist.

"Don't." Her voice was harsh, and any arousal that still lingered in my body seeped away. "Just go inside. Please." I couldn't see her expression but I could hear the emotion in her voice. Not exactly anger, but a disappointment much deeper than being denied sex would warrant.

"I'm sorry," I said, and when she didn't answer, I unlocked the front door with shaking hands. As the door swung open, I turned to apologize again, but Ryan was jogging back to the truck.

I stepped into the house and shut the door behind me. I dodged Pepito's attempts to greet me and peered through the window. Ryan was slumped forward in her darkened truck. I had the fleeting thought that I should run out there and tell her that I had made a mistake. That I had felt more passion coming from her in those fleeting, heated moments than I ever remember having with Brenda.

The thought was shocking enough to make me step back from the window just in time to see the headlights come on. She pulled slowly away from the curb, almost as if she felt me willing her not to go.

❖

Pepito was so excited to see me that he nearly fell over twice. Both times I thought I heard his longest tooth, his left, click on the wood floor, acting as a sort of crutch. It took me a moment and two sniffs of the air to realize that he wasn't excited, he was angry.

"You little…" I muttered. "Bad boy, Pepito!"

I took a step toward him, but he was already hightailing up the stairs. I didn't have to walk far to find the little load—actually, a big one by Chihuahua standards—that he had left in the middle of the doorway to the den. "Damn it, that's just perfect."

I was on my way from the kitchen wearing rubber gloves and an apron, with a brand-new roll of paper towels tucked beneath my arm, when the phone rang.

My hello was probably a lot more abrupt than it would have been usually, so it was no surprise when the person on the other end hesitated before speaking. "Did I catch you at a bad time?"

I could have said yes and explained that I had to clean up dog shit, but I welcomed any excuse to leave the unpleasant task until it was a little less…fresh. She had said she would call, and for the most part, Brenda kept her promises. Well, there was the "till death do us part, love and honor" thing, so perhaps what I should say is she kept her less demanding promises.

"Glad you made it okay." I wished I could stop myself from sounding angry. I had been successfully hiding all the hurt of her exodus, but now, hearing her familiar voice sounding warm and relatively unchanged in my ear made me feel both livid and a little guilty about what I had just allowed to happen at our front door. And that made me even angrier. I wished that I hadn't answered the phone. "Can you hang on a minute? I just walked in the door."

"Sure, but remember the call is expensive."

I almost reminded her that she always expensed her calls while she was working, but it just wasn't that important anymore. I sat the phone down and took a deep breath. Mrs. Margolis must have dumped a pound of salt in those sugar cookies she fed me, because my skirt was now painfully constricting my waist. I unbuttoned it, reached into my purse, pulled out a Snickers, and kicked off my shoes. It wasn't quite nine yet, which meant that it was dinnertime in Fiji.

"I'm back," I said.

"So where've you been?" The question was casual and only slightly bored.

"I was at a client's. Why?"

"Oh, no reason. I called earlier and when I didn't reach you I called Christina."

"Oh?" I waited for her to comment on the button incident, but if she knew about it she didn't say anything. It didn't matter, really. If and when she did come back, if and when she did go to dinner at my parents', I was sure my mother would tell her all about it. "I haven't seen Christina since Sunday brunch, the day you left."

"You two mad at each other?"

"Look, Brenda, is this why you called? To discuss if my sister and I are mad at each other?"

"No, I called because I told you I would."

"For some reason, I thought you'd call the day you got there, not two weeks later. What, too busy to let me know you'd made it in okay?"

"I left you a message saying I had made it. Didn't you check your voice mail?"

I winced. I hadn't checked the voice mail. Brenda had always checked the voice mail and told me if I had a message. "No, I forgot."

"I see. I left a message when I got here and I said I would try you again in a few days. Tonight was the first night I had free."

I found myself wondering why her nights were so busy and the dull pang in my gut kept me from asking her. "Well, I'm glad you made it. Thank you for calling me."

"Mia, can we talk, please?"

"No," I said as firmly as I could.

"No?" Brenda sounded shocked.

"You left, Brenda. You made the decision without talking to me about it."

"So, I guess you meant it when you said that you wouldn't wait for me, huh?"

I hate to admit to this, but I liked the sound of bewilderment in her voice. I liked it because it meant that I wasn't the only one who was hurt and confused. "I wasn't the one unwilling to talk. I wasn't the one waiting till the last minute to spring a five-month trip halfway around the world on you."

"I know I could have handled that better."

"Better? You didn't handle it at all."

"You're angry."

"I'm pissed," I corrected and I realized that it wasn't an exaggeration. I was pissed at Brenda, so pissed that I didn't even want to talk to her. "Look, let's not do this. Thank you for calling me. I'm sorry I missed your message from earlier this week, but right now I have to clean up the temper tantrum your dog left on the floor."

"Mia..."

I said good night, pushed the end button, and stood staring at the wall. I couldn't help feeling I should be more hurt, more angry, and more heartbroken. Instead, most of what I felt was embarrassment. Embarrassment for the things she had said to me before she left. *That's not right, is it? I should feel something more, shouldn't I?*

I was still holding the phone, and when I pressed the receiver to my ear, sure enough, I recognized the broken dial tone that was supposed to alert me to the fact that there were messages. The first was from the gardener informing me that he would be out later that week to drop off his invoice. I assumed said invoice was still in the mailbox since I had neglected to pick that up too. The next voice mail was from my sister, asking if I wanted to go shopping tomorrow. Just as she was about to hang up, she hesitantly tacked on that Ned's eye was fine and she hoped I wasn't embarrassed, because no one blamed me for anything.

Had she not heard what I told her husband? How could she not notice the way we couldn't be in the same room together without him gawking at my chest? Had she just let Ned off, or was she in denial? Even as a small child, my sister never held a grudge. One minute she would be mad at me about something, and the next she wanted me to play with her. I supposed I should be thankful she wasn't blaming me.

I was pretty sure I wouldn't be so lucky with Ryan. She had every right to be angry with me, but I didn't regret stopping things before they got out of hand. I wasn't Goody. I would never be able to handle a one-night stand.

I dropped the phone back into the cradle and was halfway to the bathroom before I remembered that Pepito had left me with one more chore to do before I could slip off into solitude.

Chapter Six

I abhorred the mall on Saturday afternoons. It wasn't just the fact that it was teeming with kids wearing clothes that cost too much and attitudes that make me want to hurt them on principle, it was the smell and the noise, and the fact that I was beginning to be treated differently.

Case in point: Christina had gotten to the mall before I did. Instead of waiting in her car as I would have, she decided she would mosey on in. I knew where to find her. Christina was predictable. Her first stop was Gap Kids and her last was Nordstrom. I didn't mind either of those stores; it was the ones in between that gave me the trouble. Sure enough, I spotted her curly blond head bobbing amongst the racks in Anne Clipper. If you've been in that store more than once, then you already know what my problem was. They hire freshman coeds, who probably couldn't afford their clothes without the employee discount and a red tag sale, to stare down their noses at the customers who pay their wages.

I considered waiting outside in the hope that some demon would possess Christina and convince her to release whatever garment she had latched on to and leave the store without prodding. *Yeah, right.*

A chime sounded as I walked across the threshold of the store, but neither Christina nor the young sales clerk helping her looked in my direction.

Christina's back was to me, but I could see that she was holding a garment out in front of her. The sales clerk, Tiffany according to her badge, was listening with grave seriousness to something my sister was saying.

"Yeah, I've tried that one on. It does run a bit big." She took the hanger from Christina and held it up to her own chest. "I could bring you a zero too."

Christina looked at the handkerchief-sized dress a little bit longer. "I would hate for the waist to be too big, so maybe you should."

A two? And who the fuck wears a size zero? That's fucking ridiculous. I rolled my eyes and folded my arms in front of my chest. My stomach was growling and Christina hadn't even started trying on clothes yet.

"Uh, excuse me, I'm with a customer here. If you'll wait for a few moments, one of my coworkers…" The look of utter annoyance on Tiffany's face rankled. If I were Goody, I would have given her a piece of my mind. If I were Christina…well, she probably wouldn't have ignored me in the first place.

I was about to tell her I was waiting for my sister when Christina turned around and saved me the trouble. "Oh, Mia! I was wondering where you were. What do you think of this?" She snatched the hanger from Tiffany and held the dress out in front of her for my review.

I'm not sure if she didn't realize I was still looking or she just plain didn't care that I saw her, but Tiffany looked at me from the tips of my shoes to the top of my hair, the expression on her face as clear as if she had pulled out an Etch A Sketch and written it there. *What is she asking her for?*

I took the dress from her and pretended to contemplate my words. "To be honest, it looks like something someone half your age and with little education would wear." I handed the dress back. "Where's Justin?"

"Mama's keeping him." Christina twisted her mouth. "You're probably right, I bet this color would make me look fat."

Tiffany didn't bother to hide her glare, which pleased me.

"Oh wait, take a look at this." Christina ran away from me and was back a few seconds later carrying a dark brown suit. The cut was nice enough, but the color was all wrong for my complexion. It would make me look washed out. I took it from her and glanced surreptitiously at the tag. It should fit.

"Okay, I'll try it on," I said even though it was the last thing I wanted to do. I had learned a long time ago that the quicker I had a bag—any bag—in my hand, the sooner we were kicking back in the food court snarfing down burgers.

"We have some larger sizes in the back," Tiffany said in apparent innocence.

"That won't be necessary. This should fit fine."

"I'll be right back. I saw a blouse that would look great with that suit." Christina ran off and I followed Tiffany into the fitting room and shut the door behind me. A few moments later a brown silky thing was tossed over the door and Christina slammed into her own narrow little box.

I stood in front of the mirror and looked hard at myself. Why had I come to the mall on a Saturday when all I really wanted to do was curl up on the couch and watch a good movie? *You know why you're here. Because that house is getting lonely and that dog gives you the willies.* I unbuttoned my white shirt. There was something heavy sitting on my chest. It had been there since the conversation with Brenda. It wasn't so much that I missed her. I did, sort of. But more than anything, it was that shadow of a doubt that was there. The feeling that maybe she was right…about everything.

I yanked my shirt off and glared at my double D's. It didn't matter if she was right; she was wrong in how she handled it. She was wrong in every aspect and she cheated on me. *Did she? You don't know that. You just accused her of that because you needed to believe that she was leaving you for a reason.*

"How's it going in there?" Tiffany actually sounded concerned. *Probably scared I'm going to have a heart attack in her dressing room.*

"Fine," I bit off as I pushed off my slacks. Brenda had cheated on me; I could sense it. There was no point talking myself out of it now.

"Oh, damn it. The waist is too big on this one too," Christina said just loud enough that the people in the next store would have heard.

"On the zero?" I said incredulously as I tried to pull the skirt up over my hips.

"Clothes are getting so damn big these days," she said with a note of satisfaction that made my skin crawl.

For a brief instant I hated my sister. I would have given anything for it to have been her standing in front of the mirror, avoiding her own reflection. I wanted her to know what it felt like to have to look at herself with a skirt stuck halfway up her thighs and her tits billowing up and out of a bra that had fit fine the week before.

"Do you have it on yet? Let me see."

"I'm fine and I'm already out of it. I'm going to take it."

"Why didn't you let me see, Mia? That's why the button popped off the last dress." I thought I heard someone snort, but it was so soft that I could have imagined it. I tossed the suit jacket on the chair and gritted my teeth.

"It fits fine. I was bloated and PMSing; I told you that."

I heard Christina quietly telling Tiffany that she couldn't fit her dress, but that I would be taking my outfit.

I found myself thinking of Ryan's lean frame as I dressed. Not only would she never shop in a store like this, but I doubt she would allow herself to be shamed into wearing clothing she didn't like. I found myself wondering what she did with her Saturdays. I would bet dollars to donuts she didn't spend it shopping with her younger sister. No, Ryan was probably languishing in bed somewhere. Or at the gym working out, or shopping at Whole Foods or some such place.

"You almost done in there? I'm getting hungry."

"Yeah, I'll be out in a minute, Christina." My voice had grown sharp with frustration. After I heard her leave, I opened the dressing-room door to let air cool my moist face. As I sat down to put my shoes on I told myself, a little less salt and a lot more water, and that suit will fit.

I stayed in the dressing room until I felt reasonably calm. When I came out Christina was looking at a rack of clothing close to the front door of the store. Tiffany didn't ask me if I had found everything okay, nor did she ask me if I wanted to sign up for a store credit card. Too bad, I would have liked to have gotten ten percent off $569.

"I'm going to run over to Abercrombie," Christina called out.

"I'll meet you over there." I reached in my pocket for six one hundred dollar bills and set them on the counter. Tiffany took the money as chimes signaled that Christina had left the store.

"Fourteen days," I said.

"Fourteen days?" she repeated.

"That's how long I have to bring this suit back before they pay you your commission. Right?" I got little pleasure out of seeing her mouth fall open, but I pretended to smile as I thanked her. I took my bag and tucked the receipt into my pocket. "I'll be sure to write in to the store and let them know how *helpful* you've been."

I rushed out the door so fast that the chimes barely had time to register my exit. I made myself hold my head up, content in the fact that, from behind, she couldn't see the one angry tear I was unable to confine.

❖

When I look in the mirror I see all of my imperfections. A dimple here, a pooch there, maybe the slightest hint of a wrinkle. But Pepito, with his skinny shaking body, his cross-eyed glare, and his oblong teeth, didn't suffer from any of my issues.

I stayed in my bed, transfixed, five minutes after I should have already been in the shower. Why? I'll be frank; Pepito was scaring the shit out of me. Even before Brenda left he had been a source of strife between us. The fact that he was a gift from one of her model friends was one thing, the fact that he was not an attractive dog made things even more difficult. Calling him ugly made me feel bad, but Pepito was pretty hard to look at.

Brenda wanted to let him sleep at the foot of our bed. Because I secretly feared he would creep up and bite me, or worse—lick me on the lips while I was sleeping—I had put my foot down. We compromised by allowing him to sleep under our bed on one of our fluffiest towels. My mother would keel over and die if she knew one of her housewarming gifts had become a pallet for a dog.

With Brenda gone, I was tempted to lock him out of the bedroom. I had contented myself with placing a cashmere sweater in a box for him to sleep on. The sweater was one of Brenda's favorites. I hoped he ruined it. Pepito was the reason I was going to be late for my appointment. He was standing in front of the mirrored closet door, shivering. Maybe it was swaying; I couldn't tell. He would also periodically lick his lips. I let this behavior go on for as long as I could before I forced myself to interrupt.

"Hey?" He turned around so fast that I could tell he had forgotten I was there. He whined a little and looked at me with the desperate eyes of a meth addict before turning back to the mirror.

"This is ridiculous," I groused and forced myself upright.

Pepito began to prance like he did for Brenda when she came home to give him his evening treat. He never pranced for me; hell, he really only did it for Brenda when he wanted something.

"What is it? Do you want to go in there? Brenda isn't in there. Trust me, she's so far out of the closet it's not even funny." I slid the closet door open and Pepito skittered to the side so that he could continue to look at himself. "Okay, so what do you want?" He licked his lips. "Work it out, Pepito. I've got to pee."

I gave him a wide berth but kept the door open as I entered the small bathroom. I was sitting on the toilet, wishing I had closed the door, when it dawned on me that Pepito was gazing—no, making goo-goo eyes—at himself. My jaw dropped as the most unattractive dog I had ever seen gazed ardently at his own reflection. I would have laughed if there wasn't something so *not funny* about it.

"You're weirding me out, you know that?" I kicked the door to the bathroom shut despite the fact that by doing so, I would turn the small space into a steaming-hot hell.

I showered quickly in order to make up for time lost lying in bed. It wasn't just Pepito that had caused me to loiter. After drowning my sorrows with french fries and a double-patty cheddar cheese hamburger from the mall food court, I had driven home and called the gym to schedule a free consultation. I then spent the rest of the weekend feeling sorry for myself and trying to ignore the fact that a six-hundred-dollar suit—a suit I didn't particularly like, nor fit into—was hanging in my closet.

By the time I went to bed I had made up my mind that I was not going to take that suit back. I was going to lose the weight. I was going to wear that suit back into that store and show Tiffany that she had been wrong when she hinted that I might need a larger size. I wanted Brenda to come home and see how much better I looked when she wasn't around. And most of all, I wanted this feeling of self-pity to leave me the hell alone.

After showering and dressing, I took one last look at Pepito as I walked out the door. He had lain down, his scruffy chin resting on the few wispy hairs covering his paws. I really didn't want to leave him in my room; I had a strong suspicion he had been getting busy with one of my shoes, despite the fact that Brenda claimed he had been fixed. He whined a little as I padded by, but I ignored him.

The bus ride downtown took all of ten minutes. I tried to return the cheery "have a nice day" from the driver, but my stomach was tied in knots. As I approached the doors to the gym, I saw two women jogging on the treadmills through the large glass windows. Both of them looked great. That, at least, was comforting. They were in there jogging on those damned treadmills pretty much every day and I couldn't help but wonder, *Is it worth it? Do I really have to run in place for an hour every morning to look like that?*

Neither of them looked happy. They looked resigned. Not even a happy resigned, just a tired kind of *I'm here, might as well do it* resigned. Surely there had to be a happy medium, a—

"Miaaa, hiiiii." The woman I assumed was Selena Sanchez—no relation—walked up to me with her hand out. Sanchez had to be her married name because Selena looked about as Hispanic as lunch at Taco Hell. "I'm so glad you made it. I left a message with your assistant this morning, but he said you hadn't come in yet."

Ah great, now that Goody knew I was working out, he would ride my ass daily about how it was going. "Oh, no. I came straight here." I already regretted making the appointment with the trainer, but I figured I'd let her tell me what to do, then do my own thing with the equipment I had at home.

"No problem," she said with too much enthusiasm. "Why don't you get changed and I'll show you the gym."

I pushed into the women's locker room. The gym, as Selena called it, was about the size of my new office. I'm exaggerating, but not by much, which meant the locker room was about the size of my coat closet. I was grateful no one else was in the room because we would probably end up bumping elbows as we tried to change. The fear that the door would swing open, leaving me bare assed and visible to anyone walking by, motivated me to get into my gym clothes in record time. My forehead was already damp when I returned to Selena.

"I was starting to worry about you in there," she gushed and led me to a seat in a tight little corner, behind a tree of coats and sweatshirts that had probably been hanging there since winter. "First thing we're going to do is get some info about you, okay? If you'll just sign here and here first." She handed me a clipboard. "This is just saying that you have no known heart conditions or physical problems that you aren't telling me about."

I squinted at her white teeth and considered telling her I wasn't feeling well. "I, uh, don't want to sign up or anything yet. I just want to try things out, see if I like it."

"I know, but we have to do this for insurance purposes. You know, in case you keel over and die while you're working out, so your family can't sue us."

I looked at her until her smile faded. "My family wouldn't believe I was in a gym in the first place."

She tittered as if I had made a joke, and I felt bad. This woman was offering me her services for free. It's not as if she had forced me to come in here, I had called her and asked for an appointment. What could it hurt to at least make the best of it?

It's not as if a little exercise was going to kill me, right?

CHAPTER SEVEN

"That bitch tried to kill me!"

"Stop exaggerating," Goody said and frowned at some imagined imperfection on in his right thumbnail.

I stopped dumping Equal into my coffee long enough for him to see the look on my face, the soggy wet hair, smudged mascara, and lipstick that no doubt looked like it had been applied by a three-year-old. "Do I *look* like I'm exaggerating?"

I could have scripted his reaction. One well-manicured hand clutched at the break-room counter as he doubled over, laughing. Goody did nothing halfway. When he laughed at you, he really made sure that you felt like a total idiot. *Great, my day is now complete and it isn't quite seven a.m. yet.*

"She sounds so nice on the phone," he said between guffaws.

"Nice, my ass. Do you know what she had me do? She had me run on the treadmill for, like, twenty minutes. I'm up there loping along like a giant fool, my tits were…" I stopped mid-sentence because a female broker named Irene came in and put her lunch in the refrigerator. She looked at Goody and me, rolled her eyes, and walked out of the break room.

"What's her problem?" Goody asked.

I shrugged. "Large stick up her ass. All brokers are like that the first couple years in the business."

"You weren't."

"Yes, I was. You just didn't know me then." I searched the cabinet for a box of Pop-Tarts I had tossed there when I was in my last "no sugar, no flour, no white rice" phase. I grinned like crazy when I found the box. Strawberry, my favorite.

"You know, I wouldn't have minded so much if I wasn't running next to two skinny girls with track suits on right in front of the window on Fourth Street. I mean, who in the heck puts a gym in a fishbowl where the whole damn world can see you?"

"I don't know, I think my gym is like that too. As a matter of fact, every gym I've ever been to has been like that." Goody looked like he was having a hard time keeping himself from laughing at me.

"It wouldn't have been so bad if I hadn't seen someone I know."

"Who?"

"Ryan," I admitted after some hesitation. I wasn't going to tell him about the kiss. If I did, he would hound me, wanting to know what I was going to do about the situation. The truth was, there was nothing I could do. Ryan had made it clear when she walked away from me that she wasn't interested in baggage, and against my will I had acquired lots.

"She was standing out front. I think she might have caught the bus in because she was walking from that direction." I frowned, remembering how my heart had swelled when I saw her, making me think I was truly having a heart attack. Selena's voice had faded into the background, and I grunted my answer to one of her inane questions about my job as I watched Ryan walk toward me.

The way a woman walks is usually not the first thing I notice. But Ryan had such long legs and such a beautifully shaped body, I found myself trying to dissect what it was about her that had made me want that kiss so badly.

"Wow, you're really picking it up there," I heard Selena say, but I wasn't really listening. Even though Ryan wasn't looking in the window of the gym, I realized that she would have to walk straight toward me to get into the building. My heart rate increased two notches.

"So what is it that you do, exactly?" Selena asked.

Ryan would look up at any moment now, see me running on this treadmill, and she would think what? Maybe she would smile and I would wave with casual indifference and try not to go flying off the back of the treadmill.

"I'm a financial advisor," I said between huffs.

Ryan wasn't looking my way, but I could see that she would probably do so at any moment. She would have to look up in order to open the door and then she would see me trotting along. My thoughts were interrupted when a guy who had been walking behind her sped up, as if to catch up with her. The idea that he was hitting on her made me grip the bars of the treadmill harder.

"Let me know if you feel like you're going to pass out," Selena said.

I wanted to tell her that I had passed that stage ten minutes ago, but I kept running. Sweat rolled down my temples and a twinge was beginning in my knee. And of course my chest, even with the sports bra, hurt. When the man reached out as if to grab Ryan's arm, I almost stopped running; Ryan jerked her arm away and turned around, her body tensed for a fight. I don't know who was more relieved, me or the guy who was about to get slugged, when her body relaxed. He laughed and said something to her that elicited a hug. The guy pointed, and instead of continuing toward me, Ryan walked off with him. The machine beeped, telling me I had completed my run. Selena was so impressed that I had finished, I almost believed she had placed a bet on how long I could survive.

Goody made a little jumping move that reminded me of Pepito. "I think you're stalling. What happened when she took you to Mrs. Margolis's? What did you two talk about?"

I was saved from having to answer because Jackson's assistant, Robin, walked into the room carrying an empty water bottle with red lipstick and God knows what else crusted around the opening. "Excuse me," she said and pointed with the bottle toward the sink.

I moved out of her way, tucking my Pop-Tarts box protectively against my breast.

"You still eat that crap?" she asked while sticking her bottle beneath a stream of water.

"Yup." The question would have annoyed me, normally, but I was grateful we'd moved on from the topic of Ryan.

"So?"

"So what?" I tried to keep the annoyance out of my voice, but I don't think I was successful. One of the reasons we didn't hire Robin when Henry's longtime sales assistant Eleanor retired was Robin's propensity for gossip. A broker has to be able to trust her or his sales assistant implicitly. I trusted Goody with two exceptions: his taste in men and his taste in friends.

"Goody told me that you went home with that construction worker?"

"I didn't tell her that." Goody's denial was too feeble to be believed. "I just said she gave you a ride home."

"Same thing," Robin said.

"Glad to hear I'm all you can talk about when you're off work, Goody."

He shrugged, unperturbed by the scathing look I shot his way.

"The 'construction worker' was kind enough to take me to my client's house because I had taken the bus to work," I informed both of them. "And yes, she did take me home…"

"You mean she waited for you?" Goody did his little excited jumpy thing.

I didn't want to answer, I really didn't, but something about the way he was looking at me kind of made me feel proud. "Yeah, she did."

"So what's she like?" Now Robin was looking at me the same way Goody was. I felt like I did when I was thirteen years old and everyone at school found out that the popular boy had asked me to the dance. Later, I discovered that he had bet his friends that I would let him touch my, by then, 32D's. He had lost that bet and that was the end of my popularity.

"She's very nice. Kind of quiet." My Pop-Tart devoured, I got on tiptoe trying to find something else to shove into my mouth.

"Is it true she was a fashion model?" Robin asked. "I hope it's true. I love pageants!"

"Are you freaking serious?" I abandoned my search for more sugar in order to turn and glower at Robin. "Where would you get a crazy-ass idea like that?"

Robin looked at Goody, who had the sense to blush.

With a hint of defensiveness, he said, "Cathy, in the cage, said they heard her talking on the phone about not being in pageants anymore."

"We think some crazed fan stalked her and cut her face to stop her from competing. You know those Texans are serious about their pageants," Robin said.

"Look, I don't know her well. Hell, I barely know her at all. But I can't imagine her being in any kind of beauty pageant. Did you see the size of the woman's tool belt?"

"That doesn't mean anything. They've got this chick on Fine Homes Network that used to be a fashion model, and now she can build a house in, like, two days," Robin said with the surety of an expert.

"Fashion models and beauty pageant contestants are two different things." I was trying hard not to sound condescending. "Figure out which one she's supposed to be and then ask her about it. Don't blame me if you end up with a screwdriver broken off in your…"

I caught my breath because Ryan had just walked past, probably on her way to the new office space. She glanced casually into the room, so she must have seen me standing there, but she continued on without speaking.

I pushed past Robin and Goody and walked out into the hall. Fashion models didn't move like Ryan; strong, purposeful, not the least bit interested in a man's approval.

"Hey, Ryan," I called out. She turned around and I was acutely aware of Goody and Robin behind me. Part of me was glad that they were there—that is, until both of them joined me in the hall like two children waiting to see a fight on the playground. I tried to smile at her, but I saw Goody give a quick shake of his head in my peripheral vision. At best, I had lipstick on my teeth; at worst, bits of Pop-Tart were stuck between them. "I just wanted to, you know, thank you again for taking me to Mrs. Margolis's."

"You're welcome," she said.

After a long pause Ryan pointed toward the room she had been working on for the last few months. "I should probably get to work."

"Oh, of course." She turned away and I heard myself call out to her again. "Ryan, I was wondering if I could take you to lunch some day. You know, to thank you." *And to apologize for leading you on and to find out if there's any possibility of a repeat and to find out how you got that scar…*

Her face went from surprised to unreadable.

"You don't need to do that, I enjoyed myself."

Later I would think of all sorts of snappy comebacks, but right then I could think of absolutely nothing to say. Robin's ridiculous theory about Ryan being a beauty pageant contestant seemed so, well, Christina. Still, I couldn't help wondering what someone like Ryan would do for the talent part of the competition.

I must have stared at her too long because Ryan's next words were rushed, as if she wanted to get away from me. "It's going to get loud in there today, but after that, it's just painting and a few touch-ups. I'll be out of your hair in a week or two."

"Good," I said, and then almost choked on my words. "I don't mean good you'll be out of my hair. I mean, you're not in my hair at all."

"It's a nice office. I understand why you would be excited to move in."

"Thanks for letting me know about the noise."

"You're welcome," she said and walked away.

I had almost convinced myself that I had imagined the awkwardness of our conversation, the curtness of her tone, and the fact that she walked away faster then I thought humanly possible. But then I turned around and saw the look of false compassion on Robin's face and the embarrassed flush on Goody's. I felt like I had just been dumped in front of my entire senior class. The worst part of it was, I couldn't exactly blame her.

❖

A week and a half later I was forced to admit that Ryan was going out of her way to avoid me. I saw her, of course. She was working right next door, but the door was often closed, even though I heard no loud hammering inside. The wonderfully accented "hi's" had been replaced with strained smiles or dips of the head. It was as if the kiss we'd shared at my front door had never happened.

"I rescheduled your appointment with Selena for one thirty today," Goody announced from the doorway. He didn't come in and sit down as he normally would have, probably because I had been in a foul mood all morning. I removed the pen clenched between my teeth.

"I didn't mean for you to reschedule it for today. I meant," I waved my hand limply, "you know, some other day."

Goody frowned and leaned his shoulder against the door frame. "You want me to call her back?"

"No, I should go." The thought of Selena's constant prattle set my teeth on edge, but I was reluctant to admit that I hated the gym; Goody never missed a chance to work out.

"Hey, what's with the sad look?" Goody's voice sounded

concerned, which made me think that some of what I was thinking had become evident on my face.

I shrugged. "I just feel so inept. Everything she asks me to do just feels like…I don't know, such a trial. I can't believe you love this stuff."

Goody walked into the office and shut the door behind him. "Is that what's really bothering you? You've been quiet since Monday."

He sat down in the visitor chair across from me, his customary perch during our gossip fests. But he didn't pull out his nail file as he usually did; for once, I had his full attention. "Something else happen with Ryan?"

"No, how could it? She's been avoiding me all week. I can't say as I blame her."

"I knew it." Goody leaned forward and stage-whispered, "You slept with her, didn't you?"

"What the hell do you take me for? I hardly know her." But my face heated because he wasn't far from right. In fact, if it wasn't for my own guilty conscience, I could have slept with her. The idea was so unexpected, so unlike me, so unbelievably hot, that I bit my bottom lip.

Goody caught his breath. "Oh, my God. Was it good?"

"Okay, listen to me. I—did not—sleep with her."

"I don't believe you." His eyes were wide now. "I think you slept with her and you're ashamed to tell me."

"Goody, I swear to you on my aunt Virginia's homemade enchiladas, I didn't. I wanted to, but something happened and it didn't work out."

Goody sat back in his seat and I stood up, and walked to the window. I hadn't done anything with Ryan, but I felt as guilty as if I had, and I was still thinking about the what ifs. The fact that she was treating me like a one-night stand didn't help matters.

When I finally turned, Goody was looking at me with such pity that I regretted telling him. "Sweetie, I'm so sorry. I'm sure she won't tell anybody."

"What are you talking about?"

"Hang on a second. Maybe I'm missing something here. Why are you upset, exactly?"

I took a deep breath. "I don't really know why I'm upset, but I can't help feeling like…I don't know, I messed something up."

"Okay, so I'm going to ask you straight up. Did you try to have sex with her and fizzle out?"

"Lesbians don't fizzle out. Damn it, all I did was kiss her. Hell, I don't even know if I was the one doing the kissing. I think I just stood there and she did all the work. Things got heated so fast I must have gotten scared. I told her about Brenda."

"Was that before or after cunnilingus?"

"I didn't have sex with her," I repeated through gritted teeth. Goody would never understand. To him, Brenda and I were separated; there was no reason for me to feel guilty, no reason for me to even have called off what no doubt would have been great sex. Why had I called it off? "I could have, I wanted to but—I just couldn't."

"You got scared, huh?"

"Yeah."

"Did she come on too strong? Start acting like she wanted to get married? What?"

"No, none of that. She just...I don't know. We were standing in front of my door and she kissed me and...I just forgot about everything...nothing else mattered. I just wanted—"

"Sex?"

"Yeah, but..." I almost said, *Something more than sex.* "Things cooled off fast when I told her about Brenda."

"She get mad?"

"Yeah, she kind of stormed off. I felt horrible."

Goody shrugged. "At least you told her. It's not like you slept with her and then told her, or you were lying there after, all hot and sweaty, and then told her; or worse, you were in the act and Brenda walked in or—"

"Goody, I get it. I'm sorry those things happened to you, but that would never happen to me."

"Really? Why is that? You weren't thinking about propriety when you were letting a woman you hardly know kiss you in front of your house. Anyone see you?"

"No, of course not." But of course I couldn't know that for sure. What if nosy old Mr. Gentry saw me, or Mrs. Ferguson down the block happened to be out walking her dog? What then?

"Sorry I'm not much help, *chica*. You should try to look at the bright side. If it gets back to Brenda, you can always remind her that you two were on a break. No such thing as cheating when you're on a break. Damn," Goody rose in one abrupt motion and started for the door, "I wish you had told me earlier. Lunch is going to be awkward."

I could tell he was waiting for me to ask. So I did. "Why?"

His shoulders rose in a sigh. "I asked Ryan to have lunch with me today."

"What? Why would you do that?"

"Because I want to get to know her. We rode up the elevator together and I noticed she wasn't carrying her lunch like she usually does, so I asked her to have it with me."

"You can't go to lunch with her. Tell her you can't make it."

Goody stared down his nose at me. "I will not. I want to go."

"But why? She's a she. What could you possibly—"

"Have in common?" Goody shrugged. "You're a she and we go to lunch all the time. I can have friends that are women, friends without benefits. Novel idea, huh?"

"If she says something about me, will you tell me?"

The question must have sounded pathetic, because Goody took pity on me. "Why don't you try to ask her to lunch again in a few days, you know, after things have cooled off? Maybe you're taking it the wrong way."

"If I am taking this the wrong way, I'm not the only one. You and Robin looked embarrassed when she turned me down."

"We weren't embarrassed for you, we were embarrassed—"

"*With* me. I know. It was like being turned down for the prom."

"Didn't you tell me you ended up making out with a girl at your prom?"

"Helena, my parents' gardener's daughter, she acted like it never happened the next day." I covered my mouth with my hand. Surely if it was a bad breath thing someone would have told me? I was about to do a puff and sniff, but I realized just in time that Goody would never let me live it down if he figured out what I was doing.

Goody looked at me oddly, but shrugged. "For what it's worth, I didn't ask her out to spy on you or to be nosy. I think she's a nice person and I don't have enough friends. Besides," he looked uncomfortable, "I think her boss is interested in me and if he asks me out, I want to make sure he's not a player."

I pulled my thoughts back into the present long enough to get the gist of what Goody was saying. Something about Ryan's boss. Had I actually ever seen someone who looked like they could be Ryan's boss? The only other person I had ever seen was… "Wow, he's very different from your usual pretty boys."

Goody shrugged. "Maybe a little."

Maybe a lot, I thought. It wasn't that Ryan's boss was unattractive. He was just different. Not as refined as Goody's usual. Maybe only a couple inches taller than Goody, never clean shaven, and in dire need of a good haircut. He was also thin. Where Goody's normal bedmates were well dressed, Ryan's boss wore the same attire as Ryan, T-shirt and jeans, right down to the tool belt. "So you think he's going to ask you out?"

"Yeah, I do. But I'm just starting to feel comfortable sleeping alone. I think it's going to be a while before I share my bed with someone again." Goody's face became serious. I had never seen him look that way when discussing a potential new date. "It's got to be something more than a fuck this time. You know what I mean?"

"Yes, I know."

Before I could step back into my office Goody said, "You don't need to worry about me having lunch with her. You know I would never say or do anything to hurt you, right?"

I nodded. I did know that Goody would never intentionally hurt me. He just had different ideas about privacy and dating than I did. I smiled and shooed him away from my door. "Have fun."

For the next few minutes I shifted back and forth between anger and annoyance at the knowledge that Ryan had accepted a lunch invitation from Goody and had turned me down flat. I pulled my compact from my briefcase to touch up my makeup. I moved the mirror to my lips and pursed them.

Ryan would be the second person who'd basically stopped speaking to me after one kiss. If I didn't know better, I'd think I was a bad kisser.

Surely someone would have told me after all these years if I was…right?

❖

All I wanted to do after my workout was sit behind my desk and kick off my high heels.

But when I spotted Jackson standing outside my office, reading from a piece of paper, I had to ask, "Can I help you with something?"

Jackson dropped the paper into Goody's in-box and leaned against the desk, his arms folded in a falsely casual pose. "Yes, I want to know how you did it."

"How I did what?" I said, not bothering to hide my exasperation.

"How you managed to go Business Formula and the rest of us keep getting turned down."

"The rest of us? Who else tried?"

"That's not the point. What do you have over Ralph Knight that he let you—?"

"Jackson, he didn't *let* me do anything. The Business Formula guidelines are clearly posted on the internal Web site. If you met the requirements, Knight wouldn't turn you down. Now if you'll excuse me." I turned toward my office only to have Jackson's hand on my shoulder bring me to an abrupt stop.

"Don't walk away when I'm speaking to you."

I had had enough. I dropped my bag and reached up to knock his hand away when I spotted Goody walking toward me with Ryan close behind. Even from a distance I could see the scowl on her face.

She pushed past Goody and in a voice powerful with emotion said, "Get your hands off of her."

Everything stopped. Even Goody was struck speechless. I lowered my hand and stepped away from Jackson. He stared at Ryan. That nasty little wormlike vein was working on the side of his head. "Mind your own business. You can start with my bookshelf if you need something to do."

"Don't tell her what to do," Goody said, after finding his voice. I don't know what possessed him; perhaps he didn't see what I did, that Ryan wasn't to be toyed with and that she meant what she said. I didn't sense that he was going to hurt me; or perhaps I was just so stunned that Ryan had gone from avoiding me to swooping in as my savior that I found myself a little numbed to the situation. But as Jackson stepped toward me, his finger rising again as if to continue his tirade, Ryan dropped the bag she was carrying, spun him around, and pushed him down the hall.

"Apparently no one ever taught you to keep your hands to yourself," she said.

"Oh shit," Goody whispered. I was incapable of speech myself.

Rick Parish, the young broker with the office closest to ours, came around the corner, probably on his way to the kitchen, and promptly changed his mind.

"So let me speak slowly," was the last thing I heard Ryan say before she pushed Jackson out of view. I heard a door slam and then there was utter quiet. "I wonder what that bastard did to her," Goody murmured from behind me.

"Who, Jackson?"

"No, whoever hurt her."

I couldn't guess the extent of the damage, but based on the little Ryan had told me about her father, I had a good idea who the "bastard" was.

Chapter Eight

I trudged down to Dynamic Body Fitness for my third and final workout of the week. Selena was with someone on the treadmill, but she stopped talking long enough to wave at me. Having to listen to her prattle while running on that treadmill was pure torture. As if she realized that I was about two seconds from darting out the fire exit, she kept watching me right up until I pushed the door to the women's locker room open and walked inside.

I was greeted by the sound of running water and female laughter. The scent of women's sweat and hand lotion assailed my nose, and my heart sank as three women, none of whom appeared the least bit disturbed by the fact that I had just walked in while they were undressed, did the "hello, stranger" bob of the head. I returned it and immediately locked my eyes on the floor. I sat down on the nearest empty bench, my gym bag beside me.

"I tried to get Linda in accounting to do it, but I think she's scared of Selena." A tall African American woman with legs I would kill for bent over to place a piece of clothing in her bag. She did so without bending her knees. I'm certain that if I ever tried to pull a maneuver like that, I would fall ass over teakettle. A shape like mine did not lend itself very well to balancing acts.

A woman I recognized as one of the assistants from the accounting firm on the same floor as Goldsmith walked into the lone bathroom stall and shut the door. It sounded like she barely had time to pull her workout shorts down before her pee came out in a rush. I listened with envy; I have what my mother calls a shy bladder. In other words, I have to wait until everyone is out of the bathroom before my bladder will allow me some relief.

I removed my jacket and hung it on a hook in one of the lockers. A quick look at my watch told me that I probably had five more minutes before Selena was done with her current client and came in search of me. I tried to look like I was in no rush while I gritted my teeth and prayed they would just hurry up and leave.

I heard Bold Bladder pounding on the huge roll of toilet paper until it must have turned around enough for her to tear off a few squares.

"Selena is a pussycat compared to the woman who used to teach boot camp before her. God, she was seriously ex-military and the biggest bull dyke ever." I glanced up at the speaker, a hippy brunette in tight leggings and a dingy T-shirt. She was walking away from me and therefore missed my offended look.

"What the hell was Selena's problem this afternoon? I think she was really trying to kick our ass."

"That's why they call it boot camp, girlfriend. 'Cause they're supposed to put a boot in your ass," the long-legged African American woman said matter-of-factly.

The two nearly dressed women showed no signs of leaving as their friend walked stiffly into the shower, giving credence to the idea that she still had a boot wedged firmly in her ass.

I jumped as she slammed the shower door shut. *Note to self: stick to mornings.*

I stood up to remove my pantyhose just as Bold Bladder stepped out of the stall and ripped her T-shirt over her head. I got a flash of a surprisingly toned tummy before I turned my back. What was it about this situation that made me so uncomfortable? I bit my bottom lip. It wasn't that I found any of these women even remotely attractive. I think most straight women would be shocked to find that the majority of gay women look at them as if they are another species, and therefore not really mating material. What made me uncomfortable was the fact that these women didn't know I was gay and would no doubt have thought twice about how easily they appeared nude in front of me. There was also the fact that I had trouble taking my clothes off in front of my own partner, let alone these strangers.

"We need to find another person. These prices are killing me. If we find one more, shit, maybe even two more, we could split the cost." I turned my back on the pair and reached beneath my sweater to unclasp my bra. I could take that off without any problems, but when I was left with only my sweater and the skirt I was wearing, I had no choice but to pull the sweater over my head. My back felt cold and I found myself wishing one of the women would continue with their mindless conversation so that the room wasn't so quiet.

I had almost finished dressing, and Bold Bladder and Bull Dyke Hater were primping in the mirror when African American Woman with the Long Legs came flouncing out of the shower. In one hand she had her white towel pressed primly against her chest and in the other she held a small bottle of something I avoided looking too closely at.

I stooped to tie my shoelaces, but not before noticing that she made no effort to cover herself, nor had she really bothered to dry her feet.

"All right, girlfriend," said Bull Dyke Hater, "we'll see you upstairs."

I gave the women just enough time to get out the door before I scurried after them to avoid making inane conversation with a naked woman.

Selena's male client had left and she appraised me for a moment, and then walked over to me with her hand outstretched. "Congratulations. You'll make it through your two-week trial membership. I was scared you weren't going to come back. I'm glad I was wrong."

"Yup, you were wrong. Here I am. So what are we going to do today?" I slapped my hands together. Run on the treadmill for a few minutes again? The balance ball? Whatever it was, I was ready. I had undressed in front of three women. Granted, they were very helpful in that they didn't show me the least bit of interest.

"Great, we can finish filling out your paperwork."

"Paperwork? I thought we did that already?"

"This is different. It's how we're going to measure your progress. Step into my office." Selena tittered at her own joke. Her office was a small corner of the gym that, although somewhat hidden by a shoji screen and a coat rack, was by no means an office. "We're going to start by measuring your body fat."

"Why do you need to do that? I already know I'm fat. That's why I came in."

Selena laughed. She had transformed from silly to all business in the space of a few seconds, and it was doing my head in. "You're not fat, just out of shape. We just need to know how far out of shape so we can create a game plan. Here we go." She moved the coat rack aside and revealed my worst nightmare, a scale similar to the one I had to step on for my annual Pap smear. "Why don't you hop up there and we can see where you're at."

"Do I have to? I mean, is that necessary?"

"I can't help you if you're going to hide from the scale."

"I'm not hiding from it. I don't need to see the number to know I need to lose the weight." What I didn't tell her was that I knew what the number was, I just didn't want her to see it. I had been watching that number creep up for months, right up until I trashed my scale in frustration.

"Okay, so if you already know the scale isn't going to be kind, why does it matter if you see the number?"

"I just don't want to see it and get discouraged."

This must have sounded reasonable to Selena, because she acquiesced. "I'll just measure your body fat, but hiding from the scale is never the way to go. At some point you need to get on it, if only to measure your progress. These are body fat calipers." She held up two plier-like devices that made me squirm much the way Dr. Rider did when I saw her approaching me with those cold-ass things she used for the Pap smear.

"Let's get your body fat measured and then we'll get going on the treadmill." I let her crimp, pinch, and measure to her heart's content. I was already dreading my workout, as I remembered that Bull Dyke Hater had implied that Selena wasn't in a good mood. I had probably made that mood that much worse by my refusal to cooperate.

"Okay, if you're ready, I'm going to step things up a notch today." I watched her walk away. *She's going to step things up? Oh boy.* I glared at the scale and followed her slowly toward the treadmill.

❖

It was almost three o'clock when I returned to the office. I hated exercise. I hated exercise on an empty stomach, and most of all, I hated Selena with a passion I usually reserved for the anchovies that Brenda insisted we add to our pizza. The only thing that brought me a glimmer of joy was the fact that it was Friday. I would have the whole weekend to veg out on the couch and eat whatever the hell I wanted.

My thoughts turned to Ryan as I tucked my gym bag beneath my desk. I hadn't seen her since the confrontation with Jackson on Wednesday. The new office space had been quiet with the exception of two electrical contractors who had come and gone.

I was actually happy when my phone rang, because I was beginning to feel morose. Before I could even utter my standard greeting, I detected the strains of tropical-sounding music and laughter. I toyed with the idea of hanging up and letting voice mail pick up when she called back. Instead, I gave my customary if not unenthusiastic, "Mia Sanchez."

"Hi, it's me. I've been trying to reach you at home all week." Brenda sounded annoyed.

"Sorry, I've been busy."

"Are you going out? I thought you were just avoiding me. Good for you, I'm glad you've finally got some kind of social life." She sounded so genuinely pleased that it rankled.

"Brenda, I have a meeting that I need to prepare for, so, do you need something?"

Brenda had either turned down the music or walked away from it, because the line grew so quiet that I wondered if we had been disconnected. "We really haven't had a chance to talk, Mia, and it's been almost four weeks since I—"

"Since you left? Walked out?" I filled in helpfully.

"Mia, let's not be childish about this."

"I'm being childish because I'm telling the truth?"

"I thought maybe you had gotten over being mad. I had hoped we could discuss things like adults."

I rubbed the bridge of my nose. I felt and looked, I'm sure, worn out. I had taken a long shower to help ease what I knew would be some sore muscles come tomorrow and I had yet to put my makeup back on. My hair was damp and my back felt like I had neglected to dry it completely when I put on my blouse. My pantyhose were still balled in my bag and my feet were moist and cramped inside my heels without them. I wanted to go home and I couldn't, not without explaining to Goody and not without blowing off quite a few phone calls.

"What in the world do you and I have to talk about? You left me, remember?"

"I didn't leave—"

"Brenda," I interrupted, and then I felt all the anger ebb from me as the realization of what I was going to say hit me like a ton of bricks. "I loved you. Our relationship may not have been perfect, but if we had problems you should have told me. Instead, you ran off to Fiji."

"Mia, I couldn't turn down this opportunity."

"Yes, you could have. You could have done a lot of things. You could have asked me to come for a little bit. You could have asked my opinion. But that's not what this is really about anyway. Fiji was just an excuse to do something that had obviously been on your mind for a while. You took the coward's way out of the relationship."

"I didn't know what else to do."

"You should have talked to me." I realized then that tears were coming down my cheeks. "You should have told me the truth. You should have told me you didn't like the person I had become."

"That's not true."

I ignored her vehement denials because I needed to get the words out. "You should have told me that it was over."

"Is it over?"

Now Brenda's voice sounded soft, almost pleading. For what, I wasn't sure. I didn't realize that this conversation would happen until just now. Or maybe I had; maybe that was one of the reasons I had been avoiding her phone call.

"It's been over for a while for you, hasn't it?" I asked.

"I never wanted it to be. I still remember how much fun we used to have when we hung out with Saundra and Nora."

I glanced at the photo on my bookshelf. How long had it been since I had talked to them? Well over a year. Brenda had been right, we had lost contact with most of our friends. I had become so engrossed in my work that there had been no time to really do anything together, let alone have a social life.

"Can't we, I don't know, discuss things when I get back?" Brenda asked.

Now she wanted to have a discussion? I felt the ache in my neck, the throb in my shoulders, and a worrying dull throb in my shins; but in my heart, I felt nothing. "I don't know that we have anything else to talk about."

"Maybe you could come down for a few days next week. We can talk about this in the evenings." I heard something in her voice, but it wasn't the desperation of a spurned lover, it was fear. I had forgotten how much Brenda hated to be alone.

"I can't. We're about to move into the new office space and I've picked up several new clients."

"Can I call you tonight?"

"I don't know what time I'll get home, Brenda. But you can try the house. I need to get back to work and you probably should too."

"Okay, I'll talk to you later. I hope you're around tonight." Her voice had dropped to low, sultry tones that, in the past, would have had me pinned to the couch, waiting for the phone to ring.

I still felt nothing. Perhaps I was just stunned or weary or something, but I responded with, "I can't say for sure, but I'll talk to you soon." I hung up the phone before she could say anything else.

I was grateful that Goody was gone from his desk, because if he had questioned me about the exact origins of my tears, I wouldn't have been able to give him a good answer. I pulled my compact out of my purse and began to reapply my makeup. What had just happened? What was wrong with me? When did the woman I spent four years of my life with turn into a stranger? I closed my eyes to try to calm myself; my whole world felt like it was on a Tilt-A-Whirl and I just wanted off.

❖

"That bastard got her fired!"

I looked up sharply. "What bastard? Who are you talking about?"

Goody marched into my office, his face flushed with anger and his fists gripped together in a tight little ball. "Jackson."

"Jackson is trying to get Robin fired?" Tension eased from my shoulders. I'd never understood why Jackson had hired Robin in the first place—the two seemed as mismatched as night and day—but I had never heard of any problems between them. I couldn't help but think that dislike of me was the one thing that they had in common.

"No. Ryan."

My face went slack. "Ryan? How can Jackson get Ryan fired? She doesn't work for him. She doesn't even work for Goldsmith." I remembered the altercation in the hall. *Oh, God no. Jackson couldn't be that fucking petty.* "What happened?"

"I don't know. I just overheard her arguing with her boss Steve, and then she just stormed out. She took all of her tools."

I'll never see her again. I was shocked at how distressed I was that

Ryan was about to walk—no, be pushed out of my life. "So she just left? Damn it, Goody, why didn't you come get me!"

"I tried," he wailed, but I was already running down the hall.

I skidded to a stop just outside Goldsmith's doors, and my heart threatened to leap out of my throat like a suicidal goldfish when I spotted her standing at the elevators. Her back was to me, her arms folded, a toolbox at her feet, and her head was down.

I heard the distant pinging of the elevator as it approached our floor. "Ryan?"

She turned away quickly. My heart stopped trying to escape from my throat and instead sank. She wouldn't look at me. This was my fault. No, this was Jackson's fault. In that moment I was closer to hating another person than I had ever been.

"Ryan, please let me talk to you."

"You already know? Bad news travels fast in your office, huh?" She was still avoiding my eyes, and from the sound of her voice, she had been crying.

"I'm so sorry. Please let me try to fix this."

The elevator slid open. Five or six people stared at me over her shoulder.

Her face had paled, making the scar on her right cheek appear vivid and cruel. Her eyes were red and swollen from tears and probably rough rubbing. The two swatches of nearly white hair that always worked their way out of her rubber band were in her face, and my fingers itched to push them gently back. She beat me to it.

"I am not a thief," she said with vehemence.

I didn't have to look to know that the bored faces inside the elevator had probably changed. This was different from the grind; this was drama, and they had front-row seats.

"I know you're not," I said. "I'm sure this is just a misunderstanding."

"A misunderstanding? How could it be? Something is missing in his office, and I was in there when he claims it disappeared."

"Let me talk to your boss. Explain to him what happened with Jackson; that you were only trying to stand up for me. He'll understand." The elevator door shut and I thought I heard laughter, which made me angry that someone would find Ryan's pain amusing.

"How can he, Mia? Any whisper of impropriety and my company has to react. Steve had no choice but to send me home. I can't work here anymore. Even if that paperweight thing shows up. The damage is done."

"But Jackson lied."

"I know." Ryan took a deep breath. "Thank you."

"For what?"

"For believing me."

"Of course I believe you. You don't strike me as a thief. And I know what an asshole Jackson is, especially when he feels he's been slighted. I had no idea he would stoop to this level to get back at you. I mean, it makes no sense."

"Revenge never does." Ryan's voice sounded calm now and the anger had receded slightly. Goody's words about revenge being the best way to get even came flooding back to me. I thought about Brenda then, and realized that I didn't want revenge or anything else from her. I just wanted Ryan to stop looking so devastated.

"Ryan? I never got a chance to thank you. You know, for telling him off for me. But I'm so sorry this happened to you."

"Don't worry about me, but you should be careful. Maybe have Goody take you home instead of catching the bus."

"He can't threaten my job," I said. "And I don't think he'll try anything physical. He's an asshole but harmless."

"He isn't harmless, Mia. I think that's obvious now." Her face softened. "People like that rarely mean to hurt anyone at first. They're just angry and reacting to it. If you don't tell them, if you don't make sure that they understand that there are repercussions for not controlling themselves…just promise me you'll be careful."

Her concern warmed me. "I promise. Please. Let me talk to your boss. Even if you can't work here, maybe he'll let you work at another building."

Ryan was shaking her head. "I can't. I got so mad that I said some things I shouldn't have. I doubt Steve will want to work with me again."

"But you're his best worker." My outrage surprised even me, and Ryan's smile, though brittle, lightened the heaviness in my heart.

"How do you know I'm his best worker?"

"I can tell. He trusted you there alone, and you do most of the work yourself. I figure you'd have to be his best worker."

Ryan sighed. "I used to be. Now I'm on leave until further notice."

"Don't you have a union or something?"

"I don't want to make Steve go through that. This isn't his fault. I should probably start looking for odd jobs until I can find something permanent." Ryan pressed the elevator button again.

She was already pulling away from me, her thoughts turning inward, making me feel powerless and empty inside. "Ryan, I have a cousin who owns a construction business. Let me call him. I also have some work that needs to be done on my house."

I could tell she was about to object even before the words reached her lips

"It's not charity," I said. "You're going to do some work in my house and I'm going to pay you. I'd rather you be in my house than somebody I don't trust. Wait right here."

Before she could refuse, I left her and hurried back into the office. I could tell by the flurry of motion that the receptionist and Robin had been watching us through the smoked glass. There would be stories, but I couldn't care less. Right then, all I cared about was keeping Ryan close; I would figure out the whys and hows of it later.

I rifled through my desk drawer until I found my extra set of house keys. Goody looked as if he were about to speak as I ran past, but I stopped him with a quick, "Be right back."

As I approached the double lobby doors, the idea that Ryan might be gone when I stepped out into the hall made me hesitate, but I could feel the stares at my back so I pushed on.

She was still standing in the hall, and she didn't return my smile.

"Here." I pushed the keys into Ryan's hesitant hands. "There's wallpaper that needs to be torn down, several rooms need to be repainted, I'd like built-in shelving in the closets in the master bedroom, and the floor needs to be replaced in one corner. The water pressure is awful throughout the house and the toilet leaks and"—I took a deep breath—"the back door sticks."

She did smile at me then, and I thought I heard some amusement in her voice when she asked, "Anything else?"

"Yeah, I live at—"

"I've been there. Remember?"

I blushed. *Of course I do. How could I ever forget?*

"Are you sure about this?" she asked.

"I'm positive. You'd be doing me a favor."

"I've just been accused of stealing and you give me the keys to your house? For all you know, it could be true. You don't know me from Adam."

I barely stopped myself from saying, *But I feel like I know you.* Instead I said, "Maybe not, but I know Jackson, and I don't trust him as far as I can toss him. Come on, Ryan. We've discussed this and you thanked me for believing you. End of story."

Ryan shrugged. "I can head over to your house right now."

"Okay, I should leave here in about an hour."

"No problem. I'll only need half an hour or so to take a look and leave you a quote. Do you have other keys or should I—"

"Those are my spares. You can leave them inside the house."

"All right." The moment grew long and inexplicably awkward. The elevator pinged and slid open. Ryan stepped inside. "Don't call your cousin. I can get other work myself."

"Okay."

"I'll put my cell-phone number on the quote."

"Okay," I said with a little more energy. "Thanks."

For an instant I saw the look that I had longed to see again—raw, unhidden lust. The kiss at the front door hadn't been a dream.

"Thank you," she murmured as the door closed, severing our eye contact.

CHAPTER NINE

"Wow, Mia, who knew you could run so fast?"

Normally, I would have kept walking, holding my anger inside; today I stopped. I could see Robin's eyes widen. "Your boss is the biggest asshole I've ever met. You two were meant for each other."

The anger that had simmered under the surface now threatened to boil over. I was stomping toward Jackson's office before I even realized that I was going to confront him.

Robin chased after me. "Mia, don't make things worse. She was stealing."

I reared around so quickly that Robin ran into me. "You know as well as I do she didn't steal from that bastard."

"He said she did."

"He also said you looked like a tramp not a month before he asked you to become his assistant." Robin looked so hurt that it brought me up short. "You're sleeping with him, aren't you, you idiot?"

At least three heads poked out of their offices. Within minutes all twenty-five assistants and at least half the brokers would know that Robin was sleeping with Jackson.

"That's crazy. I'm not sleeping with him." Robin was shaking her head, but her eyes gave her away.

"I hope you're being careful, because Jackson would rather let you drown than get his hands wet. And another thing. You want to know why Henry and I didn't ask you to be our assistant after Eleanor retired? It was because of what you were doing up there at the front desk. I bet you couldn't wait to tell the receptionist that Jackson had Ryan fired."

"That's not true. I was relieving her for a bathroom break."

I had reached Jackson's closed door now. I could see him on the phone, with his back to the door, looking out the window.

"Liar," I said and pushed into his office.

Jackson turned around with a scowl on his face. The minute he saw me, that nasty little vein began to writhe like a maggot. "Dave, can you hold on a moment? I have something irritating in my eye."

He had only just finished what I'm sure was meant to be a jab at me, but I had already snatched the phone from his hand and dropped it in its cradle.

"That was an important call," he said mildly.

"Really? Setting up a tee time?"

"How did you know?"

"Cut the bullshit, Jackson. Why'd you accuse Ryan of stealing that thing you called a paperweight?"

"How do you know she didn't steal it?" His mouth turned up in what I guessed was supposed to be a smile.

"Because the pen in your hand probably cost more than what you accused her of taking."

"I'll have you know my mentor gave me that paperweight."

"Before or after you stole his book while he was on vacation?" Jackson smiled, his eyes telling me what his lips didn't. "You were mad at me. Why'd you go after her?"

"If someone does something to me, I can't let it go unpunished."

"You got her fired because you wanted to get back at me?"

The poor excuse for a smile disappeared. "This has nothing to do with you."

"I think it has everything to do with me. She was defending me and you didn't like it."

He shrugged. "She learned a lesson today, then. She should really be careful of the company she keeps."

"Funny, I just told your bed buddy the same thing. One day, Jackson, someone's going to come along and wipe that smug look off your face."

Jackson canted his head as if giving me a point. "Perhaps. But it won't be today, Ms. Sanchez. And it won't be you." The tolerant, amused look left his face and was replaced with an emotion that chilled me. "Shut the door on your way out."

He picked up the phone and dialed. I stood there shocked by what I had seen in his eyes. Jealousy was one thing, but hate? Over a book that rightfully belonged to me anyway? I left the door open as I stormed from his office.

Robin was back at the front desk and stopped speaking when I walked by.

I did my best to ignore her and spoke directly to the receptionist. "Would you let Goody know I'm not feeling well and I'm heading home early?" From the corner of my eye I saw Robin open her mouth as if to speak. I raised a finger and pointed at her without looking at her. "You would be smart not to talk to me right now." I heard her teeth clack together as I walked away.

❖

I was grateful that the MAX wasn't as crowded as it usually was on a Friday evening. I sat with my eyes closed for a few minutes, and by the time I got off, I had let a lot of my anger go.

I walked faster than usual up the street and then up my drive. As I stuck my key in the door, I heard Pepito yip. Shit, how in the hell had I forgotten to tell Ryan about him? I walked into the house and set my bags on the floor. I took a few minutes to pet Pepito's stomach before I searched for Ryan's quote. I found it on the kitchen table along with the keys. She wrote in a clear block style. The letters were all uppercase and perfectly spaced.

> *Mia, your dog looked like he needed more water and food so I fed him. Hope you don't mind. He's a sweet little thing.*

I glanced down at Pepito. His pink tongue hung between his long front teeth in what I imagined was his version of a grin. "You have a friend over? She couldn't possibly be talking about you."

> *Here is the quote for the work you said you needed, as well as a few other things you may not have known about.*

Please let me know if the amount is too much and I can find different materials. The ones I have listed are of quality and would give you a better finish. Ryan.

Pepito had long since lost interest in me and had high-stepped over to his bowl. I read the rest of the note.

P.S. Your dog was taking out his frustration on a throw pillow when I came in. I cleaned up the mess and tossed it into the trash.

I growled and took what was meant to be a menacing step toward Pepito. Instead of hightailing it up the stairs and under the bed, he turned his back to me as if hiding his bowl from my view. I left him to the rest of his meal and went in search of my own throw pillow to thrash.

❖

Saturday morning I awoke to snoring. Not the cute, my nose is stuffy, morning snoring, but the deep man snore that comes with being overly tired or a smoker. I leaned over the bed and looked down at Pepito. He had finally decided to use the box outfitted with Brenda's cashmere sweater rather than sleep under the bed.

"Sweet little thing, huh?" I repeated Ryan's comment. "I bet she wouldn't think so if she had to sleep next to that snoring."

Pepito's pink tongue crept out to moisten his lips. His stomach rose and fell as he sighed hard. His belly looked like a dark brown mini-football. I ran my finger along it and he lifted his leg. I hesitated, then rubbed him more; a sound similar to a cat's purr emitted from his throat. *Maybe he is a little sweetie*, I thought. Pepito raised his head looked at me with angelic innocence, closed his eyes, and sneezed. Dog snot flew out of his nose, misting my arm and hand. Both Pepito and I froze. There was a moment in which I honestly considered faking a sneeze of my own just so that I could spit right back on him. But I could see by the way he lay still and tense that he expected retaliation, and I couldn't get further than the inhale.

Without touching anything, and with my hands out in front of me, I walked into the bathroom and turned on the shower. I could hear

Pepito's nails clacking on the floor as he got up to go downstairs and hopefully out the pet door.

Somewhere between washing my hair and shaving my legs I had decided that it was perfectly acceptable to call Ryan. I managed to dry my hair, get dressed, put some food down for Pepito, and dial Ryan's number before I realized that someone newly unemployed might not appreciate a phone call so early in the morning. She answered after the first ring.

"Hello?"

"Ryan? Hi, it's Mia." I took her silence for confusion. "Mia Sanchez?"

"I know. I was just surprised. I guess I didn't expect to hear from you until Monday, if at all."

"No, I wanted to call you last night, but I was too tired." The truth was, I was too nervous. I went on before I could lose my nerve. "I want you to start the work as soon as possible. Could we meet to discuss it? I know it's Saturday, but..."

"That's fine."

"Great, how about the Japanese place near Nordstrom at one?"

She hesitated, but agreed. I said good-bye and hung up before she could change her mind.

I spent most of the morning either contemplating a drive to Krispy Kreme or feeling sick to my stomach. 12:50 brought the guilt, 12:52 brought the anger caused by the guilt, and by 12:55 I was calling myself all kinds of fool. The kiss could be explained away. A moment's indiscretion, even temporary insanity. But now I was going out of my way to continue the contact when I should be avoiding her.

My qualms ended the moment I spotted her waiting in front of the restaurant. She looked downright edible in her jeans, starched white shirt, and leather jacket. Our eyes locked; she looked away first.

"Hi, have you been waiting long?" I asked.

"No, not long."

We stood, not looking at each other, for a few more seconds before I felt like I had to say something since it was my idea to meet. "Are you hungry, should we go in? This place is pretty good."

I half expected her to turn me down based on the frown on her face. When she said sure and opened the door for me, I was hard-pressed not to show my surprise.

I had chosen to wear the black suit that I had picked out some time ago. To my surprise, it didn't feel quite as tight as the first time I'd worn it. I hoped Ryan didn't hear the swishing of hose as I walked. I waved to the lady behind the counter and headed to my normal table.

"I come here a lot."

"I figured."

"This table okay?"

Ryan nodded and I glanced up to order green tea. "So anyway, here's the extra key back."

Ryan took the key and put it in her jacket pocket as if I had just handed her a vial of cocaine. The tea arrived and we busied ourselves drinking it. I picked up the menu even though I always got the same thing, tempura. I felt awkward around her now, nothing like the night she took me to Mrs. Margolis's.

"How are you feeling today?"

"You mean about not having a job?" Ryan shrugged. "I've had a job since I was fifteen years old. It's hard. I'll get another one, though, and thanks to you, I'm not without work. Things will be fine."

"I really am sorry."

Ryan suddenly covered my hand with hers. "Would you stop apologizing? None of this is your fault. I'll admit, I was furious at first, but never with you. Okay?"

The waiter appeared at our table, and Ryan moved her hand away. I pretended to consider other entrees before ordering my usual. "What are you going to have, Ryan?"

I could tell by the way she flushed when our eyes met that she had been studying me, not her menu.

"What would you recommend? I'm not really that hungry."

"When's the last time you ate?"

She blinked before answering. "Yesterday at lunch."

Before all hell broke loose. "How about we share, then? I never finish mine."

"That's fine." Ryan handed her menu to the waiter and he walked away. "You might be taking most of it home with you. I don't have much of an appetite."

"No problem." She was starting to look as uncomfortable as I felt. "So, I guess we should get down to business. I'd like you to start as soon as possible, so I thought—"

"Mia, there's something I need to say first. I want to work on your house, but…"

"But?"

"But I don't want what happened after we left Mrs. Margolis's to happen again."

I looked down because I didn't want her to see how her words affected me.

"Okay. Can you tell me why?"

"Can you tell me where your girlfriend was the other day?"

I was too stunned to answer.

Ryan was busy scratching a line in the table cloth with her short fingernail. "No, on second thought, don't tell me. Even if you weren't in a relationship, it wouldn't change things. I'm in no position to—"

She looked up at me then, her eyes candid, honest. Any sexually charged looks that had passed between us were either gone now or had been a figment of my imagination. "I can fix your house. I'd like to do the work. But that's it, nothing more. Deal?"

"Deal," I said.

When the food came I busied myself dipping my tempura in the sweet sauce, while Ryan, true to her word, ate very little and spoke even less. By the time we went our separate ways my emotions were so conflicted that I felt like crying. Deep down I knew she was right. Neither of us was in any position to explore a new relationship. But knowing it to be true didn't make it feel any less painful.

CHAPTER TEN

"Ho, there, Mia."

Mr. Gentry could talk the ears off a jackrabbit, and if he had been privy to the look on my face, he would have been as offended as he probably had been when he realized two lesbians had moved onto his street. But he was standing behind me and I was not six feet from my front door. I wiped the exasperation from my expression before I turned around.

"That girl of yours is here at eight o'clock on the dot every morning," he said. "Leaves right at five o'clock too. She any good?"

I was about to tell him that Ryan wasn't my girl, but I realized that Mr. Gentry was just being sexist, not assuming a relationship where there was none. I was trying to figure out how to reply when he tapped at his hip.

"I'm not as young as I once was," he continued, sounding slightly miffed, "and there's some things around the house that I'd like fixed up."

"Oh, yeah. She's very good. Makes sure to pick good materials."

"Good materials are important," he said. "My father was a carpenter, you know."

"No, I didn't know that."

"Yup. In my younger days I wouldn't think to have anyone do work in my house." He looked so sad I considered revising my opinion of him. "My father would be fit to be tied if he knew I had a woman in my house fixing things."

I stiffened. "There are lots of handy*men* in the phone book..."

"Nah, I like your girl's work ethic. My log says she's been

working on your house for the last four days. She gets here right on time even though you wouldn't know if she was late or not. I make sure she doesn't see me, just in case she ever knocks off early, but she never does."

"Mr. Gentry, as much as I appreciate knowing that Ryan puts in a full day's work here, I don't pay her by the hour. She can come and go as she pleases. You don't need to spy on her."

He looked offended. "I wasn't spying. What with all of the break-ins and everything, I'm part of the neighborhood watch. I'm the only one that don't work, so I—"

"What break-ins?"

Now Mr. Gentry looked exasperated. "Don't you read the paper? Hell, we even stuffed flyers in everyone's mailbox." He walked, stiff legged, over to my mailbox, opened the flap, and pulled out a mass of papers and envelopes. I would have been amazed at his audacity if I hadn't been so embarrassed by the fact that I couldn't remember the last time I had checked it. *Note to self: talk to Ryan about putting a mail slot in the door.*

"If you're going to leave your mail in the box like that you should put a lock on it. Gima Samisen across the way there has had her identity stolen four times this year." Mr. Gentry held a flyer up to my face and I obediently scanned it. "I noticed your girl because she was a stranger. I almost called the cops. She had a toolbox when she came, but she went in with a key so I figured I'd just watch to make sure she didn't take anything out when she left."

"Thank you so much for looking out for my place. Says here the burglaries started a couple months ago. I had no idea."

Mr. Gentry nodded. "Yeah, two houses were hit just last week. We thought it was some kids at first because it was in the daytime. But one of the fellas on the next street over came home while his place was being hit, and the guy punched him while trying to get away. Broke his nose. That's why I figured your girl was okay. No woman could deliver a blow like that."

The comment made me want to prove him wrong. I held up the flyer instead. "Thanks for this."

"Just be careful. Wouldn't want that guy to figure out you're a single woman living alone."

I thanked Mr. Gentry again and escaped as fast as I could. I was already well past the time I had told Ryan I would be home. My key was in the doorknob when I realized what Mr. Gentry had said about me being a single woman living alone. He was extremely nosy and he lived next door, so it wasn't much of a surprise that he figured out that Brenda hadn't been living here. But was that what I was now? A single woman living alone? Could years as a couple be wiped away in less than a month's absence? Shouldn't I feel something other than a low-grade confusion?

The moment I opened the door, Pepito was there scampering wildly. I was about to call out to Ryan when I heard her speaking. I frowned, not completely certain I liked the idea of Ryan bringing people into my house. I followed Pepito and the sound of Ryan's voice to the den. The door was open and Ryan was sitting on the floor with a cell phone to her ear. The ravaged walls and the piles of wallpaper on the floor were proof that Ryan was working hard. Not that I needed any.

She scooped Pepito up with one hand and set him on her lap. He snuggled down as if it were something he did all the time. Almost as if jealousy made noise, he glanced back toward the door and his mouth opened in what I could have sworn was a taunting grin.

"I know, Mother, and I am working. I'll send you money as soon as there's something to send."

I backed away from the door; I didn't want Ryan to think I was listening in on her phone call.

"I'll try to find a cheaper place. Maybe a room instead of an apartment, but it might take me some time. I'll send you something by the end of the week. I know. I will. I don't know. I haven't seen him. Half the time I don't even know where he sleeps. I thought Aunt Lynne was looking in on you every day?"

Ryan went quiet for a long moment and then said. "Mother, I should let you get some sleep." I looked at my watch. If Ryan's mother was in Texas, that would mean it was six p.m. And she was getting some sleep?

I returned to the front door, opened it, and after a few seconds, shut it again. Ryan walked out of the living room with Pepito by her side. I slipped off my heels and let my briefcase slide to the floor. Pepito let out a loud, piercing bark and I looked at him quickly to make sure he wasn't preparing himself to do something icky and embarrassing.

"Give me time to talk to her, Pepito," Ryan said. Her fathomless eyes sparkled as she looked from Pepito to me. "I was wondering if you would mind if I took him for a walk. He seems a little depressed."

"He does?" I frowned. Now that I thought about it, Pepito had been a little more mopey than usual. I thought he was still mooning after Brenda or just vibing off me. "You think something's wrong with him? Should I take him to the veterinarian?" Pepito stopped prancing around us and stared up at me his eyes squinted in suspicion. He didn't know the words "no, don't" or "bad boy," but he knew the word "veterinarian."

"No, he just spends a lot of time inside, so he's happy when he can get some fresh air."

"He goes out in the backyard all the time."

Ryan smiled. "Not the same." Brenda used to take him out for a walk almost every day. It never occurred to me that I should do the same. I must have looked sheepish because she became serious. "I'm not putting you down or anything. I've just always had dogs. They all act like that."

"Is it obvious that I'm not a dog person?"

"A little."

I stifled a sigh and articulated an irrational impulse. "I'll come with you." I looked down at my dark suit, hose, and bare feet. I was definitely dressed inappropriately for walking the dog. "Mm, it'll only take a minute to change."

Ryan, to her credit, only hesitated for a split second. "Sure. I had a few other things to do before I was going to take him, anyway."

"Great, I'll see you in a few." I hurried to my room, telling myself that it wasn't because I was afraid that she would change her mind. But the truth was I damn near ran out of the den. All so I could walk around the block with an ugly little dog and a woman with a voice like warm honey. Damn, I had no right to feel as good as I did.

It took twenty minutes to track down a pair of jeans that fit and a cotton top. Another ten to find shoes that I could walk in and that also went well with jeans. I refreshed my makeup and was on my way out of the bedroom when I caught sight of myself in the mirror above my dresser. If I stood far enough away I could get a head-to-shin view of myself, which was reason enough to avoid looking into it on most days.

I winced as I caught sight of my love handles spilling from the waistband of my jeans. My breasts looked swollen in the cotton shirt. I considered changing into a loose-fitting button-down, but I could hear

Pepito's shrill little barks reminding me that he had been waiting long enough.

Ryan was standing at the front door, studying a piece of paper when I came down the stairs. She was frowning, but I was learning that didn't mean that she was upset or anything, just concentrating.

"Hi, I'm ready."

"Great." It took her a moment to look up. "Are you thinking about doing this?"

I moved closer so that I could see what she was looking at. What I had assumed was the notice for the burglaries was actually the entry form for the PDX Challenge. I was going to point out that the application was probably addressed to Brenda but I decided against it.

"I was thinking about it, but I need to get in better shape." *A little white lie won't hurt, will it?*

Ryan handed me the application. "I could help you if you like. It is grueling, but totally doable. I can't commit to doing the Challenge with you until I get a full-time job and know what my schedule will be like, but I can help you get into shape if you need a buddy."

"Are you sure? I wouldn't want to take up your free time," I said, but the idea of spending time with Ryan set off a little thrill at the pit of my stomach.

"I don't mind at all. Besides, I could use a workout buddy."

"Well, if you don't mind...when are you available to start?" I felt a little like I had when I blamed Christina for eating the last of my mother's Christmas peanut brittle. The lying sucked, but the brittle sure was tasty.

"I can wait around after I'm done working, or if you're a morning person I can come before you go to the office."

"I'm never sure what time I'll get home, but I try to be at my desk before the stock market opens at half past six."

"That should work. I'm up way before then, anyway."

"You are? Doing what?"

Ryan shrugged. "Whatever needs doing."

The comment brought a vision of Ryan in the early morning sun doing...well, me. She was looking at me oddly and I feared that my face was giving me away.

"I don't think I've ever seen you in jeans," she said. "You look real nice."

"Thanks." I blushed.

Ryan bent down and attached the leash and collar to Pepito. "We should go. I think he's been holding it."

Ryan opened the door and Pepito shot out as far as his leash would allow. "Holding it?" I shut the door behind us and decided to lock the dead bolt with my key in deference to Mr. Gentry's warning. "Why wouldn't he go out his pet door?"

"Because he knows we're going for a walk. I told him. He stores it all up so that he can leave his scent in more places. See?" I watched Pepito prance over to the mailbox pole, lift a leg, and let fly three short streams.

"Oh, that's nice."

Ryan laughed. "Don't worry about it, the sprinklers will take care of it."

"If you say so," I said. "I'm thinking about putting one of those slots in the front door anyway; it's supposed to help with identity theft."

"It's certainly a good idea. Want me to add it to my list of to-dos?"

"That would be great, thanks." I couldn't help but notice the way her bicep bulged when she lifted her arm to gently encourage Pepito against "marking his scent" on one of my neighbors' newspapers. "So, do you work out a lot?"

"Not as much as I used to. I try to make sure that I'm doing some form of exercise every day, though."

"In the gym?"

"Nah, I can't really afford a membership, and the gyms around here are so expensive."

"Did you see the equipment downstairs?" I asked, perhaps too quickly. "Why don't you use it? It's probably not as good as a real gym, but there's no membership required."

"It's pretty good equipment. It looks brand new." Ryan sounded curious. "It looks like you paid a lot for it. Why buy it and not use it?"

"I go to the gym in the building. I train with Selena." Now, that wasn't exactly a lie. I did work out with Selena, for about three days last week.

"I know Selena."

"You do?" *Great, nothing like trying to impress someone and getting caught in a lie.* I stared up at the sky as I tried to figure out how to extract myself from the hole I was digging. There was only one large, fluffy cloud above us, which, for Portland, meant that the day was picturesque.

"We aren't friends or anything. I used to see her around a lot when I first moved here. Not so much anymore."

I wanted to ask her more, but since she had respected my privacy by not asking about Brenda, I decided to do the same. "He sure does stop a lot, doesn't he?"

Ryan laughed and looked down at Pepito fondly. "Yeah, he does. I think he does it to make the walks take longer. He loves being outside."

He was kind of cute if you looked at him sideways and squinted with the eye still viewing him. "Ryan, have you noticed anything…odd about Pepito?"

"No, like what?"

"Have you been in my bedroom yet?"

Ryan didn't reply at first. "I haven't gotten to the items in your bedroom yet."

"I was just wondering if you've noticed him staring at himself in the mirror?"

Ryan looked askance at me.

"No, I mean he kind of gazes at himself."

"Gazes? Like how?"

I looked at Ryan as if I were longing for something, which wasn't exactly hard. "Like that."

"Poor baby must have gas."

My jaw dropped and I would have been horrified if I hadn't noticed Ryan's smile. God, the woman had a wonderful smile on her.

"I'm sorry, but you should have seen the look on your face." Ryan was laughing so hard that I was starting to get offended.

"It wasn't that bad and besides, I was just mimicking Casanova here."

Pepito's tongue appeared from between his two front teeth as he looked at me, his hind leg arched high above a dandelion.

"No, I can't say that I've seen him doing that. But if he is, good for him."

"Good for him? What do you mean, good for him? Don't you think that's weird? He might be psychotic or something."

Ryan laughed again, that strangled, uncontrolled kind of laugh that hurt about as much as it felt good. I was secretly proud of myself for eliciting that kind of response. I vowed to try to make her laugh more often.

After she quieted I became serious. "Thank you for paying him so much attention. I have no idea how I ended up with a dog." *Sure you do; Brenda abandoned him just like she abandoned you.*

"I like him. He's always so excited when I come in. He follows me around and he doesn't ever get bored with me. He's always so appreciative when I feed him and he listens when I talk." Ryan shrugged. "What more could you ask for in a companion?"

"Length-appropriate front teeth?" I ventured. "Use of a washcloth instead of his tongue to clean his bitty parts? Fresh breath?"

She was laughing again and I was eating it up.

"You know what I mean," she choked out.

"I guess, but Pepito doesn't like me half as much as he likes you," I said. "He tolerates me, like I tolerate the cashier at Burgerville. You know, a means to an end. I can just see him thinking 'hurry up and give me my food, bitch,' every time I'm getting his dinner ready."

"Is that what you think when you're standing in line at Burgerville?"

"Yeah, doesn't everyone?" That set her off again and I felt like high-stepping alongside Pepito.

We had reached a small neighborhood market that was too expensive to shop at regularly, but was perfect for special occasions.

"Speaking of dinner? Would you mind walking him around the block while I run inside?"

"Sure, go ahead."

"I won't be long."

"I got all the time you need," she said, and I could have sworn there was a caress in her voice.

By the time I walked across the threshold of the little store, I had convinced myself that I had imagined it. I grabbed a couple stuffed chicken breasts, enough salad fixings for two, and a box of oolong tea, and didn't even blink over the fact that Ryan had thus far refused to have dinner with me at the house. I walked out of the store with my paper bags just as she and Pepito came around the corner.

"Ready to head back?" She took one of the bags and I was heartened by the fact that although the smile was gone, her eyes still had the residual glow of laughter. She seemed less guarded, relaxed. *Oh, what the hell. If she says no I'll just have leftovers.*

"Hey, I know you're probably busy, but I have enough here for two. Pepito and I are getting tired of talking to each other. We'd love it if you would stay for dinner."

This time there was no hesitation. "Sure, I'd like that."

"Really?" Thankfully Pepito tugged at his leash and she allowed herself to be pulled away from me. I hurried to catch up. "It's just that I've asked you before and you always said no."

"Maybe I wasn't hungry."

She wasn't hungry then, but now she is? What does that mean? It means she's hungry. It means she's going to have dinner with you. Don't question it and don't question the fact that you're positively giddy with excitement at the prospect of being able to spend more time with her.

I slowed and let her walk ahead with Pepito. I loved the way she walked. The way she murmured little words of encouragement to Pepito as he stopped, sniffed the ground, turned in circles, and decided not to release his precious cargo just yet. I loved the way she paid no attention to the surprised, even horrified looks of passersby as they got a good look at the dog she was walking. I loved the fact that she dressed so simply and wore no makeup. Yet I couldn't imagine there was a time when she didn't turn heads.

She really was quite stunning. My thoughts had just turned to a place that made me feel uncomfortable and a little scared when she seemed to realize that I wasn't at her side. She looked back, her brow raised, her lips turned up in a quizzical smile. My heart was already beating a staccato against my rib cage even before I quickened my pace to catch up.

❖

What the hell was I doing? The woman made it clear she wasn't interested, why was I working so hard to be her friend? *Because you don't have enough friends. Or as Brenda so eloquently put it, "you have no friends."*

I can do this. I can do this. The mantra was almost enough to convince me that I was overreacting, that Ryan didn't look half as good as I thought she did and the tingling at the back of my neck was because of the brisk walk home.

Back inside the house, Ryan unbuckled Pepito's leash and he ripped down the hall, into the family room, through the kitchen, and out his pet door. We had barely shut the front door when we heard the sound of him crashing back through the kitchen. He ran back down the hall and veered up the stairs. I grimaced as I imagined him diving onto my bed and rubbing his snot-moistened nose up and down my duvet.

"Guess someone's had a good day," I said.

"Mmm-hmm. Want me to take the bags in the kitchen?" Ryan asked.

"Sure." I caught my breath and followed her, pausing at the doorway to watch her from behind. Her hips twisted slightly as she set something on the counter. A throbbing ache started between my legs as I imagined what it would feel like to touch her.

"Ryan?"

She glanced toward me. "Yeah?" Her face was sad, contemplative. I thought about the conversation I'd overheard earlier and decided she was probably worried about finding enough money to send her mother.

"Why don't you let me do that? You've been working all day."

"So have you." She seemed confused, and again her reaction made me smile.

"You have the most expressive face in the world. Has anyone ever told you that?"

"Hmm…yeah." Ryan turned back to the bags. "It's gotten me in a lot of trouble over the years. I try to hide it, but people mistake that for disinterest. My mom used to say 'you can't win for losing.'"

"Here." I took the chicken from her hands. "Wash up and grab a mug. I'll make you some of this…" I held the box out in front of me. "Oolong tea. Does that sound good?"

Ryan smiled; this time the smile reached her eyes. "Thanks for, you know, doing this. You didn't have to."

"I know, but I wanted to. I can handle this. Relax. Have your tea."

She looked at me for a long moment. "If I can't help with anything, I'd rather go get some work done on the house."

"Do you have a hard time just relaxing?"

She smiled. "I just prefer to help." As if she were trying to understand her own impulses better, she said, "I guess when you're busy, it's easier not to worry about things you can't control."

I was probably just trying to keep her close to me, but I really wanted to understand her better. I took her mug and poured bottled water into it. She unwrapped the tea bag while I put the mug in the microwave. Ryan was quiet for so long that if I hadn't felt her presence, I would have wondered if she had left. I noisily pulled a pan from the cabinet and searched the cabinet for foil.

I heard the click-clack of Pepito's nails; he stopped and whined a little and I watched Ryan scoop him up and sit down with him on her lap. *Good, she's going to stay.*

"Do you have a lot of things you don't want to think about?" I asked finally.

"Don't most folks?" For some reason, that phrase sounded more Southern than anything she had ever said to me.

I wanted to tell her I don't know many "folks." But I didn't know how to voice it in a way that didn't offend her. I had my own circle, but the people Brenda called our friends—none of them felt real, not what I suspected Ryan meant by "folks." She was honest, hardworking, caring, and one of the sexiest women I had ever laid eyes on. I wanted to tell her all that, but what I said was, "You act a lot older than you are."

She made a small sound that I took for a laugh and I glanced at her face. Her eyes were red rimmed as if she had been crying or missing sleep. "Thanks a lot."

"You know what I mean. I'm not talking about your looks. You look good. I can tell you take care of yourself." The microwave beeped and I pulled the mug out and handed it to her.

"So you're keeping busy to keep your mind off not having a job?"

I made a point of seeming distracted with my kitchen activities so she didn't feel as though I was giving her the third degree. I sometimes had to employ this tactic with my older clients so that I could get a better feel for their worries and fears. Older people sometimes hide financial problems behind bravado. The old lady with so much money she has to hide it in her mattress is not a reality that I've come across.

"No. Well, maybe a little. My job was a means to an end. I liked working with Steve, but it's not what I see myself doing years from now."

"What do you see yourself doing?"

I could sense the shrug in her voice. "I want my own business. I like the idea of rehabbing some of the homes in less desirable neighborhoods. You know, for low-income or single-parent homes."

"You mean like Habitat for Humanity?"

"Sort of, but I'd do it with existing houses instead of building new ones."

"Do you know what's involved in doing something like that?"

"I've done a little research, and there are grants that you can apply for. I could do most of the work myself and I'd probably live in each one as I worked, so the overhead would be low."

"Would you do that here, or go home to Texas?" I kept my hands busy putting the chicken on the foil as I waited anxiously for her response.

"I don't think Texas is my home anymore."

"And Portland is?"

"I don't know yet. I keep telling myself that I'll know when I find the right place. I do know there's something about this city, this state, that I really like. It's great being able to go to the beach and hike on the same day."

"You hike?"

"Almost every weekend. You?"

"I don't even own hiking boots."

"Too bad, you're missing some gorgeous trails. I hike and camp up near Mount Hood."

"Do you do that alone or with friends? I heard that could be dangerous alone." *Damn, Mia, if she doesn't see that as a thinly veiled attempt to find out if she's seeing someone, then she is a lot more innocent than she looks.*

"I usually go alone." With nothing else to do, I put my own mug of water in the microwave and washed up the counter space where I had been working with dinner. I was stalling because I felt a little nervous about sitting down and having a conversation with Ryan.

"Mia?"

"Hmm." I opened the microwave door before it could ping.

"You look tired. Why don't you sit down?" Her voice was soft; not sexual, but concerned.

"Okay." I took my cup of hot water from the microwave and walked toward the table. I could feel her eyes on me the whole time and it should have made me nervous, but it didn't. Instead I felt well cared for. "This last week has kicked my butt."

"Really? What happened besides me getting fired?"

"I had a couple of clients leave recently. They were older clients that I inherited when my senior partner, Henry, retired a couple years ago. Anyway, they left, and it bothers the hell out of me that I don't know why. All of them were making money, not a lot, but nothing to be ashamed of."

"Can't you just call them up and ask them?"

I started at the question because I couldn't ever remember discussing my job at home and it was disconcerting to feel free to do so now. "You know, that's the weirdest thing. Neither of them called me directly. They called the manager of my firm to ask that their accounts be transferred to some brokerage firm I've never even heard of." I frowned. "They aren't returning my calls. I asked Goody if he had heard from them, but..." Realizing that I had stopped speaking, I added, "I'll just have to try again tomorrow."

"Was it a lot of your business?"

"No, not at all. But it bothers me that clients would leave me like that. If I did something to upset them, I'd like to know so I don't do it again."

"I'm sure it's not anything you did. They probably got some flyer in the mail or something that enticed them over to this new company."

"I thought about that too. I hope no legitimate firm is out there trolling for elderly people. Either way, I just want to make sure they aren't getting taken advantage of."

Ryan sipped her tea, her eyes searching my face as she did so, and I looked down into my cup. The stuff wasn't half bad. I certainly wouldn't give up my hot cup of espresso roast, but it wasn't bad.

"You're a really nice person, aren't you?" she asked.

I couldn't help, it. I laughed. "No, not at all."

"Really?" Her expression was hard to read. "You could have fooled me."

"I keep the mean stuff to myself."

"Do tell?" I told myself that the smile on her face was not an invitation.

"It wouldn't be keeping it to myself if I told."

When Ryan laughed her face transformed, making her look less tired. I told myself it was the tea and not my company.

"When people walk in front of me with strollers I think about kicking them," I confessed.

Ryan choked on her tea. "Kicking strollers? With babies in them?"

"It isn't the babies I'd be kicking, just the strollers. Besides, I never did it. But I think they are such a pain in the ass, and God forbid you should walk in front of them. It's like the world should stop just because they can breed."

She tried to look shocked. "Okay, I give you one point for that one. What else?"

"Let's see. I once saw one of the girls in the cage write on a broker's car with a permanent marker."

Ryan laughed again. "Nah, that one doesn't count. You were just the innocent bystander, she was the mean one."

"Okay, how about this? I once told the school nerd that this girl who dumped me for the football jock was secretly in love with him."

Ryan gasped. "You did not."

I nodded sagely. "I am not to be trifled with. He followed her around for a year. Even told a few people we knew that they were together. She spent most of senior year hiding from him."

"She ever find out what you did?"

"She probably suspected." I stood up and searched the drawers next to the oven for a towel to remove the pan.

"What happened to her?"

"She married the prom king, they have four beautiful kids, and she works part time at a bank in Southeast."

"You know a lot about her. You still keep in touch?"

I pulled the chicken out and set the pan on the stove. The aroma was mouth-watering and I was pleased with how well the chicken had browned. "Her father owns the landscaping company my parents use. She tries to reach out to me sometimes."

"But you're not interested in being her friend?"

"It's not that I'm not interested, it's just that I don't have much in common with her anymore. I was sixteen years old. I thought she loved me and we would spend the rest of our lives together." I gave a self-deprecating smile.

"She must have hurt you really bad."

Note to self: Ryan can make you cry with a look, so tread carefully.

I took down two plates. "The sad part is, I still believe she's gay. Puppy love like ours doesn't often survive, but it makes me sad to think that she might have married him because of her family's religious beliefs. My parents aren't as devout as they used to be when we were kids, but I thought they were going to disown me there for a while after I came out to them."

"I think some people have trouble dealing with their sexuality. Especially if family is involved."

"Did you? Have trouble telling your family, I mean."

Ryan looked sad, and the scar pronounced and jagged. "My mother hasn't left her bed for longer than two hours in years. My brother has a habit of hanging out with the wrong crowd, and my father has a gambling problem. My family was so messed up that my sexuality failed to make a blip on the radar screen."

"Sounds like you had a hard time growing up," I said carefully. "If you ever need to talk…"

She either looked down or nodded. Either way I took the gesture to mean "thanks, but no." I busied myself with placing our food on the plates. She had opened up to me more than I could have ever dreamed.

"Everything looks really good," Ryan said from behind me.

I jumped because I hadn't heard her get up. "I can't take credit. It's just heat and serve. But yeah, it does look good."

She was standing at the sink, watching me. She said, "I'll help you set the table after I wash up." It felt nice to have someone interested in doing something so mundane as putting food on the table together.

I kept quiet as Ryan tucked into her meal as if she hadn't eaten in days. Five minutes of silence is a very long time, especially when you have something monumental to say, which I did, and I kept framing my important question and backing out before I committed myself.

It was Ryan who broke the silence. "What's on your mind, Mia?"

I swallowed and took a sip of my tea, grimacing at the flavor combination of chicken stuffing and oolong. "Why do you ask?"

"You're usually not this quiet."

I finished chewing. "It's kind of awkward."

"Just say it. Is there something wrong with my work? You can tell me—"

"No, oh no, Ryan. Everything is wonderful."

"Good." She relaxed. "Then please go ahead and tell me."

"It's not…it's not that I need to tell you anything, I want to ask you something."

"Okay, ask."

I could tell my stumbling-idiot act was making her nervous, so I took a deep breath and said quickly, "I want you to move in with me." I didn't need to be a psychic to know the word "nutball" was floating through her head. "Wait, just hear me out. It's not what you think. You know Mr. Gentry, the guy next door?"

"Yeah, he accosted me when I was coming in to work on that first day."

"Yeah, him. He says there have been break-ins in the neighborhood." I could see Ryan's tension ease.

"I saw the flyers."

"I thought it might help you out too, you know, until you found something more stable. I know I couldn't possibly be paying you a quarter of what you made with Steve, so I thought…we could help each other out. Besides, Pepito loves you."

I could tell that Ryan was considering my proposition, but I couldn't tell how she felt about the idea. "Look, I don't want to make you feel awkward by having you answer me now. Just think about it. I have the extra room upstairs, and I wouldn't expect you to pay me anything…"

"No, I'd pay."

"But I want to—"

"No. I would pay something."

"We can talk about that later, maybe work something out with the work you're doing for me."

Ryan looked down at her plate.

"Ryan, I didn't mean to make you feel uncomfortable. If that's what I'm doing, I'll rescind my offer. But I'd do this for any of my friends, and I'd like to think of you as a friend." When she still didn't look up, I reached out and covered her hand. "Please look at me." I waited until her gaze met mine. "There's nothing else to this, okay? I really just want to help you, and if I'm being honest, I'll admit that I feel some responsibility for your getting fired."

"What about your girlfriend?"

"Brenda?" I said her name and the air between us became thick. "She's not here and she won't be for a very long time."

"Will it cause problems between you two? Will she believe that you and I are just friends?"

"I don't know, but she isn't here, and according to her, she hasn't really been with me for a long time. So I'm done considering her feelings when I plan my life. As far as I'm concerned, I'm alone. And right now, I really want to help a friend while I help myself in the process. Will you at least consider it?"

It felt like forever before Ryan spoke, and when she did, the words came out slowly. "I'll consider it," she said, but the warmth had left the room and it didn't return until after Pepito and I walked her to the door after dinner.

I stood there for a few minutes after she'd gone, then engaged the dead bolt and walked slowly up the stairs, Pepito at my heels. For reasons I couldn't put my finger on, I felt as if I would never see Ryan Benson again. The thought made my chest ache so bad that it kept me up long into the night.

CHAPTER ELEVEN

My phone rang at four thirty the next morning, about an hour after I finally fell asleep. My hello was unintelligible, but Ryan must have understood because she chuckled.

"I woke you up, didn't I?"

My first reaction was to make a smart-ass comment, but the warmth of her tone and the memory of the way she had looked when she left the house kept me from getting cranky. "I was just getting up. Do I hear your teeth chattering?"

"Yeah, it's cold out here."

"Out where?"

"I'm outside."

"You're outside? Outside my house?" I sat up in bed and looked toward my window. Pepito grumbled, got out of his box-bed, and crawled beneath mine. "What are you doing out there? I thought you didn't come until around eight."

"That's what time I get here to work on the house, but you said you wanted to work out so I came early. Did you forget?"

My hand was on my forehead, trying to remove the fog of sleep. "Yeah, four thirty, but why are you standing outside? Did you forget your key?"

"No, I didn't want to scare you. I'll come in now, okay?"

"Okay." I pulled myself out of bed as I heard her put the key in the front door. The question felt oddly intimate. I pressed the phone tight against my ear and tried to imagine her asking me if she could come inside in a different context.

"Mia?"

"Hmm?"

"I asked if you usually drink coffee before you work out?"

I could have told her the truth. I could have told her that I usually just cursed before I worked out. "Yeah, I usually have a cup of coffee," I said.

"I'll make some while you get dressed."

"Wait, I should probably shower first."

"Before you work out?"

"Not a good idea?"

"Nope, you're just going to work up a sweat and have to take another one."

I'm sure I waited a split second longer than I should have, because Ryan sounded embarrassed when she said, "But if you feel more comfortable…"

"No, you're right. I'll be down in a few minutes."

I sat blinking into nothingness for a few minutes after Ryan had said bye. I clicked on the lamp at my bedside table and grabbed my old terry cloth robe from the foot of the bed. A quick search of my gym bag netted me perfectly clean workout clothes that just didn't quite work.

I was going through my dresser drawers when I caught a glimpse of myself in the mirror. What was I doing? Ryan was here as a friend trying to help me work out for a challenge that I wasn't really planning to compete in. Sports bra in hand, I let my robe drop to the floor and appraised my reflection the way a stranger would. The way Ryan would if she were here. I saw the thickness around my middle that had been easily hidden just last year. I saw the fuller breasts, the rounder face, and I quickly turned my back to the mirror and donned my bra, a pair of black Nike shorts, and a T-shirt. It wasn't sexy, but it was the best I could do on such short notice.

The scent of fresh-brewed coffee greeted me as I approached the kitchen, and my mood improved immediately. Brenda never left for work before I did, and neither of us ever bothered to set the pot. It was easier to stop at Peet's Coffee on my way into work than to bother grinding beans or setting the pot the night before. Besides, they had the best lowfat coffee cake in Portland.

"Morning," Ryan said from the table. Her cup was almost to her lips, and her eyes were hooded from the heat from her tea or some thought that I would never be privy to.

The way I felt just looking at her almost made it worth waking up an hour earlier than usual. Almost. She had already poured a mug of coffee for me and I picked it up without sitting. "Morning. Thanks."

Ryan smiled and pointed at me with her mug. "You can sit down and enjoy your coffee if you like."

I smiled and slid into a chair at my own kitchen table. I felt like a stranger offered a seat in an unfamiliar diner. I fell back on the old "keep your mouth full so you don't have to talk" trick. I realized too late that there was a flaw in that plan. The sooner I was done with my coffee, the sooner I had to go work out.

"I'm ready whenever you are," Ryan said after I had finished my second cup.

All of my nervous energy drained from me like a leaking balloon. I set my mug aside. "Right behind you," I said with what I hoped passed for enthusiasm. Ryan bent down to pick up a boom box that I hadn't noticed when I walked in. I followed her through the wooden door and down the steep flight of stairs.

The basement was simply a carpeted square room with four floor-to-ceiling mirrors. The equipment consisted of a huge weight rack, a treadmill, and a weight bench.

"You have enough equipment here to get a good workout," Ryan said.

"I do?"

I had never considered it, really, but all of the equipment I had used during my few workouts with Selena was represented here. Both of us did some stretches; she looked natural and I'm sure I looked awkward as hell.

Ryan hit the Play button on her boom box and I heard the CD player whir to life. She walked over to the weight rack.

Here we go.

"Do you know how much weight you can lift for a full set?"

"Tens, I think."

She took the weights off the rack and handed them to me. I expected her to release them, but her fingers seemed to linger over mine. At first I thought she was just making sure that I had a firm grip on the weights, but when her eyes met mine I thought she was searching for something. Something that I found myself looking for in hers as well. Assurance that the spark was there, that it hadn't faded away just yet. She must have seen it the same way I did, because when she said, "Let's get started," I was certain I recognized relief in her voice.

❖

When I walked into the office, I was sore and happier about it than I had any right to be. Ryan had been exceedingly patient with me, coming close when she needed to and even going so far as to help me lift the weights correctly. As tired as I was after the workout, I still felt like I could tackle anything life threw at me. Right up until I saw the look on Goody's face.

"Brenda's holding. This is the second time she's called. She said you weren't answering your phone at the house. What's going on with her? She was kind of rude."

"I don't know. Let me find out what she wants." With a sigh I did not bother to hide, I shut my office door and picked up the phone. "Hi, Brenda."

"Mia, I've been trying to reach you all morning."

"So Goody tells me. What's wrong?"

"Nothing, I just didn't like the way we left our last conversation. You sounded, I don't know, a little dispassionate."

This was one of the things I hated about Brenda; if she felt I wasn't reacting the way she thought I should, she would dig until she got the reaction she was looking for.

"Mia, have you…thought about seeing other people?"

Perhaps it was guilt over the fact that I had been doing more than just thinking about it—I had been fantasizing about it and with someone specific—but the question pissed me off. "Brenda, what in the hell is wrong with you? I mean, really, did you track me down this morning to tell me that you think I should see other people?"

"You're taking this the wrong way."

"How else am I supposed to take it?"

"I just want to make sure you're okay. I do love you."

That was it. All the anger, all the frustration that I felt with her came to a head and I blew up. "You don't love me. You love the home I made for you. I am not some place you can just park your shoes whenever you get over this…this thing you're going through."

"I didn't say you were. I'm the one telling you you shouldn't wait."

"I don't need your permission."

Brenda went quiet. "I can't say anything right anymore, can I?"

"Please, just tell me why you're calling."

"I don't know. I just felt like…I should. I was standing on the beach the other night and the moonlight was glinting off the waves and I realized I was wishing you were there to see it too."

There was a time, hours, even days after she left that I would have jumped on that tone, begged her to come home, maybe even taken some time off so I could go see her. Here was an opening; I could mend my relationship if I wanted to. The realization that I didn't want to, that it was truly over between us, stunned me.

"You haven't said how the photo shoot's going," I said in an effort to get the conversation on steady ground.

"It's going well." There was no enthusiasm in her voice, just weariness and regret. I wished I hadn't heard it; I didn't want to start the conversation I knew we had to have.

"Mia, are you still there?"

"Yeah, sorry. I was thinking about something."

"I should get going. Can I call you when I have a little more time to talk? Maybe in a few days?"

"Yeah, you probably should." I marveled at how frozen my heart felt as I hung up the phone. *Damn it, Brenda. Why is good-bye the only civil thing we can say to each other?*

❖

It wasn't like Goody to be so quiet. Well, "quiet" wasn't the right word. I could hear the sound of his emery board as it rasped slowly across his nails. But he hadn't said a word since he plunked himself down in the chair opposite my desk.

"All right, spit it out," I said after two grueling minutes of scraping. "Please. I have a lot to do and you're obviously pissed off about something, so just spit it out."

He stopped looking at his perfect crescent-shaped nails long enough to glance at me. "I'm not pissed. I'm just a little hurt," he said and went back to filing. His voice had a petulant quality that drove me insane on the best of days. I didn't hear it often, and I suspected, if other people reacted to it as I did, it could factor into his chronic state of singlehood.

"Hurt about what?"

"That was Brenda on the phone?"

"You know it was, you were the one who told me she was holding."

"Selena Sanchez called while you were on the phone with her."

"Okaay?" I dragged the word out in the hopes that he would get to the point.

Goody's brow rose. "How long have we known each other?"

"Two years, plus the lifetime it's taking us to have this conversation. What's your point?"

"My point is, I tell you everything." He rubbed his nails on the front of his immaculately starched shirt. "I thought our arrangement was mutual."

"What do you mean?"

"I mean, all of a sudden you have three women calling within a five-minute span, looking for you. Something is going on and you aren't telling me about it."

"Wait a minute, Goody." I laughed. "I have no idea why you're getting all upset because Brenda called, and Selena was probably just checking to see why I haven't made another appointment."

"Then why'd she ask me if you were seeing anyone?"

"She what?" My eyes grew large as I caught on. "But she's—"

"As gay as you are."

"She doesn't look gay."

"And you do?"

"Yes, damn it, I look really gay. What did you tell her?"

"I told her she should ask you," Goody said with an affronted look on his face.

"So she's gay? I mean for real?" Envisioning the length of Selena's fingernails, I shuddered. "You said three women. Who was the third?"

"Ryan called too." Goody stared at me intently and I'll be damned if my face didn't heat up.

"She did?" I tried not to sound too excited. "So what? She's working on my house."

"Yeah, but she called to make sure you were feeling okay. Why wouldn't you be okay?" He stood up. "I mean, it's not like you had some rough sex that you aren't telling me about."

"Goody, you've got to be ki—"

"Wait a minute, let me finish. Don't I tell you about every sexual encounter?"

"In graphic detail, yes. Every time."

"So, do I have to spell it out?"

"Goody, there's nothing to tell. We worked out. She offered to help me train for the PDX Challenge."

His mouth twisted. "Then why do you have that guilty look on your face? You didn't do anything embarrassing like ask her to be your lover, did you?"

"Goody, what do you take me for? I'm not crazy. I just told her she could stay with me while she…"

"Oh, my God. It's true."

"What?"

"You already called the moving van. You did it, didn't you? You had sex and it was so good that she's moving in so you can…screw on your lunch."

"Okay, now you're being ridiculous." I was nearly shaking because, well, it did sound good, and I would if I could. But I couldn't and, damn it, I was not too happy about that fact. "Look, I feel responsible for what that asshole Jackson did to her, okay?"

"So you ask her to move in with you? That goes a bit beyond guilt. What are you going to tell Brenda?"

"I'm not going to tell Brenda anything. It's not what you think. I feel safer having someone around when I'm not home. There's been a rash of burglaries in my neighborhood."

"So you get a burglar alarm, you don't ask a stranger to move in with you."

"She's having money problems. Problems she wouldn't be having if Jackson hadn't gotten her fired after she stood up for me."

"So you write her a letter of recommendation. Hell, you've already given her a job. Lord knows, I've ended up giving money to what I thought was a nice free one-night stand."

"Neither Ryan nor I are the one-night-stand type, okay? It'll never happen. We've become friends. I need help fixing up the house. She needs to save money until she finds a new job. I need a workout buddy. She can't afford a gym membership. It benefits both of us. Let's not make more of it than that. Anyway, she's really good."

"Oh, I'm sure."

I gave him a look. Something made me want to prove my point, to convince him that I was completely in control of the situation and not kidding myself about anything. "She's had this great idea about pulling up the carpet in the den to see what condition the floors are in.

She thinks they might be in excellent condition, but she's worried about the asbestos."

Goody leaned forward and glared at me for a long tense moment. Finally he leaned back and nodded. "All right, now that I've had a good look at you, I believe that you haven't slept with her. You don't look like you've had sex in a year."

"Oh, well thank you very much, Goody."

"Don't thank me for that."

His expression turned from sulky to serious. "You may not have slept with her yet, but you really like her, don't you? You got this big old smile on your face just now when you were talking about her."

I wanted to continue the happy fiction about my platonic detachment, but I couldn't hide my feelings that well. "Goody, she doesn't want anything to do with me, and I can't say as I blame her. She knows that I have unfinished business with Brenda. If she didn't need the money, I doubt she'd even be working for me right now. But I don't know…there's something there that I've never experienced before. I like being around her. I wonder about her life before we met…"

"You never felt that way about anyone else? About Brenda?"

"If I did, I don't remember," I said to be diplomatic, but I knew that I hadn't. "Please tell me this is normal, that it's infatuation."

"It's infatuation."

"Good, so what do I do about it?"

"You ignore it."

"Goody."

"Shit, I don't know. The only thing that ever worked for me was letting them break my heart, and I don't recommend that one."

"She won't even have the decency to break my heart. She just wants to talk paint and carpet and wood ants."

"Wood ants?"

"Yeah, apparently I have wood ants as big as my pinky finger." I shuddered just thinking about it. "I was going to bring some in and put them in Jackson's office, but I changed my mind. All I need is to have him accuse me of purposely giving the office ants."

Goody laughed. "You know, I haven't seen him since the day you two had it out."

"Good. Hopefully they fired his ass."

"Nah, Robin would have said something, and she's been coming in to work like she normally does. When he goes on vacation she always comes in later and leaves earlier…you know?"

I nodded, even though I really didn't know. I came to work early and stayed late. At least I had before Ryan started working on my house. "I guess we'll see soon enough."

I logged into my computer and pulled up my date book in the hopes that Goody would get the hint that I was done discussing Ryan Benson.

"May I ask you one more question? Then I'll leave you alone."

"Yeah, go ahead."

"Are you sure you aren't just lonely? I'm asking because I like Ryan. I would hate for you to get involved with her because you're missing Brenda. You could end up hurting her a lot."

"Do you really think I'm the kind of person that would do something like that?"

"I think a lot of people aren't that kind of person. But then someone nice comes along and likes you so much that they end up inadvertently letting you walk all over them."

"I would never do that to anyone, least of all Ryan. I don't have that kind of pull."

Goody stood up. "Uh-huh. Don't forget to call Selena and Ryan back," he said as he walked out of my office.

❖

"Thank you for agreeing to have lunch with me." Selena smiled and I wondered what chemical could possibly make teeth that white. "I wasn't sure if you would come at all."

Since I had been very close to calling her back and lying my way out of the invitation, I said, "I have to admit you caught me off guard, but why wouldn't I come?"

"I saw you leaving one evening with Ryan…oh, I can't think of her last name—beautiful if she didn't have that horrible scar. Are you two seeing each other?"

"No, we're just friends. How do you know Ryan?"

"Let's just say we had a brief but mutually pleasing time together, and then we went our separate ways."

It would have been unreasonable for me to believe that a woman as attractive as Ryan would not have had affairs, but having that affair sitting across the table from me was asking too much. I wanted to reach across and wipe the smirk off Selena's face. Instead, I kept my smile bland and concentrated on my plate.

"I didn't ask you here to talk about Ryan, though."

"Okay, why did you ask me here?" I tried hard not to show how cranky I was getting.

"I wanted to know why you stopped coming to the gym. Come on, tell me the truth. I don't bite." Her teeth gleamed as she smiled so wide I thought I heard her jaw crack.

I had expected her to ask, but I still winced. "It had nothing to do with your training, it was because—"

"Because you felt it too." She covered my hand with hers. We were sitting in the deli in our building, so the public displays of affection made me just a tad uncomfortable.

"I felt it too?"

Apparently Selena missed the question mark at the end of my sentence, because she did a little high school cheerleading move and clapped her hands twice. I looked around the restaurant to make sure no one from the office was around.

"I knew it!" she said too loudly for comfort. "I thought it was just me. I could never date someone I worked with, but now that you're not coming to the gym, I thought I would ask." I stared at her, speechless.

"I asked Goody about you, of course...because he's gay. I wanted to make sure that you were actually gay and somewhat open to the kind of relationship I'm looking for."

"What kind of...relationship is that?"

"I'm not looking for marriage or anything, just a friend."

"Just a friend?" I repeated.

"Yeah, a friend with benefits." Selena laughed at her own joke and clawed gently at the top of my hand.

"You asked Goody if I would be open to that."

"He said that he couldn't answer for you. He sounded unsure, though."

Oh, Goody, I'm going to break my foot off in your scrawny ass.

"So what do you say about us, you know, hanging out as friends? Maybe catching a movie, I could cook us some dinner, that kind of thing."

"Sure, but I'll have to check my schedule and let you know when I'm free." I picked up my sandwich and she picked up her fork, beaming at me as if we had just agreed to an orgy.

If there was one thing I had learned, growing up in a family like mine, you keep your mouth full and you don't have to answer awkward questions. My lunch hour couldn't end soon enough. I watched Selena nibble at her salad. Why had I agreed to lunch? The fact that she had asked Goody if I was available had tipped me off to what was coming. Why hadn't I called Ryan back first?

I knew the answer without really needing to ask the question. I hadn't called Ryan back because I was afraid she had been calling to turn me down. Lunch with Selena had been a diversion. Goody was right, even someone like me could use people unintentionally.

CHAPTER TWELVE

Henry, hi! I haven't heard from you in ages. I was beginning to think you had forgotten about me."

"Aw, Mia, you know I could never forget about you, doll. I think about you almost every day."

"Before or after you tee off?"

"Before and after. You're like my favorite daughter."

"You only have one daughter and you two argue all the time."

"Exactly," he said and we both laughed.

"Listen, Mia, you know I'm not one to put my nose where it doesn't belong, but I ran into Stan Wallace over at Lone Oak Golf Club and he mentioned that he had just switched his accounts to another broker."

"I know, Henry. I've been calling him to find out what happened. He's up…" I pulled up Stan Wallace's accounts. "He's up something like thirteen percent on the year. I called him last month to make sure that he was happy with our services and he said no complaints. Did he tell you anything?"

"He told me enough, that's why I'm calling you. I hate to tell you this, but you have a weasel in the henhouse."

I tensed. "What do you mean?"

"Someone, specifically Brad Jackson, is stealing your clients."

"That's not possible. He works here. How could he…?"

I stopped speaking because I knew the answer, the same as Henry did. "That arrogant bastard left the company and is trying to take my clients with him? What in the hell?"

"Stan is my friend. He didn't want to tell me because he knows how I feel about you, but Jackson is claiming that you've been putting him in a bad portfolio mix."

"What? And he believed him? He's up thirteen percent, Henry. It's not even September yet!"

Henry cleared his throat. "Jackson also claimed you were charging too much in fees. Stan said that Jackson was undercutting you by half."

I inhaled. "So that means Jackson is only charging half a percent? What company would agree to that unless he got some kind of exception just to steal my clients? I haven't changed my fee structure. It's still one percent!"

"Good," Henry said. "I can call a few more of my old customers, but I'm assuming Jackson got a hold of your customer accounts and is quietly stealing them. You had no inkling that Jackson was going to leave Goldsmith?"

"None," I said, rubbing hard at my forehead. The On Hold light was flashing, signaling that Goody had another call waiting for me. I ignored it. "I haven't seen him since last week, but I didn't think anything of it. Scratch that, I was happy about it. He's always been an ass to me, but after you left, he just became intolerable."

Henry grew quiet. "I'm afraid that might be my fault."

"Your fault? How?"

"I talked to Jackson about coming on board with me when you were still in the training program."

"You did what? But Henry, he's sleazy."

"He'd been in the business a lot longer than you had. Besides, I didn't know you that well, and even after you became a full-fledged broker, I didn't know you would be able to take over as fast as you did. I already had retirement in my crosshairs and I worried that some of my older male clients might have a problem relating to such a young woman."

"So he had reason to think your book would go to him."

"No, he didn't. I never once promised him anything. And as you know, we never partnered. The fact that he assumed that's what I was going to do is his own fault. Jackson has always had a chip on his shoulder. That man was born into money and he still wants more. I didn't get that, and when all was said and done, it came down to one thing—who could I trust with my clients. Yours was the only name I came up with."

"Thanks, Henry. Your confidence means the world to me."

"No problem, doll. You want me to call up Stan, see if I can figure out who else that ass tried to steal?"

"No, I'll take it from here." I already knew of two because they had transferred their accounts just recently. I didn't need to worry Henry with it any more than I had to. I said good-bye, hung up, and considered bumming an antacid from one of the other brokers. But I dialed Ryan's cell number instead.

"Hello?" Her voice had the surprised, worried tone of someone receiving a call at two in the morning rather than two in the afternoon.

"Hi, Ryan, it's Mia. Sorry to bother you, but before you leave tonight would you mind putting food out for Pepito? I wouldn't ask, but I don't know what time I'll be leaving here and I don't want him to be hungry."

"No problem. Is everything okay?"

"No, not really, but it will be."

"Okay, don't worry about Pepito. I'll look after him."

"Thank you." It was amazing how such a small gesture could make me feel better. Even with everything going on, I still felt tempted to ask if she had made a decision about moving into my extra room. But I didn't have time to start that conversation now. I said good-bye and went out to give Goody the bad news.

"Brenda is parked on two," he told me.

"Of course she is. I need another kick in the cooch today."

"What's going on?"

"Did Robin say anything to you about Jackson leaving the company?" Goody's chin dropped, which answered my question. "Me either. Would you believe I actually thought he was avoiding me because he felt guilty about Ryan? Not only is he gone, he's gotten hold of some of my client information."

"Those accounts we just lost?"

"Yup, might be the tip of the iceberg, I'm afraid."

"But why those? I hate to see them go, but they aren't our big… you think he's going after all of them?"

"Yeah, I do," I said grimly. "I think his last 'fuck you' is going to be an effort to make me look like a laughingstock. The only Business Formula with no business. He's undercutting my fees by half."

"How in the hell could he afford to do that? What firm would agree to let him do it?"

"I don't know, but I'm going to find out. Until then, I want to keep the number of people who know about this to a minimum, understood? I'm going to break the news to Knight now. Goody, don't say anything to Robin."

I was already walking toward the branch manager's office when I heard Goody gasp. I turned to find him with his hand over his mouth. The whites of his eyes seem to glow against his light caramel skin.

"My God, poor Robin," he said. "She relies on Jackson to supplement Goldsmith's shitty base salary. The two other brokers she works for don't pay her squat."

I was angry enough to consider pointing out that Goody should be more concerned about himself. One of the stipulations of Business Formula was that a broker paid for their own rent, their own supplies and equipment, and *all* of their sales assistant's salary and bonus. Instead I said, "I wouldn't be surprised if Robin knew more than you think."

Goody shook his head in denial, but I pressed on because the more I thought about it, the more Robin's involvement felt like a given. "Would there be any reason Robin would have had access to any of my accounts?"

"Well, yeah. We relieve each other. She's helped me on a couple of occasions. Remember when I had jury duty?"

"Shit." It would have been so easy for Robin to give Brad Jackson information about my clients without Goody's knowledge.

"Mia, she wouldn't have," Goody said, but I could already see the seeds of doubt forming in his mind.

"I'm not saying she did, but Jackson couldn't have done this by himself. I've caught him skulking around your desk before, but it would take time to gather all that information. So, not a word until we get this thing worked out."

Goody's eyes grew wide again. "Jackson bought her a PalmPilot."

I went still, not because I was interested in gifts that Jackson would have given Robin, but because Goody seemed to think it was a valid piece of information.

"He gave it to her last Friday. I remember because it's the first time he ever gave her anything. She can tap into free Wi-Fi from the coffee shop downstairs to check her personal e-mail without using the company computers. It has a camera on it." Goody's voice was dull and he looked as hurt as he had when he'd been dumped by Mr. Sure Thing number one hundred and four.

"Don't jump to any conclusions, okay?" I was just saying the right thing. It was obvious Goody had already reached the same conclusion I had; Robin was Jackson's accomplice. That wasn't the most troubling part. As disreputable as it sounded, stealing another broker's clients wasn't illegal. What was disturbing was that Robin might have been left behind for the specific purpose of stealing confidential information. If she had made copies of my documents to give to Jackson, that could be a federal crime.

As I stomped toward the office of our branch manager, Ralph Knight, I remembered that Brenda was parked on two, and detoured to pick up a courtesy phone.

"Mia Sanchez," I barked into the receiver.

To my relief, I was greeted by a dial tone.

❖

Cool air hit the back of my neck and sent a shiver down my spine as I walked. I was so tired and hungry that I could barely force one foot in front of the other. The streets seemed deserted, and all along my neighborhood sprinklers chirped as they drenched lawns already preparing themselves for an early fall. I just wanted food and my bed, in that order. I was done with worrying about Jackson, my clients, or my ex-girlfriend, at least for tonight.

I put my key in the lock and nearly screamed when the key was pulled from my hand. Ryan stood there looking so tall, so beautiful, and so concerned that I almost cried. "You're still here," I said.

"Yes. I'm sorry, I didn't mean to scare you. I was worried about you." Ryan moved away from the door and I walked into my own house like I was a visitor. The air smelled like water-based paint and seasoning.

"You cook something?"

"Yeah, I found some stuff in the kitchen, I hope you don't mind. You sounded so tired when you asked me to look after Pepito that I…" Ryan shrugged.

"No, of course I don't mind." I stepped out of my shoes. "And yes, I am really tired."

"I made broccoli beef and brown rice."

"I had brown rice here?"

"No, that I had to buy. But you had the rest."

I followed her into the kitchen, my mouth watering as I tried to remember what I had eaten that day. The best I could recollect, I'd had about nine orange Tic Tacs, a leftover pack of saltines that I had found in my desk drawer, and a Diet Pepsi. "It smells heavenly."

"It is. Pepito and I tasted it for you."

"Oh, you've already eaten?" I was disappointed that we wouldn't be sharing another meal together.

"Sorry, I got hungry a few hours ago."

"So where is the little devil?"

"I pulled his bed into the kitchen so he could watch me. He napped while I cooked. Not sure where he is now, though. Why don't you sit down and I'll play hostess."

As I slumped into a chair I heard the clickety-click of Pepito's nails on the floor and then felt a warm, bony body lean against my shin. I leaned back so I could look under the table. Pepito blinked at me, then closed his eyes.

"He's been waiting at the door for you all night," Ryan said.

"Funny, he barely tolerates me when I'm here."

"Maybe he has a hard time showing his appreciation."

"Ryan?"

"Hmm?"

"Thank you for doing this and for being here."

"You're welcome. I'm going to dish this up so you can eat and then I'll get out of your hair." When she slid the plate in front of me, I felt my eyes well up. "Would you like some water?"

"No, but I'd love a Diet Pepsi. Mind grabbing me one from the refrigerator?"

"That won't keep you up?" she asked, but she was already pulling at the refrigerator door.

I tucked into my dinner. "I don't think anything will keep me up after the day I've had." I forced myself to stop chewing long enough to grunt a thanks when Ryan slid the can in front of me.

"I'm heading out. You gonna be okay?"

I stopped chewing long enough to be embarrassed by how fast I was eating. "Ryan, can you…would you stay? I mean, are you in a hurry?"

"No, I can stay. Let me get some water going and I'll have my tea while you eat."

"This is so good. I doubt there will be any left by the time your tea is ready."

"There's plenty left on the stove. Do you want to tell me what's going on, or would you rather not talk about it?"

I stopped shoveling food into my mouth long enough to note the concern in Ryan's eyes. For the most part, I hadn't had many problems at work. But even if I had, Brenda thought that it helped the relationship if we kept work and home separate. I never got the impression she cared about what I was doing at work anyway.

I intended on giving Ryan the short version. Instead, I found myself telling her everything Henry had told me about what Jackson had done, right down to the part that had been the most difficult. Knight had given Robin five minutes to gather her things and leave the office, and he had called the company lawyers. Not only was he going to press charges against Brad Jackson's new employers, but he was naming Jackson and Robin in the suit. Robin had been teary-eyed and full of denials as she left the office. Even Goody had refused to speak to her; he looked like he'd been kicked in the chest.

I pushed my mostly empty plate away. "I can't imagine ever being so pissed off that I would go to the lengths Jackson has to get even."

"So now what happens?"

"Knight will make him an example to other brokers, and unfortunately, that means that I'll probably have to deal with this for years to come."

"How so?"

"He stole confidential information about my clients for the express purpose of soliciting their business. That's against the law. He might not have wanted their Social Security numbers, but he got them. Therefore, he's in more trouble than he ever imagined. The SEC will have to go after him, and as the broker for these people, I may have to testify against him."

"It's amazing that he would think he could get away with that."

I shrugged. "He's so arrogant it probably never occurred to him that he might get caught."

I stifled a yawn and Ryan did too. "I should get going," she said.

"Your mail is on the table near the front door. You probably didn't notice, but I got the mail slot put in the door."

"Ah no, I'm sorry, I didn't." I limped to the front door and admired the job she had done. The mail slot looked as if it had always been there.

"I saw that your entry form for the Challenge was still on the table when I brought in your mail. I think that has to be in by next Monday if you're still thinking about doing it."

"Thanks, I'll take a look at it in the morning. Will I see you Monday?"

She smiled. "As long as you have the energy to work out, I'll be here."

"I have a feeling I've got a lot more late evenings in store, but I want to keep up the workouts. I was wondering if you had decided, you know, about taking the room?"

Ryan looked embarrassed. "I was going to mention it to you tonight, but with everything going on, I figured it was the last thing on your mind."

"I haven't forgotten. The first of the month will be here in a few days, so if you're going to make a decision, now would be a good time."

"I decided. If the offer still stands, I'd like to take you up on it, but only for a few months...if that's okay."

I was too sleepy to do anything but smile. "The offer still stands. You can move in whenever you want. Just let me know so I can help you."

"So that's it? No contract or anything?"

"I'm too tired to be businesslike. We can work out the details later."

Ryan met my eyes as she pulled the door shut. I felt like reaching out and wiping the apprehension from her face. I didn't, of course. I was afraid that it might mess up the progress we had made. I engaged the dead bolt and followed Pepito up the stairs. My whole body ached from the workout life seemed to be giving me.

CHAPTER THIRTEEN

I wish I could say we spent a lot of quality time together once we were living under the same roof, but the truth is, I was getting home well after nine o'clock and Ryan was an early to bed, early to rise kind of girl. In other words, the only time we saw each other was during our morning workouts. I looked forward to those twice as much as my evening workouts alone. I loved the extra motivation of showing her that I was making progress. I was trying hard not to be disappointed that we were still far from bonding. I had no right to be disappointed, though. She had made it clear that we were just friends.

At work, the Jackson situation moved relentlessly toward a court date. We got the client exoduses stanched after a couple of weeks. My personal clients wouldn't even talk to Jackson, and the smaller accounts that we did lose we agreed to chalk up to a learning experience. It took a while for Goody to stop blaming himself for being gullible. I was sorry that Robin took advantage of him, but it was past time for him to stop beating himself up over it. The best way to get even is to move on, so I reminded him that it was my turn to host poker night.

"You might want to tell her about it as soon as possible," Goody said. "I hated when my roommates brought people into the house without telling me first."

"I'll just ask her to play." I stretched a few muscles, distracted by a slight cramping in my shoulders. "I just realized why I'm so damn sore. I've worked out for eight days straight. Two was my record."

"You, addicted to exercise? I'm impressed."

"Ryan wants to go hiking."

He gave me a long look. "No comment. Now, getting back to more important matters. The poker game. Same crowd?"

"Christina might not come, since Brenda isn't here. We don't need the extra person to make the pots even."

"She'll come. She'll never admit it, but I think she needs the break from that husband of hers." Goody swept out of the office, more like his old self than I had seen him since the day Robin was escorted out.

I picked up the phone and called Christina first. She seemed surprised that I wanted to have poker night without Brenda but enthusiastic nonetheless. I caught Amy in the car and had to wait for her to pull over, put me on hold, and call her very pregnant partner, Dominique, before agreeing to come to play. I could hear the same unasked questions in her voice: *Have you heard from Brenda? Are you really just going to go on with your life?* The last call I had to make was to Ryan. I could have waited until I got home, but I couldn't pass up an excuse to hear her voice. My fingers hovered over the dial pad as I realized that I had just inadvertently volunteered myself for a fun-filled evening of explaining to my poker buddies why I had a woman I hardly knew living in my home seven weeks after my girlfriend left me. *I'll pick up some wine. If I get them drunk enough they might not even notice her.* I shook my head and smiled. I couldn't imagine anyone not noticing Ryan. I started dialing my home number. "This is going to be fun," I said as the phone began to ring.

❖

Ryan had made me promise to take a break from working out this morning so that I wouldn't burn out. So why was I wide-awake at 4:30 a.m. on a Saturday morning? I'll tell you why. Because I heard her get up and after a few moments open her door. I heard her shoo Pepito away from my bedroom door and I heard both of them walk downstairs, where I imagined her sitting at the table to have her cup of tea. I tossed and turned for another forty-five minutes before I gave up and stomped into the bathroom to take a quick shower.

The poker night was one of the reasons I had awakened on the wrong side of the bed. I would have to spend my Saturday morning in the grocery store because there was no food in the house. My Saturday afternoon would be spent unpacking—translation: hiding—

the remaining moving boxes still stacked in the family room, and my Saturday night would be spent explaining my new, attractive roommate. To top it all, I had had sexual relations with myself three times in the last five days and I still felt like I could hump the hell out of anything firm and willing.

I didn't have any warning that Ryan was done with her workout until the door swung open. I had found a box of biscotti hidden in the back of the cabinet and I was nibbling on one. Great thing about biscotti, you can never really tell if they're stale.

"Morning, Mia."

"Morning." I didn't hide the fact that I was grouchy. Why should I? I *was* grouchy and she looked good. I mean deliciously good, and she did that smile thing and my heart thumped so hard in my chest that I almost dropped my biscotti. But I didn't; it was a good one and I was damned if I was going to waste it, so I just scowled at her.

She grinned at me and sat down with her legs wide open. My mother would have been horrified. *Don't look, Mia. Don't you dare look.*

"What do you have planned for the day? I expected you to sleep in," she said.

Don't look, don't look. Aww, God damn it, I looked. I snatched my eyes away quickly, but I could have sworn she had an "aha, gotcha" look on her face. That made me hate her so bad that I could have just thrown her ass on the floor and ravished her, which pissed me off even more.

"Poker. I got poker, remember?" I turned my back on that grin so I could finish my biscotti over the sink. I deserved the biscotti, and she probably wanted to say something to me about it but wouldn't. She got her revenge by looking sexy; I got mine by eating my cookie. *Who's having more fun?* I stopped eating and turned around for a peek. *Oh good Lord, she is.*

"Uh-huh. I didn't know you played, by the way." She stood up, dragging a sweatshirt off the counter.

Thank God. Yes, please cover yourself. I kept waiting for the relief, but it never came. "The girls and I are playing poker. You can play if you want."

"No, thank you. I'm not much for gambling."

"It isn't gambling, really. It's a twenty-dollar buy-in..." I trailed off as I remembered that money was tight for Ryan.

"Thanks for inviting me, but no." Her words were firm, much as they had been when she had told me there would be no further intimacy between us.

"Okay," I said. I was about to leave the kitchen with my tail tucked when she did something really weird. She reached out and touched my arm.

"Hey," she said. "Don't do that."

"What?"

"Look at me like that. You look like I just kicked you in the stomach."

I laughed a little. "No, I think you did that yesterday, and it was a little lower down and to the back."

She smiled but it didn't go further than her lips.

"I know you said that you didn't want…" I backed away from that particular topic. "I just thought we could at least be friends."

She was shaking her head. "We are friends. You're misunderstanding. My father was a gambler."

"Shit, I'm sorry. He really did a number on you, didn't he?"

Ryan shrugged. "He didn't do as much of a job on me as you would think."

"Did he lose a lot?"

"That's just it. He was really good. Until he drank too much beer. When he drank he lost and he did destructive things. Like gamble with money that should have been used to pay the rent."

I don't know why I did it, but I reached out and rubbed her arms through her sweatshirt. She was watching me carefully, as if she was trying to figure out what I was playing at. Hell, even I didn't know. What was I doing? Why couldn't I keep my damn hands off her? "You've had a hard life, haven't you?"

"No more than anybody else," she said, but I instantly knew that that was a lie. "What time is your company due tonight?" Her voice was quiet, her words tight and controlled.

I dropped my hands. "Seven, and it's just my college roommate and her partner, my sister, and a friend of a friend. Oh, and Goody, of course."

"Thought you said it was girls' poker night."

"He squeals if he wins fifty cents. It's amusing."

"I'll make sure to be out of the way by the time they get here. I'm going to go grab a shower."

I stood in the middle of the kitchen just long enough to ensure that Ryan wasn't going to come back, and then I tossed the rest of my half-eaten biscotti into the garbage disposal.

❖

"Naomi, I hope you brought more than twenty bucks, because I am not loaning you any money this time." Goody swept past me followed by Naomi, Christina, Dominique, and Amy. I somewhat reluctantly shut the front door behind them. Goody stopped in the living-room entryway, causing a logjam. "Ooh, did you clean up for us? The place looks great. No boxes. Where's—"

"Goody." I shook my head in warning.

"Wow, so this is it?" Naomi pushed past Goody and turned in a small circle, looking around with the air of someone trying to find fault at every turn, but she smiled and said, "Great house. Do we get a tour?"

"We don't have time for that," Goody answered for me. "I need to beat you bitches and get home for my beauty rest before midnight."

I gave him a grateful look because a tour would mean I would have to explain why one of the rooms upstairs was off-limits. "The rest of the house is a mess. How about next time?"

"Next time will be six months from now, and who knows where you'll be liv—"

Amy's words were cut off when her partner Dominique socked her in the arm. "What?" she asked, then her eyes grew wide in realization and she immediately stuttered an apology. "Oh, my God, I'm so sorry. You know I didn't mean anything by that. It's this pregnancy thing. My hormones are all messed up."

"If you were the one with the huge belly, that might be a halfway plausible excuse," Naomi said.

I waved my hand. "Girls, please. Do we play, or do we sit here trading sewing patterns?"

"Let's play. But first, where's the spread?"

"Where's the spread?" was Dominique's standard question since she had become pregnant. She had embraced her own round pregnant body with a passion that only a naturally skinny girl could appreciate.

"Right through here, sweetheart." I was already holding my breath. Besides my biscotti debacle, I really was trying to eat better, so I had created a spread that consisted of fresh fruit, lower fat cheeses, and cold cuts. With the exception of Goody, who was notoriously healthy, all the other girls provided chips and dips. I needn't have worried; my guests descended on the food like vultures.

"So how's it going?" Goody asked me while everyone else was busy devouring food.

"We worked out together every day this week and I'm sore as hell."

"You know that's not what I mean."

"I know. But honestly, things are fine. Great, even." *Who am I kidding? "Great" is pushing it.*

"There's a 'but' in there," Goody said.

"No but. I just wish I could stop wanting more. She's obviously gotten over any attraction for me, so why can't I?"

"You think Ryan's not attracted to you anymore?"

"Well, she doesn't seem all that perturbed by us just being friends."

"And you are?"

"I don't know, Goody. Do we have to talk about this now?"

"No, of course not." Goody put his arm around my shoulder, something he only did outside of work. I let myself lean into him. "Poker is just the thing to get your mind off your troubles. So where do we play?"

"Easy for you to say. In the family room." I led the way, which was a good thing because no one saw the surprised look on my face. All of the boxes had been moved to the corners, the table had been pushed into the middle of the floor, and my poker set had been placed in the middle of the table and opened.

"This is what I'm talking about, right here," Dominique said. "You see this, Naomi? This is a real poker setup. Not that itty-bitty card table with dinky-assed chairs you had us sitting at."

"If you hadn't eaten all those cream puffs, that chair wouldn't have broken," Naomi retorted and I would have laughed if the statement wasn't somewhat true.

"She's pregnant, you ass." Amy was quick to come to Dominique's defense.

"So, whose fault is that? You're lesbians. Breeding isn't required."

I let the arguing go on around me. Ryan's gesture had touched me, and I found myself wanting to talk to her, wanting to ask her why she did these things for me and yet refused to even talk about how close we had come to falling into bed together weeks ago.

"Guys, where's the cheat sheet? I can never remember what the color is for the twenty-five-cent chips," Christina said.

Goody groaned and rolled his eyes. "It's the blue ones. It's *always* the blue."

"It's the ones he has the most of," Naomi said.

"Hey, I may have had a lot of blues, but I left with more money than you did last game."

"That's because you did a re-buy. I was still playing with my original twenty bucks."

"Don't you mean the twenty bucks I loaned you in the first place?" Goody said.

"Would you two stop? Are we going to play or what?" I snapped.

"Ooh, someone's touchy. What's the matter? Brenda forget to call or something?"

The room fell silent and I glared at Naomi. "Who in the hell keeps inviting you?" I looked at Goody and he shook his head. I went around the table to Christina, Amy, and Dominique.

Finally Amy said, "We let her come so that we can take her money."

"Oh, okay." I shuffled the cards. "Not that it's any of your business, but I talked to Brenda yesterday morning."

"So that explains it," Naomi said.

I wanted to ask her what exactly it explained, but I didn't want to get into it with her. I dealt the cards with a flourish, then picked up my own hand. I found myself thinking of Ryan in her bedroom watching TV or whatever it was she did in there. Maybe working out, or worse, taking a shower.

"You going to play or fold?" Naomi's annoying voice cut across my pleasant thoughts. "Don't make me call the clock on your ass."

"This isn't Pictionary, fool," Goody said.

"Don't engage her, Goody," I said and mucked the hand.

"I'm going to go get some water." Dominique stood up and her stomach bumped against the table.

"Oh, sweetie, did you hurt yourself?" Amy asked with a hand on her belly.

"Oh, for God's sake," Naomi said. "She's got more padding than the Michelin Man."

"Naomi, if you say one more thing about my wife…"

"Hey, I'll get the water, okay?" I stood up. My muscles groaned in protest and my head pounded with every step I took toward the kitchen. All I wanted was for everyone to get the hell out of my house.

I poured a glass of cold water and stood with it pressed against my forehead. I could hear them intermittently cat-fighting and laughing, a normal poker night. So why was I feeling so out of sorts and spiteful? It was because of Ryan, of course. She was driving me nuts.

I froze with the glass still pressed to my forehead as the door to the basement opened and Ryan stepped into the kitchen wearing black shorts and a gray sports bra, both of which left nothing to the imagination. Her skin glistened from her workout, and the sight of it made me moist somewhere else. She stood there with her towel at her neck and I must have wobbled or something, because she walked closer, as if to catch me, then stopped.

"Mia?"

"Hmm?" I seemed to be having both a hard time breathing and tearing my gaze away from hers. Her hand went to the countertop, and the door to the basement thumped closed.

"You have to stop looking at me like that."

I blinked at the plaintive quality of her voice. "I'm sorry, I don't mean…" I looked away.

"Don't be embarrassed," she said.

"Ha, easy for you to say."

"Are you angry at me about something?"

"No, of course not." It wasn't a lie. I was angry at myself for wanting her so much and for the fact that it just felt inappropriate.

"What's wrong, then?" Ryan's eyes went to my mouth and I struggled not to chew on my bottom lip. I didn't succeed.

"You're what's wrong. You're still acting like we're strangers or something and it's driving me crazy."

"I thought we'd discussed this."

"We did. I suppose part of me was hoping that we would still get to know each other, I guess." I dropped my gaze to the floor because I couldn't stand seeing the obvious frustration on her face. *Oh, my God. Somebody please just drop-kick my ass off the side of a tall building.*

"What do you want me to do?"

"I don't know. Not pretend? Stop acting like you don't…I don't know…like me."

When she finally spoke she sounded dejected. "I do like you. I like you a lot. But you have someone else."

"She left me."

"Yes, she left you. It doesn't mean you don't have unfinished business."

"She's not here."

"She's not?" Ryan placed her hand in the space between my breasts. "Are you sure?"

I wanted to tell her that yes, damn it, I was sure. But what did that mean? Did that mean that four years of supposedly loving someone meant nothing? That someone—even a beautiful someone—could come along and my feelings would change?

"Do you know how you look right now?" she asked.

"No."

"Your eyes are so big and brown and sad. Your lips are parted and moist because you keep licking them, and I can see a pulse right in the hollow of your neck beating so fast that I just want to touch it with my fingertips." I closed my eyes and waited. I knew she was close because her breath caressed my lips as she spoke. "My moving in was a bad idea, wasn't it?"

She turned me around and the door thumped again, this time as my back was pressed against it. My chest heaved against Ryan's and I felt a groan travel from her chest, out of her mouth and into mine. Based on the way she had been looking at me, I had expected a rough, hungry kiss like the one at the front door, but what I got was soft, gentle, almost pleading.

When she tore her mouth from mine I sucked in air like a diver in anticipation of another deep-sea dive without a tank. The hands that had been everywhere slowed and so did her breathing.

"Why do you have to feel so good?" Her voice sounded sad, almost angry, or maybe it was both. "Do you know how hard it is for me to even look at you?"

Something in her tone tore at me and my desire dampened slightly until her hand reached beneath my chin. I met her eyes and saw exactly what she couldn't articulate.

"I need to touch you this time." Her voice seemed thick, as if she had been drinking.

"It's all right, sweetheart." I reached for her hand and pressed it to the front of my shirt, just below my breasts, as if she didn't know what to do. She continued to watch me as she eased my shirt from my jeans. I expected her to make short work of the buttons once it was free, but without a modicum of hesitation, she slipped warm fingers beneath my shirt and rested them on my stomach. I inhaled and she closed her eyes. I watched her face change again. The desire was there, but there was a look of discovery, of finality, and of quiet longing that sent warmth rushing to my crotch.

"Ryan?" Most of her name came out silently and when she opened her eyes to look at me, I knew that my last thread of control was lost. If she wanted to, if she wanted me, I was hers.

The hand that had been at my back was now at my hips. Her leg was between mine and I whimpered as I found myself being supported by a muscled thigh at my crotch. The seam of the jeans pressed my clitoris roughly and I felt her body jerk. I cupped her face in my hands, deepening the kiss, in case she had any intention of moving. Then I dropped from her neck down to her shoulders and tore my mouth away again so that I could breathe. Her hands were creeping beneath my bra, raising it above my breasts until they tumbled out like two eager puppies, and she cupped them.

"Jesus, Mia. I've wanted to touch you like this from day one."

I nodded my agreement. I was holding on to her sides, watching her face as she cupped and caressed my breasts reverently. The palms of her hands made chill bumps raise on my arms. I lifted my hands to her breasts; I grazed her nipples through the cloth and she whimpered. I met her eyes and lifted her sports bra until her small, firm breasts came into view. I cupped them and leaned in to kiss them only to have her press me back against the door.

"I'm sweaty."

"I don't care," I said and pressed harder against her until her arms weakened and my lips came in contact with one nipple. I kissed the firm russet-colored nipple, then took it into my mouth and caressed it with my tongue. I could feel her breath passing across my ear in soft little puffs that turned to sharp gasps as my tongue began a slow caress. She was salty, but there was something sweet about her too. Her gasps had become like soft hiccups, and if not for the two hands pulling me close, I might have stopped to make sure she was okay.

I glanced up at her briefly before tending to the other breast. The two strands of hair that never wanted to be tamed were hanging forward;

her face was a study of tormented pleasure and she was panting. I rubbed gently at the breast I had just ravished as I took the other nipple into my mouth. She was shaking and leaning against me, so I urged her to turn around and rest against the door again. I hadn't intended to kiss her as hard as I did, but when she shuddered and gathered me close, I lost all thought of holding back. When she pulled her lips away I kissed the line of her jaw, working my way back to her lips.

"We need to stop while I still can," she gasped.

Even as I heard the halfhearted plea, my hands were traveling to the damp crotch of her shorts. I realized with stunned clarity that she wasn't wearing any underwear. Not only could I feel how much she desired me, I could feel every fold, every curve of her sex. Her clitoris shuddered against my fingertips, and she let out a choked sob, which I smothered with my mouth to keep myself from crying out. I moved to kiss the scar at her cheek, her neck, and her breasts, which were still free. My fingers, of their own accord, crept beneath the waistband of her shorts and paused at the neatly trimmed hair, giving her time to stop me. Her only reaction was in the heaving of her stomach, and when I moved forward, parting her legs so that she was open to me.

My fingers sank into her warmth. She tried to straighten against the door and when she did, I slipped even deeper inside her. I pulled out my soaked finger, gliding over her clitoris twice, and then sank back into her, this time with a second finger. Her head slammed back against the door so hard that it startled me.

"Oh, sweetheart, don't." My hand, the free one, went to the back of her head to rub gently where I imagined she had struck the door.

"Mia, please…stop playing with me. Finish it." Her mouth was trembling and her body felt heavy, as if she could barely keep herself standing. She thought I was playing with her. I wanted to stop, desire be damned, and make her understand that I wasn't playing, that I had never felt this for anyone. Not Brenda, not anyone. But she was hurting and I was touching her so deeply that each breath she drew made her rise slightly off my fingers.

"Oh, God," she whispered.

"It's okay, sweetheart."

"Mia, someone's coming."

If it wasn't for the shocked look on her face, I might have thought she was prophesying her pending orgasm. I managed to pull my hand from her pants and stick it in my back pocket just as Christina, Goody, and Dominique stumbled through the door.

"Oh, hey. Sorry," Christina said. "We didn't mean to interrupt."

Ryan's breathing was shallow behind me.

"Hey, everybody, this is Ryan. She just finished working out."

"Hi," Ryan said.

I had the horrifying realization that I had left Ryan's breasts hanging out when I had turned around, but a quick glance back showed that she'd had the presence of mind to right herself before they came. I, on the other hand, no longer had a ponytail and my shirt was untucked. They would have to be pure innocents not to know what they had just interrupted.

"I guess you wanted that water, huh." I picked up the glass and tried to hand it to Dominique, but her eyes were riveted on Ryan.

Goody cleared his throat. Any fantasy I'd had that they might not realize what we were doing went out the window with that action. "Ryan, I didn't know you were here. You should come out and play with us."

"No, thanks. I was just downstairs working out. I need to get a shower." Ryan took the glass from my hand and drained it. Her eyes never left mine as she drank. She handed the empty glass back and, with a soft "excuse me" to Dominique, squeezed by everyone and escaped out the doorway, leaving me in the clutches of evil.

CHAPTER FOURTEEN

"I want her so bad."

The words cracked through the silence and sent a shiver down my back. If the voice hadn't been so irreverent, so lecherous, and if Amy hadn't popped Goody in the back of the head, I would have thought the words were my own.

"What?" Goody protested in a voice worse than the sound of a cat in heat. "I could want a woman."

"And what would you do with her?" Christina asked.

"I'd, you know, paint her toenails and play dress-up with her."

Both Dominique and Goody had expectant looks on their faces, while Christina had, as far as I could tell, avoided looking at me altogether. Her disapproval was no less evident than if she had picked up the phone and called our mother and told her what she had just caught me doing. I turned away, filled the glass with water, and downed it in the hopes of cooling myself down. Too bad the glass was still warm from where she'd held it, too bad I had the immediate vision of her lips being pressed there. Damn, even thoughts of my mother weren't cooling me down. I steeled myself and faced my waiting audience.

"Okay, so you gonna tell us about the chick you got living under your stairs?" Dominique asked.

"Ooh." Goody whipped around. "I saw that movie. It was with that cute actor that played the boy doctor…what was it called?"

"Yeah, we saw it too. It was based on a true story," Amy said.

"Shut up…for real? I had no idea," Goody said with all the reverence of a child.

"Yeah, they ended up trying to kill the husband."

Goody turned to me. "You got plans we should know about?"

"Oh, be quiet." I pushed my way past the Three Stooges. Dominique was pretending to eat a carrot stick that I knew she would exchange for the Doritos Naomi had brought once the rest of us were inebriated. I couldn't help but reach out and touch her tummy as I passed. "You look so beautiful," I said.

To my utter surprise, she blushed and put her hand over her distended belly. "Thanks."

"So are we back to playing, or are you going to stand around talking about some made-for-TV movie?" I tried to sound casual but the sooner the game ended, the sooner I could find Ryan and convince her to finish what we started in the kitchen.

"I vote both," Goody said.

I rolled my eyes and stalked back to the poker table.

"Who the hell was that?" Naomi stage-whispered. "She was hot!"

This is going to be a long night.

❖

"I'm sorry, but I can't do this." Dominique tossed down her two cards.

"It's okay, sweetheart." Amy munched on a chip while she looked at her cards. "You'll get some good ones soon."

"No, I mean I can't just act like she isn't up there."

"I see your fifty and raise you seventy-five," I said, hoping that by betting three times the blind, someone would call me. But they all folded like the scared bitches they were. I swept the chips toward me and stacked them neatly. I could feel their eyes on the top of my hair.

"So, who is she, Mia? I mean, you can't just expect us not to be curious."

Amy reached for Dominique's hand to quiet her. "Hon, let's leave Mia alone. I don't think she wants to talk about it."

It wasn't like Dominique to be so persistent, and I could tell that the others were equally interested. So I reluctantly offered an explanation that I hoped would end the speculation. "She's a friend and she's doing some work on the house."

"Does Brenda know about this friend living in her house?" Naomi demanded.

"You see Brenda here?" My words carried an anger I didn't know I was feeling. Maybe Ryan was right. Maybe my business with Brenda was too unfinished to even contemplate a new relationship.

"So I have a question," Amy said as she mucked her cards. "Is it even possible to be friends with someone who looks like that?"

"Hey," Dominique protested.

"Sweetie, you're gorgeous, but you know what I mean."

Dominique growled a response, but she seemed somewhat mollified. They exchanged a few other private remarks that were punctuated with gentle kisses. I was grateful not to be the focus of everyone's attention, because my imagination had just shifted into overdrive as I envisioned Ryan stepping into a shower. The fact that the pipes had begun their normal chorus of groans lent itself nicely to the imagination process.

Finally Dominique said, "Well, I'm just glad Mia ignored you all these years."

Christina choked and sat her glass down hard. "Did I just miss something?"

"Oh, my God, you didn't know Amy had a thing for Mia in college?" Goody said. "I thought everyone knew that."

"Are you kidding me?" Christina looked from Amy to me.

I wasn't sure if I was more annoyed with Goody for picking up on something that I had obviously missed or Christina, whose reaction had just a tad too much shock to not be insulting. Was it so far-fetched to think someone had found me attractive in college? The night had gone from fantastic to ridiculous in the span of a few minutes.

"Since when did Amy have a crush on me?" I asked. "She spent most of her time dating jocks."

"I always came home to you, though." Amy turned to Dominique, who had her bottom lip stuck out. "That was a long time ago, sweetie." She leaned over and kissed her wife.

I blinked at them all like strangers. "I haven't had anything to drink and you guys haven't drunk near enough to be acting like this."

"Sorry, Mia, but you were just getting out of that awkward stage and entering the stage you're in now. I may not have wanted to admit I was a lesbian, but having a beautiful woman, who was definitely a lesbian, sleeping right next to me was difficult."

Amy's confession floored me. I considered her my closest friend. We didn't spend near enough time together because of work and relationships, but she had never admitted to being remotely interested in me. I had spent the first two years after she came out waiting for her to change her mind about being gay. Even after she and Dominique became serious, I kept waiting for her to call me and admit that she had made a mistake in becoming serious so quickly. I'd been wrong about that, and soon I was going to have a godson to prove it.

"It would have been hard having an attractive woman as a roommate when you were trying to come out," Naomi said matter-of-factly. "When I first came out, I wanted to have sex with any woman who looked remotely lesbian, let alone like Mia."

I've had friends and people who love me tell me I'm pretty enough times that the direction the conversation had taken shouldn't have bothered me, but it did. Hell, my mother's favorite phrase was "but you have such a pretty face." Even though that was disguised under a warning about my weight, I knew better than to believe any of them.

"Thank God I grew up in a small town, because I was too young to be getting out there like that," Dominique said as she put a ridiculously small bet on the table. I immediately mucked my hand, suspicious that she was trying to lure me in with her slow play. Naomi called and I watched unsurprised as Dominique turned over two kings, clobbering Naomi's pair of tens.

"So?" Naomi was looking at me. "You gonna tell us who she is? I mean, what's the big deal? You said yourself Brenda isn't here. It's not like we're going to tell her, or—"

"You know what, Naomi?" I slammed my cards face down on the table. "Call her. Tell her if you want. I'll give you her phone number. I don't give a shit what you do. I really just want to play cards." I'd overreacted. I could see it in Goody's face and the way that Christina wasn't looking at me. "She's a contractor, okay? She's doing some work on the house."

Goody had been quiet up to this point, a fact that had me trying to figure out when he was due his next raise, until he opened his fat mouth with a nifty idea. "Why don't you just invite her down to play with us?"

"She's taking a shower," I growled.

"If that racket your pipes make is any indication, she's done now."

"I already asked her, she said no."

"Ask her again." Naomi squirmed in her seat like Goody when

he got what he thought was a decent hand. "I'd like to get to know her better if she's single. That is, if you're being honest with us about there being nothing going on between you two."

Now I was angry. "She doesn't play poker."

"Even more reason to invite her down. With Brenda gone, the pots just aren't what they used to be." Christina glared down at her hand. I folded; Christina only glared when she had face cards.

"Tell her we won't make her buy in; you're loaded, you can throw another twenty in for her," Naomi said and they all looked at me expectantly.

"Fine." I stood up. "Fold my next hand for me. I'll go ask her again just to appease you people. After she says no again, I don't want to hear any more about it. Deal?"

I stalked away before any of them could answer. I'm pretty sure they were all psychoanalyzing why I was so annoyed. It wasn't that I didn't want her playing with us. I just knew I wouldn't be able to hide my emotions with her sitting inches away from me.

I reached her door and paused, nervous and unsure. The intimacy in the kitchen had been shockingly unexpected and I wanted more, but Ryan had now had time to think. There had been no doubt in my mind that she wanted nothing to do with me other than friendship. What if she decided that she needed to move out now because of what had happened? *Maybe I shouldn't go in there, maybe I should give her time. I could just turn around and go back downstairs and tell them she refused again.*

I had forgotten all about Pepito and the fact that I hadn't seen him all evening when he gave a high-pitched bark from inside Ryan's room. Before I could react, the door opened and Ryan stood in front of me. Her damp hair, for once, was tamed by a band and she had on loose-fitting gray yoga pants, a T-shirt, and no shoes. Her eyes were soft and she smelled of soap and shampoo.

"Hi. Company gone already?"

"No, they want you to come down."

"They do? Do you want me to come down too?"

"I would love for you to come down, but only if you want to."

"Are you upset with me? About what happened in the kitchen?"

"Why would I be upset?"

"Because I told you we shouldn't and then I did."

I laughed a little. "It is kind of confusing," I admitted.

"I know, and I'm sorry." She sighed and I tensed, waiting for her to tell me that it was a mistake and it would never happen again. Instead she reached out and cupped my cheek. It wasn't the sexually charged touches we shared in the kitchen, but a comforting thing meant to soothe both of us. "If you'll give me a second to change, I'll come down with you."

"For real?" I was so surprised that I let my mouth gape open. "I thought you didn't like gambling because of your father."

"But you said it wasn't really gambling, right?"

"Well…it is, but the girls won't ask you to buy in or anything. So no, for you it isn't really gambling."

Neither of us spoke for a long moment

"You don't need to change," I said. "You look fine." She looked better than fine, but I kept that to myself.

Ryan looked down at her attire and then down at Pepito, as if to ask his opinion. He snorted, turned, and trotted out the door. "I guess you can deal me in."

❖

My grandfather once told me that the company a person keeps represents them. My company was acting really stupid. I am not exaggerating when I tell you that Amy nudged Christina when we walked into the room. Goody almost choked on his celery stick, and Naomi looked like she was about ready to go down on somebody. I wanted to kick the shit out of every last one of them, but I have to admit that the fact that Ryan was actually willing to hang out with us thrilled me no end.

"Since you people insisted on new blood, I found you some." I introduced each of them to Ryan.

"Hi, everybody." If possible, Ryan's accent thickened.

"Here, you can sit next to me." Naomi pulled the seat I had vacated not five minutes before so close to her that the chair backs formed a perfect heart.

"Don't do it," Goody said. "She cheats."

"Actually, Ryan is a novice, so she'll sit next to me." I snatched my chair back and sat it down a safe distance from Naomi. "Here, have a seat. I'll grab another chair."

"Thanks."

I couldn't help but smile at her. She looked so shy that I felt the need to protect her from the vultures. I picked up the cards Goody had just dealt; the thrill that went through my body had nothing to do with the pocket queens I was holding and everything to do with the fact that Ryan's arm had just brushed against mine. I bet four times the blind and turned to Ryan. "You know you can fold if you don't have good cards. Or you could call me or…" She was looking at me oddly, so I stopped speaking. "You probably already knew that, huh?"

"It's okay. Thank you for helping me. It's really sweet of you."

I blinked on that. Did she just call me sweet? Did she forget I had my hand down her pants not thirty minutes ago?

Two chips hit the pile in the center of the table and I had to tear my eyes away and squint at her.

"Uh, Ryan, did you mean to call me? You could fold."

"No, it's okay."

I looked Ryan in the eye. *Fold, sweetie, don't make me take your chips.*

Everyone else folded, which left me up against Ryan. I did not want to take her money, so I decided to up the ante. I almost hated to do it, but I threw in a pot-sized bet and waited for her to fold. Although I was telling her with my eyes to throw away her hand, she was telling me with hers that she never would. Me and my trip queens felt strangely disconcerted.

"Whoa, it just got hot in here," Dominique said.

Ryan smiled, and in that instant I remembered her telling me that her father was good. No, not just good. Really good.

She called me. Her chips hit the stack and I blinked. *Oh shit.*

"What do you have?" I asked softly, not breaking eye contact.

"Everything I need to take care of you."

The table around us erupted with laughter and loud comments, but I couldn't tell you what was said. I bet one and a half times the pot. Ryan raised twice my bet. I blinked, bleary eyed, and threw in the chips.

"I call." I turned over my pocket queens to show the table that I had trips.

Ryan turned over a jack king suited.

"Oh, my God. Oh, my God, she got you! She had a straight." Goody high-fived Ryan across the table. "I thought you said she was a novice?"

"She's a ringer," Naomi said with all the shrillness of a young girl yelling "witch" in the 1600s. "Mia brought her in to steal our money."

"Then why the hell did she just take my chips instead of yours, you ass?"

Naomi looked at Ryan suspiciously. "Who plays that kind of money with a jack king suited?"

Ryan shrugged. "I had thirty percent odds after the flop. I figured it was worth it."

"I thought you said you weren't good at this." I was smiling because it was so hard to be mad at her.

"No, I told you I'm not much of a gambler. I hate taking people's money."

"See? Who in the hell spouts out card odds at a home poker game? She's a damn ringer. It's a setup." Naomi stood up and Goody grabbed the back of her shirt.

"Sit your skinny ass down. I drove, remember? Unless you're planning on taking MAX, you aren't going anywhere."

"Mia, can I borrow bus fare?"

"Nope," I said, and everyone but Naomi laughed.

Ryan was looking at me apologetically. "I put you on pocket aces. I might have folded if I'd thought you had queens."

"That's good to know," I grumbled but I don't think I was fooling anyone, least of all Goody, whose smirk would have made me angry if I didn't feel so completely warm inside.

The game, if you could call it that, lasted two more hours, by the end of which the only person enjoying herself was Ryan. Dominique had heartburn, as she always did after our poker games. Christina, Goody, and Amy had all busted out, bought back in, and busted out again. And Naomi was pouting into her White Russian because Ryan hadn't so much as looked at her twice the whole night.

She had, however, looked at me twice. In fact, as the night wore on, either my drink got more potent or she just stopped trying to hide the fact that there was something going on between us. I could hardly concentrate on my hand.

Generally, when people busted out they gravitated toward the couch to wait for the game to end. Tonight, no one left the table. I had no doubt they felt the heat between us too, and I didn't enjoy being on display. There is nothing like being whipped into a sexual frenzy while having your money taken. I imagine it's like being given expensive lingerie and being told it was purchased at the secondhand store after you had already put it on.

As my guests stood and began to organize themselves to leave, Amy patted Dominique's stomach, causing her to smile. The love between the two was so obvious that it almost broke my heart. Had I ever looked at Brenda like that? Maybe. Had she ever looked at me like that? No, absolutely not. I glanced at Ryan and saw her watching my two friends, her expression soft. She shifted her gaze to me and smiled. Her eyes shone with the promises she had been sending me all night. I wished with all my heart that we were alone so that I could touch her. I breathed silent thanks that the voyeurs would soon be out of my house and I could find out if she had any intention of following through.

"Thanks for hosting, ladies. It will have to be at my house next time," Naomi said.

"They let you have poker games at the shelter?" Goody asked.

Naomi's answer was to flip him the bird.

Dominique leaned in to kiss me on the cheek and told Ryan, "I hope you come to the next game and give us a chance to get our money back."

Ryan dipped her head shyly and said, "Sure, I'd like that." I found myself feeling strangely protective again. *Wait a minute, the woman just took my money and now I'm trying to protect her. Hot damn, she's good.*

Christina hugged Ryan good-bye and I was relieved when I saw no discomfort on Ryan's face. "By the way, Ryan, will you be coming to Sunday brunch with Mia tomorrow?"

"Uh, no," I answered for her. But one glance at Ryan's face stopped my next words. It wasn't so much that she looked angry or even interested; she looked blank and I realized that was her coping mechanism.

I could see the question in Christina's eyes, but I would have to deal with her another time. "Anyway, you're invited if you don't have any other plans," she said as she went out the door. "See you both later." As soon as the door closed, Pepito let out a shrill bark. He had been sitting at Ryan's feet quietly the entire length of the game. If he had begged at all, I hadn't heard him.

"I better get him something to eat," Ryan said.

"Ryan, wait." I took her arm gently. "I'd like you to come tomorrow if you aren't busy. We don't start eating until two. It's more like a before-dinner meal rather than brunch…" I caught my bottom lip between my teeth to stop it from trembling.

"I don't want to make you uncomfortable." The warmth I had seen in her eyes when she had looked at Dominique and Amy was now gone.

"No, it isn't you. It's them. I'm embarrassed by them."

"Why?"

"I don't know. It's mostly my mother. I'm afraid she might say something to make you think I'm—I really don't know why I'm ashamed of them. When you meet them you'll understand. I'm trying to say, I'd like it if you would come with me."

Ryan smiled then, and even though her smile told me that she thought I was being silly, I was relieved she wasn't giving me the cold shoulder. She leaned closer and I thought for sure she was going to kiss me again. The memory of the first and last time flooded me with anticipation. Instead, she took my wrist and turned it so that my hand was palm up. "I enjoyed spending time with you and your friends, and I would like to come to Sunday brunch to meet your parents, if you're okay with it." She must have read the disappointment on my face because she pressed her forehead against mine and closed her eyes. "I'm still struggling with this. Things almost got out of hand in there and it's too soon for both of us. Can you just give me a little time, if I promise not to act like it didn't happen?"

She did kiss me then and I leaned heavily into her. The kiss was warm and comforting, but there was still that lightning bolt of desire behind it. Ryan broke it off just before it could turn into something more. She was jogging up the stairs when I finally realized that she had pressed several neatly folded bills into my hand, her poker winnings.

I was about to call out that I wouldn't take her money, but I realized that in a battle of wills with Ryan, I would never win.

Chapter Fifteen

I slept hard—thanks to a little help from my hand—and woke up feeling refreshingly languid. I brought my hand to my nose. My own scent all but covered the last traces of hers, but she was there and I could imagine the feel of her, warm and so wet that I had to press firmly to actually feel her skin. My clitoris jumped at the memory. There had been no time for foreplay last night. I had barely shut the door to my bedroom, swept Pepito onto the floor, disrobed, and sunk my fingers deep within myself before I was biting down hard on a corner of my pillow to keep from calling out her name.

I heard a hungry mewling noise from the direction of the door. Pepito gazed at me expectantly. He licked his lips, dampening my mood immediately. With a resigned groan, I tossed my covers back, tiptoed across the cold floor, and opened the door a crack. Pepito squirted through with the liquid flexibility of a mouse and I heard the small thumps signifying that he was bunny-hopping down the stairs. I snickered. He really was a cute little thing.

Just as I pushed the door shut, the scent of bacon and eggs wafted past me. "Damn, she doesn't play fair."

I wasn't normally a breakfast eater. Coffee and Danish was my idea of a complete breakfast if I had to have one. But the tempting scent and the knowledge that Ryan was down there pulled at me. I took a quick shower and went downstairs into the kitchen.

Ryan was sitting at the table reading a newspaper.

"Good morning," I said and went right to the coffeepot, so I heard rather than saw her lower the paper. She didn't speak for what seemed like a long moment.

"Mornin'. I made breakfast."

"Yeah." I turned around with my mug in hand.

The look on her face brought me to a dead stop. I felt something weak and small turn in my chest and I nearly dropped my mug. Arousal, the sort I had never seen associated with me, was plainly written across her face. "Ryan, about last night?"

And just like that, what I saw on her face was gone. "I told you I didn't want to play."

She didn't want to play? I hesitated and sat down across from her. The fact I had sat at the same table with Brenda only weeks before made me feel tawdry. "You mean the poker game? That's not what I wanted to talk about. You won that money fair and square." *Well, Goody and the girls might have a few thoughts on the fairness of turning them on to the point that they weren't paying attention, but it was fair.* "I was referring to what happened in here between you and me."

A muscle throbbed in Ryan's jaw. "I was hoping we didn't have to talk about that."

"You said you wouldn't pretend nothing happened."

"What good would it do to explore it to hell?"

I wanted to say it did me a lot of good in bed last night. But I didn't. "I don't know. I…"

"Mia, I think you asked me to stay here because you felt guilty."

"That's not true."

"Okay, and you were worried about break-ins too. I understand that, but at some point, I'm going to be done with the work here and you're going to have to deal with…" I realized that she was asking for Brenda's name.

"Brenda," I said reluctantly.

"Brenda coming back. I know you said things were over between you, but they aren't over enough for you to start a new relationship. I don't think enough time has passed."

"How can you make the decision about whether enough time has passed for me?"

"Mia, I'm making the decision for myself."

The fact that she said I wasn't ready for a relationship, not just sex, thrilled me. "So we just ignore what happened last night?"

"I don't think we can ignore it, but we aren't teenagers. We don't have to act on it."

"Is that what you did with Selena, just act on it?"

Ryan frowned. "Did she tell you that? You two must be a lot friendlier then I thought."

"We had lunch together one day and she mentioned seeing you and I leaving together after work, when you took me to Mrs. Margolis's."

"What else did she tell you?"

"Nothing really, just that you two had gone out a few times."

"I see." Ryan stood up. Her body was rigid, and to my surprise she looked angry. "I'm going to get dressed," she said.

"Why are you so angry?"

"Are you seeing her?"

The question was so sudden that I was shocked into answering without thinking. "No, we had lunch. Just the once."

"Are you going to see her again?" Her eyes were piercing.

I answered her carefully. "I don't know. She asked me to come with her to a charity event in a few weeks."

"You said yes?"

"I said I'd think about it."

Ryan bit her bottom lip. "Have you ever been with a woman like Selena before?"

I sat my cup down and walked over to her. "What do you mean, been with? What's with the third degree?"

"Mia, I met her at a bar when I first came to town."

"I know, she told me. She implied that you—"

"We did."

I felt something sharp hit my chest and ricochet around in there, like a bullet looking for the best spot to cause the most damage. "Okay." I was shaking my head, trying to clear it, and trying to keep myself from asking her the obvious—how could she have sex with Selena, but not me?

"Mia, she wanted to be fucked. I was lonely. It was a mutual pleasure-fest, and when she was done with me I didn't hear from her again. What did you tell her about us?"

"That we were friends." The word "friends" came out of my mouth like a curse word. What else was there to say? We weren't lovers; hell, she hadn't even had the courtesy to fuck me. The idea of Ryan fucking anyone made my face go hot with anger and a little bit of something else.

"She called me out of the blue a couple days ago to ask me if I was seeing anyone. I thought it was a coincidence, but I guess not."

"What did you tell her?" I asked in a near whisper.

"I told her I was unavailable."

I shouldn't have smiled at her, I was still mad for several reasons, but the way Ryan was looking at me made me want to.

"Selena was a bad idea, Mia." She had no reason to apologize to me, but I sensed it was an apology. "I was lonely and she offered me some companionship for a few days. She's the one who stopped returning my phone calls. I was okay with it, but that isn't my style. You want and deserve more than that."

"And I can't have more than that with you?"

"Not until you break things off decisively with Brenda."

"I can't do that until she comes home. Am I supposed to put my life on hold for three more months?"

"I won't ruin the possibility of more just so I can have sex now. Besides, you're just getting out of a relationship. Is it really a good idea to jump into another one?"

She was making a lot of sense, but it still felt wrong. My attraction to her was so thorough, I found myself envious of Selena for having been "fucked" by Ryan. But I had to admit, she was right. I did want more than that. "So what does all this mean?"

"It means we have three months to get to know each other better."

I agreed because I didn't see what choice I had.

"Good. Listen, I saw in the paper that they're having a sale down at REI. We'll be able to get you something good. They have tons of refurbished bikes and some reasonably priced new ones."

Dazed, I asked, "A bike? Why do I need a bike?"

Ryan threw back her head and laughed. My eyes were drawn to her scar and down her neck to her breasts and the hard nipples jutting out against her ribbed tank. She quieted and I forced myself back up to her eyes. I was surprised how soft, how loving and warm they looked.

"You're going to need a bike for the Challenge, darlin' woman."

I don't know if it was from the realization that I had just been called darlin', or the softness of her tone, or the look on her face when she said it, but it took me a moment to grasp what she meant by the Challenge.

"Two-mile run, four-mile ride, and then another two-mile run. Remember?"

"Of course I remember." I let out a breath only to catch it again when I realized that I was now expected to buy, and subsequently ride, a bike.

❖

"I think this one will work." Ryan and some kid in a green vest were staring at me and then the bike.

I stood with the bike dutifully between my legs, trying hard not to look hungry or bored. I was both, and had been for the last hour. I also felt pissed and self-conscious. I had armored myself by wearing the only sweatsuit I owned, a black Adidas track jacket and pants that didn't do much to hide my curves but didn't make me feel lumpy either.

The kid walked away and Ryan raised an eyebrow. "You're grouchy all of a sudden."

"Sorry, I hate shopping, and we've been here an hour. I'm getting hungry again."

"I'm not surprised. You never eat enough breakfast. But it's probably the sugar you dumped in your coffee." Ryan indicated the bike I had just tried out. "I think you should get this one."

All my anger drained from me like a forgotten ice-cream cone in a child's hand. "Okay."

"Here, I'll push this up front for them."

I watched her walk through the store with the bike in one hand and her backpack slung over her shoulder. I was used to my mother commenting on my eating habits, and occasionally Brenda, but to have Ryan notice felt odd. I wanted to ask her about it but I didn't feel comfortable. Besides, someone was telling me I didn't eat enough, for once.

I joined her at the register, handed Green Vest my card, and punched in my PIN as instructed. "What do you mean I don't eat enough?" I finally asked her.

"Don't you even want to know how much it cost?" Ryan looked troubled, but before I could ask about the price I was handed the receipt and was pushing my brand-new used $350 bike out the door.

"You ate your English muffin with jelly, half your eggs, none of your bacon. The jelly and the sugar in your coffee probably spiked your blood sugar beyond belief. You should eat more protein. Hell, even more complex carbs. Less sugar."

"Ryan, have you looked at me lately? I really don't need to eat more."

Ryan stopped walking. "I look at you all the time, so if you want someone to join you in trash-talking yourself, you're going to have to look elsewhere."

Ryan stalked away. I could tell by the rigidity in her back that she was angry, but I couldn't figure out why. "Hey!" I tried to push the bike after her, but the bike's weight and my own clumsiness made it hard to keep up.

A little old man of indeterminate race sitting on a park bench said, "You can ride those things, you know."

"No kidding," I said, but after a few more steps I decided he was probably right. *Great. Now I'm getting tips on how to chase a woman from elderly men.* I waited until Ryan was out of sight and I was pretty sure Old Helpful Man couldn't see me trying to figure out how to ride the bike in the first place, then I got on the bike. I pedaled slowly and my front tire wobbled from side to side. I had seen other people riding bikes, and they'd all seemed to be riding along smoothly.

I tried to remember if I had had a similar problem as a kid, but I couldn't remember ever riding a bike or being taught how. The thought had just crossed my mind when I spotted Ryan up ahead. She had slowed her pace and her arms were folded in front of her chest, but her head was down and she wasn't looking either left or right, which meant I had some time to smooth out my bike-riding skills.

I was so intent on following her that I was caught off guard when something gray flew at my tire. I pounded hard on my hand brakes and realized too late that the bike's front wheels would lock. I was airborne longer than I thought possible and then I was staring up through long, thin fingers. No, they were the branches of trees. My head hurt and my nose felt like I had water in it. Something was poking into my back and I could hear drums pounding in my right ear. A figure above me moved closer.

"Oh, my God. Mia, what happened?"

"Ryan, the construction worker from work?"

"Yeah, where are you hurt?"

I squinted up at her because the sun, even in an overcast sky, kept me from seeing her clearly, but it created one of those glowing halo things around her head like the figures painted on the colored glass at church. "Lovely," I whispered.

"We saw her go down. Is she conscious? What happened?"

I blinked because the construction worker had just called me sweetheart, and then I remembered. She was no longer working on the next office and my head was pounding because I had probably slammed it into the pavement when I fell off my bike. Tears spilled out of my eyes and down the side of my face.

"Mia, baby, tell me where it hurts." Ryan sounded as if she was ready to do battle with my pain. "Do you want me to call an ambulance? I have my cell phone."

"No, I'll be okay," I said, but the tears kept falling and I felt a few sprinkle on my forehead. Great, not only had I made an ass of myself, but I had done so in front of Ryan and a stranger.

"Maybe you should get her to the hospital. She looks like she's in pain," said a different, unfamiliar voice. *Great. Make that two strangers. I bet the old man'll be rounding the bend at any moment to see what all the hoopla is about.*

"What about the bird?"

"Bird?" Ryan sniffed.

"Ryan, why are you crying?"

She wiped her face. "I don't know. Because you were, I guess. You scared the heck out of me."

"I just killed a baby bird," I whispered, and to my horror more tears spilled down my cheeks.

Ryan pulled me into her lap. I knew that other people were standing around us but I really just didn't give a damn. Ryan had been scared that I was hurt and she didn't want me to trash-talk myself. Pounding head and back be damned. I'd never felt so good.

"Can we sit here for a few minutes more?"

"We can sit here as long as you need."

I glanced down the path where the old man still sat on the park bench. He had no doubt seen me take a spill. If I were the blaming kind I would say that he was at fault. But if I hadn't fallen, I wouldn't have ended up in Ryan's arms. I wouldn't have seen those tears in her eyes. She wouldn't be looking at me with a worried expression on her face.

"You could have done some serious damage to yourself, Mia. Birds usually get out of the way, you know."

"Yeah, but this looked like a baby. He flew right into my tire."

"We should head back. We need to get that scrape cleaned up."

I pressed my face into her shoulder and said, "I could stay right here forever."

Ryan either didn't hear me or she refrained from responding. She leaned into me for a moment and then she gently moved me back. I sighed and forced myself to get off her lap. As I stood, I closed my eyes against aches that were already threatening to turn into full-blown agony.

When I opened them, Ryan was watching me intently. "Let's take it slow, okay? If you feel dizzy we're taking you to the hospital, and I don't want to hear any lip."

If I had felt better, I might have asked what lip sounded like. "That's fine," I said a little more weakly than was probably necessary.

"Here, lean on me if you need to."

We passed the old man on the bench and he lifted his hand in a wave. "Split your pants, little sister?" He could have been asking me what time it was or if I was having a good day.

I frowned back at him and then twisted around so that I could see my own ass. Sure enough, there was a large rip along the seam of my track pants, exposing my yellow high-cut granny panties to the world. I recognized the feeling of my heart slamming against my rib cage as the beginnings of a panic attack.

Before I could think of anything to say, Ryan unzipped my jacket and slid it off my shoulders and down my arms. I pulled my hands out of the sleeves and her head dipped as she tied the jacket around my waist. When she was done, her fingers lingered and she was slow to meet my eyes. I looked down to see what had caught her attention.

I hadn't expected to be without my jacket, so I hadn't made sure I would be decent if I needed to take it off. I wasn't, and Ryan had noticed.

I was wearing an OSU T-shirt that I had had since college. It had been washed so many times it was practically transparent. My bra didn't offer much more by way of coverage, because I could clearly see my nipples straining against the fabric and even the brown of my areolae.

When she finally met my eyes, I could see the desire in hers. "We need to get home. Now."

Chapter Sixteen

My head, chest, and right arm felt heavy when I awakened. *Why is my chest heavy?* I forced my lids open and jumped. I was looking into the deep brown eyes of a lunatic. A lunatic who had plopped himself squarely on my chest. He leaned forward, stopping inches from my face. I froze in stark horror. A small pink tongue appeared, as if tasting the air. The slow deliberate move felt like, and probably was, a threat. I had seen Pepito lick his own ass two mornings ago. He had me trapped and, based on the toothy grin on his face, he knew it.

"You're awake," Ryan said from somewhere to my right.

"Yeah, I thought I wasn't supposed to sleep."

I turned my head and winced more in anticipation than any real pain. A general ache was the only reminder of my fall. She was sitting in a chair across from me with her feet propped up on an ottoman. *Doing what? Watching me sleep?* The idea of it should have made me feel uncomfortable, but it didn't.

"I kept you up a full twelve hours and then I let you get some sleep. Don't you remember?"

I hadn't had the heart to tell her that I thought keeping a person awake after a head injury was an urban legend. Besides, I would rather stay up all night with her than go to the hospital any day of the week. "I remember watching *Lassie* and *Green Acres*. Did we really watch those shows?"

"We did." She stood up and scooped Pepito off my chest and set him on the floor. "Sorry about that. I gave up trying to keep him off you."

I sat up a little so that I could see him. He was standing with his legs splayed and he was panting; his pissed stance.

"Great." I lay back down and touched the side of my head with my fingers. I had a strange metallic taste in my mouth. "My mouth tastes funny," I said with an accusing glare toward Pepito.

"What, you afraid he's been kissing you?" Ryan had a crooked little smile that would have been charming if she hadn't been teasing me.

I flushed and lay back down. I didn't want her to think I had been tongue-kissed by a dog, but my mouth *did* taste funny. She sat down on the couch next to me. I was hyperaware of her hip touching my waist. I turned my attention to Pepito. We stared at each other for a long moment.

"Oh, shit," I whispered, and Pepito gave Ryan one of the evil snaggletooth panting grins that he usually saved for me. His tongue rolled. He wasn't the only one falling in love with her. "Shit shit shit."

"He's laughing at me," Ryan said.

"Actually, that's his ha-ha look. I used to get it all the time. You're a fickle little bastard, aren't you?" I reached down to pat his head and tried not to be disgusted when his tongue whipped out and caressed the inside of my wrist.

"You probably bit your tongue when you hit the ground yesterday," Ryan said. "Does it hurt at all?"

I stuck my tongue against my teeth. "No, maybe I just need to go brush." Pepito, who had settled on the floor, seemed unable to tear his eyes from me. I tried to sit up but a pressure, this time Ryan's hand on my chest, stopped me.

"Hang on a second. You need to take it slow. You knocked the hell out of your head."

"I really just want to brush my teeth." One look at Ryan's face and I realized that I was being a brat. "I'm sorry. Thank you for looking after me last night. I'm just hungry and sore and it's making me grouchy."

"Want me to make you something?"

Her willingness to cook for me drained all annoyance from my body. Right up until I remembered that it was Monday and I was supposed to have brunch with my family yesterday. "Oh shit. My mother is going to make my life hell."

"What would you give me if I made it so your mother wasn't mad at you?"

I looked at her through my lashes thinking I would give her anything she wanted for a lot less than getting me out of trouble with my mother. Something in my expression must have given me away, because she flushed.

"Christina called an hour after we got home yesterday. Brunch is put off until next week."

"Yes." I pumped my fist in the air, temporarily forgetting I was supposed to be convalescing.

"I hope you don't mind, but I called Goody and told him you wouldn't be in."

"Hey, Ryan?"

"Yeah?"

"Thank you for taking care of me."

"I like doing things for you." She lifted Pepito back onto the couch. "I'll go see if there's anything in the kitchen."

"O…kay," I said stupidly. I felt a strange longing that made me want to call her back and keep her close. Pepito had put his head down between my breasts and blinked long, dark lashes. "This really sucks."

Pepito blinked again, almost sagely.

I watched her leave, wondering what I was thinking by telling her she could come next week. I lay back and told myself to enjoy my one-week reprieve. But the more I tried to stop it, the more my mind insisted on dragging me through all the horrific possibilities. Each scenario ended with the same conclusion: *they are going to eat her alive.*

❖

I agreed to let Ryan drive me to work on Wednesday because she didn't give me any choice. To my chagrin, Pepito followed us out the door and insisted on hanging his head out the window despite the early morning mist that left a chilly blanket of fog over downtown Portland. More than one early morning commuter did a double take when they caught sight of him. Instead of being embarrassed, I felt protective even though I did realize that Pepito was a bit much for anyone to take before seven in the morning. I rolled him onto his back to give him gentle scratches, deftly avoiding his lolling tongue. I could hardly look at Ryan because every time I did I felt complete lust and she just looked, well…concerned.

"I'll pick you up right here after work," Ryan said as she pulled into a fifteen-minute loading/unloading spot.

"I can take the bus."

"I can also pick you up."

"It's a madhouse down here at four thirty."

"Which is why I don't want you on the bus. Promise me you won't take the bus?" She had the most riveting gaze.

"I promise," I said as I opened the door. I slid Pepito into my seat and got out of the car. Behind us I watched a woman I had never seen before lean in and kiss a man I assumed was her husband. Ryan was watching me again, and there was nothing maternal about the look in her eyes. She quickly hid it, but not before I saw.

I stuffed down my triumph and said in a calm voice, "I'll see you this afternoon."

"Call me if you need to come home early."

"I'll be fine," I said and gave her a smile as I shut the door. I was grateful for the work that would be waiting for me. I hoped it would take my mind off Ryan and the fact that she was still fighting me with everything she had.

❖

I managed to call my remaining clients as well as follow up with the ones who had already transferred their accounts over to Jackson. As busy as I was, thoughts of Ryan were never far away. I often found myself reaching for the phone to call her, only to pull it back. What would I say? *Hey, I'm just calling see how you're doing.*

I didn't really think we had that kind of relationship, did we? I mean, she had taken care of me the last two days, and she was coming to my parents' house. And we did live together, and we did have a couple really hot moments. By the time Goody knocked at my door I was exhausted.

"Hey, you look tired, do you need me to drop you off at home? I drove today."

"What time is it? It's four already? It would save Ryan the trip if you don't mind."

"Ryan picking you up from work now?"

"I had a little bicycle accident over the weekend and she's worried I might have a mild concussion."

"Hmm, you two've grown close, haven't you?"

I shrugged. I refrained from saying "not close enough" because I didn't want to discuss Ryan with Goody. "She's a nice person."

"Yeah, I could tell that when I had lunch with her." Goody seemed like he wanted to say more, but I wasn't in the mood to discuss Ryan with anyone. The mere thought of her was leaving me feeling off kilter, or maybe that was the whack to my head.

"So how much longer before the work on your house is done?"

I hadn't wanted to think about the fact that Ryan had been making speedy work of all the repairs. "I don't know. She might stay after she's done. She's helping me with workouts too."

"Brenda's good with that?"

"Brenda and I are…"

"I know, but have you told Brenda that? I mean really told her?"

"Why is everyone so concerned about Brenda? She's the one who left *me,* remember?"

Goody didn't answer. Of course he remembered. Why was I lashing out at him?

"I'm sorry, Goody. I don't…even though Brenda left me, I wasn't looking for another relationship."

"But you found it?"

"I found…something, and I'm not strong enough to ignore it."

"You know, I keep telling myself the minute I stop looking I'll find *him,*" Goody said.

I swallowed. "Trust me, it's not all roses. I actually feel pretty confused."

"Does Ryan know how you feel?"

"Yeah, I'm pretty sure she does. Things did get a little—heated in the kitchen on poker night."

Goody laughed. "I knew we interrupted something, and it looked a damn sight hotter than just a kiss."

"It felt a damn sight hotter too."

Goody cackled and I attempted to join him. If he noticed I didn't laugh quite as hard as he did, it didn't seem to bother him.

❖

Goody pulled away from the curb, and the little flutter I felt in my chest leapt up into my throat as the front door swung open. My excitement was replaced with fear when a man stepped out of my house and shut the door gently behind him.

"Hi," I said as I cautiously approached. There was something about him that felt familiar, and it took me only a split second to realize that he was the same person I had seen Ryan standing on the corner talking to. Up close I could see a resemblance. Same shaped eyes, coloring, and nose. But where Ryan looked strong, her brother looked depleted, tired; maybe even slightly unclean.

"Hi, I was visiting my sister."

"Yeah, Brady, right? I'm Mia. Ryan's told me about you."

He reached out to accept my handshake and something heavy and solid swung forward in his coat. I had a sudden image of a gun and pushed it away. This was Ryan's brother. She lived here now. She had every right to want to invite her family over.

"Um, okay, I need to go."

"Yeah, sure." I raised my hand and watched as Ryan's brother all but ran off down the street.

I watched him until he turned the corner, uneasy and ashamed of the feeling.

I heard a growl as I entered the house, and I frowned. "Hey, Pepito. It's me." Pepito whined a little and ran up to me. I squatted down and patted his head just as Ryan came into the room with one of the four beers that had been in my refrigerator since poker night.

"Mia." She looked at her watch. "I thought you were going to call me when you…"

"Oh, I just had Goody bring me home." I studied her face for a few minutes. "Something wrong?"

"No, I'm fine. Sorry, I was going to cook something but…"

"Ryan, you do not need to cook for me. Don't get me wrong, I appreciate it, but I certainly don't expect you to cook every night." I stopped speaking because she wasn't looking at me. Ryan always looked at me when I spoke to her. She always made me feel like everything I said was the most important thing she had ever heard. I followed her eyes to the mantel.

"Something was up there, wasn't it?" she asked.

It took me a moment to remember, but when I did my throat went dry because I realized what Ryan's brother had had in his coat pocket. "My grandparents' candlesticks."

They looked more expensive than they actually were, but my mother had given me so few things from my grandparents that the loss of them felt like a punch to the sternum. Ryan walked toward the mantel. She placed her hand there as if checking to see if they had somehow fallen over.

When she turned to face me, her eyes were wide, her skin so pale I almost thought she was going to faint. "I didn't take them."

I was struck dumb by the look on her face. "Ryan, I…"

Ryan walked past me and I blinked at the empty mantel. I stepped around Pepito but I heard the door open and slam shut before I could even get out into the hall.

"Ryan?" I called out, shocked that she had just left and unable to understand what had just happened.

Pepito stared up at the door, whined a little, and then began to pace back and forth.

CHAPTER SEVENTEEN

When the phone finally rang two hours after Ryan had left the house, I snatched it up from its cradle. "Ryan?"

"No, it's Brenda. Who's Ryan?"

I closed my eyes. I didn't really want to talk to Brenda right now, but I had promised myself that I would stop putting off the inevitable. If Ryan did call, I would simply put Brenda on hold, international calling be damned. "Hi, she's a friend. Brenda, what time is it there?"

"Around four. I knocked off early so I could give you a call before you went to bed. I've been having trouble reaching you."

"Yeah, sorry. Things have been hectic."

"Christina told me."

"You talked to my sister?" I was surprised. Christina and Brenda were always cordial, but I'd never call them friends.

"Yeah, I called her when I couldn't reach you." Brenda's voice sounded accusatory, and I didn't like it one bit. "She told me some other things too."

I rubbed hard at my forehead. "Brenda? I had an accident, which is why you couldn't reach me at work. My head is killing me right now, so if you don't mind finishing this conversation later…"

"Mia, hear me out. I know I was wrong to leave. I should have talked to you first, but I was scared. I didn't understand why things just felt so wrong between us. Can you try to understand what I was going through?"

The plaintive quality of her voice got to me and I felt a deep sadness. "No, I can't. I would have tried if you had told me these things a couple of months ago."

"But you can't try now?" The sadness was replaced by something that sounded a lot like anger. My hackles rose.

"What do you want me to say? That I'm not angry? That I understand completely? I can't do that because no matter what, I wouldn't have done that to you. Call me naïve, but I believe in loyalty and if I had thought we had a problem I would have told you."

"So you're telling me you had no clue?"

"Maybe I should have. Maybe subconsciously I knew things were falling apart, but no. I don't think I wanted to know."

"So what do we do?"

I took a deep breath. There it was out there and on the table. "Brenda, I don't like what you did. But I'm not angry with you anymore."

"That's a good thing, isn't it? It means you're already starting to forgive me."

"Forgiving is not the hard part. It's the forgetting. It's regaining the trust."

"So what are you saying? Are you trying to tell me it's over?"

"You told me it was over when you walked out of this house."

"I just explained."

"I know, but I can't go back there. I'm not that person. I can't wear blinders and accept our relationship as what was meant to be."

"You've found someone else, haven't you? This Ryan? Christina says you told them you're just friends, but it's more than that, isn't it? I hear it in your voice."

"Isn't that what I accused you of?"

"Well, have you?"

"Does it really matter? Whether I'm alone or with someone else, what we had is over. You knew it before I did. I'm not exactly sure why you've changed your mind about it now, but I've made my own decisions."

"I…I don't know what to say. I guess we should talk to lawyers."

"If that's how you want to handle this. I'm willing to buy you out of the house or whatever you want. We've always had separate accounts, so…"

"So you're serious about this Ryan person?"

I frowned, not liking the fact that she sounded so shocked. Had she really thought I would just take her back? After the way she left, after what she'd said?

"You're not just looking to get back at me because of what I said before I left, are you?"

"Brenda?"

"Yeah?"

"Good night." I hung up the phone. Tears of anger burned the corner of my eyes. I felt like I had wasted four years of my life and I wondered if I had any luck with women at all.

Pepito whined from his post at the front door. I called him and a few seconds later he jumped onto the couch next to me. I turned on the TV for background noise. Like I'd told Brenda, I was loyal, and as angry as I was with Ryan for running out, I was still going to wait up for her. I needed to make sure she was safe.

❖

Pepito woke me around two in the morning with his whining and snuffling at the front door. Ryan had not returned. Ryan hadn't called or come home, and I felt like someone had stuffed a whole cotton plant, nodes and all, down my throat.

I slowly untangled myself from the couch and dragged into the hall. Pepito's little butt was stuck in the air and his nose was glued to the space between the floor and the bottom of the door.

I squinted out the peephole, but I could see nothing in the cone of light cast by my front door lamps. I would have walked away if Pepito hadn't continued his obsessive sniffing at the door. To appease him, I opened it and found Ryan huddled in the corner, her arms folded and her eyes red rimmed. The distress on her face broke my heart.

Leaving the door unlocked, I stepped outside to sit next to her. The early morning air ripped through my blouse and slacks. I leaned forward with my arms tucked between my chest and thighs. She was staring out at my neighbor's lawn, so I did the same.

To my surprise, other than a few seconds more of clicking, Pepito didn't put up much of a fuss about not being allowed out with us.

I realized if I expected a conversation I would have to start it. "What are you doing out here without a coat?"

"I couldn't get them back."

"That's not what I asked you."

"I didn't bring my keys with me."

"Why didn't you ring the damn doorbell, Ryan?"

"I didn't want to wake you up."

She shivered and I placed my hand on her arm. She moved away as if I had burned her. I tried not to feel hurt by the fact that she obviously didn't want me touching her, but I was. *Stop it, Mia. This is obviously not about you.*

"As if I could sleep not knowing where you were."

"I didn't take them."

Now I was angry, which was a whole lot better than feeling rejected. "Did I ever once accuse you of taking anything?"

"No, but—"

"But nothing. You ran out of here without talking to me, damn it." My voice was raising and if I was being honest, I was angrier about how Ryan had left than the fact that my grandparents' candlesticks were missing. "I didn't know where you had gone or if you'd be back."

"I was trying to catch…my brother."

"I know. I saw him leaving the house."

"He was still here?" Her face paled further. "I thought he had left at least five minutes before you got home. I was working in the back. I should have walked him out but he said he knew the way."

"Did you invite him over?" I kept my question gentle because Ryan had already been crying.

"No, and I didn't give him your address."

"Stop, I'm not accusing you of anything. You live here too. You have every right to invite whomever you want over. I'm just curious why he was here if you didn't invite him or give him the address."

"For money, of course. That's the only time I hear from either of them." Her voice was bitter, and distant. She was quiet for so long that I was tempted to suggest that we go inside. I reached for her arm, the memory of her pulling away still fresh. She shivered but didn't reject my touch this time.

"I sent my mother some of the money I got back from my deposit on my apartment. She must have given Brady the address. I was so happy to see him that I didn't ask any questions."

Her eyes were so wounded that I decided to risk rejection and enfold her in my arms. Her whole body quaked and I held her tighter.

"I'm so sorry," she said.

"You don't have to apologize. You did nothing wrong."

She shook her head against my shoulder. "He's never stolen from me." She sounded so heartbroken that I had to fight back my own tears. This wasn't about candlesticks; this was about being betrayed by someone she loved. "He looked so much better the last time I saw him that I had hoped he could kick it."

"What's he on?" I asked even though I was sure I already knew the answer.

"Crystal for sure, but I don't know what else he's doing."

"His baseball scholarship?"

"Long gone. For a while the school was willing to let him come back, but…"

"How long has he been like this?"

Ryan drew back slightly, but stayed close, probably because she was cold. "Since his senior year in high school. He held it together for a while, but once he was on his own he self-destructed. I came here to get him back in school. I had no idea how bad he was until I saw him. My mother refuses to believe her little boy is so strung out on drugs that she wouldn't even recognize him."

Ryan had relaxed enough that she was looking at me. I expected the pain in her eyes but not the guilt.

"You're not blaming yourself for this, are you?" I asked.

"He's my brother. My mother is in no condition to help anyone. I'm all he has."

"What about your father?"

"He's dead." The words were so heartbroken, so garbled with tears that it took me several long moments to understand what it was Ryan was trying to tell me. "He…I didn't realize he had cut me at first. I was struggling to get the knife away from him, and Brady and my mom were screaming. He was yelling about how he was going to kill me. It was so loud that the neighbors started pounding on the door. He fell on me and…"

"Oh, sweetheart."

"I hated him, Mia. I hated my father. But I didn't want him to die. He was always…I should have just left the house, stayed with a friend, but I just couldn't. He was so drunk and he was waving that knife around. I knew he would kill them if I didn't get it away from him."

"It was an accident, Ryan. Please look at me?" As horrified as I was, the only thing I wanted to do was comfort her, to make the raw pain that I saw in her eyes go away forever. "You have to know this wasn't your fault."

"Justifiable homicide." Ryan could have been reading the

newspaper aloud for all the emotion her voice held. "It never even went to trial." She looked at me, her eyes pleading for something I couldn't give her. "The neighbors told investigators that they heard screaming and fighting coming from our house all the time. Can you believe that? We'd lived in that house for most of Brady's life. They never said two words to us. Never even let on that they'd heard what was going on. If they knew, why didn't they do anything to help? Why did it have to come to him dying to get him to stop?"

I bit my bottom lip to keep from ranting about the police and neighbors who didn't give a shit. "You did what you had to do to protect your family and yourself. He could have killed you, Ryan. You were brave to do what you did." I pulled her close to me again, trying to imprint my warmth on her body.

"He never laid a hand on me until that day, but Mom and Brady just couldn't seem to stay out of his way. I got so tired of watching him terrorize them. If I had just left the house…"

"He might have killed both of them and you would still be playing this what-if game, only with a different ending," I said, but Ryan went on as if she hadn't heard me.

"After everything calmed down, my mother stopped getting out of bed and Brady started doing drugs. I had to be the breadwinner and the parent to both of them. I tried, Mia, I really did, but it was like they were hell-bent on destroying their lives and I couldn't stop them."

"You can't make people want to live, Ryan."

"I had to try. But I don't think I can stand this anymore. He stole from you and regardless of the fact that he had never met you, he had to know how that would make me feel. And I only hear from my mother when she needs extra money."

"I'm so sorry that you're feeling like this."

"He gave the candlesticks to some drug dealer, Mia. I tried to find him but I—"

"You did *what*?"

"I tried to find the guy, but he had already left."

"Ryan, Ryan what were you thinking? You have to promise me you won't do anything so crazy again. They were candlestick holders, for God's sake."

"They were your grandparents'."

"I don't care. They aren't worth your life. Do you know how dangerous going into a place like that could have been?"

"I've been in places like that more than once looking for Brady."

"Do you know how I would have felt if you had been hurt? The only reason my mother even gave them to me is because they had no monetary value. And even if they were worth money they would never be worth your life."

"They may not have been worth any money, but I figured you had them up there because they reminded you of your grandparents. I just thought if I got them back and explained, things would be okay between us."

"Things *are* okay. They're better than okay, but you have to promise me you won't do anything like that again. You ran out of here without talking to me. I understand that people get angry or hurt, or they need space, but I had no idea where you were. I was scared you would never come back."

"I guess I just reacted."

"I saw him leave, Ryan. I could tell he had something heavy in his pockets. I didn't know what it was until after you noticed the candlesticks were missing. I never once thought you had anything to do with it. And I would have never been okay with you trying to get them back. You mean more to me than that."

"I won't do it again. I promise." And her eyes, though still tired and hurt, did promise something that knocked any residual chill right from my body. I hugged her again, and if I held her too tight, she didn't protest. She smelled like she had been running, and her skin, though slightly warm, had a feverish feel to it. "Let's get you inside. It's freezing out here."

When I opened the door, I heard a small yelp and scampering claws. Ryan dropped to her knees and picked Pepito up. He was shaking and trying to lick her face as she stood with him in her arms. She was about to say something when a jaw-cracking yawn caught her off guard.

"We can talk more tomorrow. You're exhausted. You should get some sleep."

Ryan seemed reluctant to climb the stairs but she did so, and after shutting off the lights I climbed the stairs as well. My own exhaustion weighed heavier and heavier with each step that I took. I found Ryan standing in front of her bedroom door, her hand resting on the doorknob. Pepito was looking up at the door as if waiting for it to open miraculously.

"Ryan?" She blinked, her face slack with exhaustion. Courage made the words that I was thinking come easily to my lips. "Would it be uncomfortable for you if Pepito and I stayed with you tonight?"

Gratitude flickered in her eyes. "Are you sure?"

"Wouldn't have offered if I wasn't. I do have to get up and work out in about three hours, but I'll try not to wake you." Ryan opened the door and before I could take a step into the room, Pepito scampered in and jumped onto the bed.

Ryan bit her bottom lip and took a deep, shuddering breath. She stepped into her room and held the door open. When I walked past her I thought I felt her inhale, but I wasn't sure.

"I want to take a shower first. I feel dirty." She seemed hesitant, uncertain of herself. "I haven't had to tell the whole story since it happened."

"I'm glad that you felt comfortable enough to talk to me."

She didn't speak for quite some time, and when she did, her voice sounded warm and caressing. "You're a real sweet person, Mia Sanchez."

There are so many things I wish I had said, but words eluded me. She saved me from any embarrassment by heading for the bathroom. Feeling warm and a little bit bewildered, I sat down on the edge of her bed and absently smoothed the cover. My grandparents had shared this bed for most of their married life. Anytime I'd mentioned the possibility of sleeping in it, Brenda had objected. She never understood how magical this bed was to me. It represented the kind of marriage I wanted for myself—sixty years of living, loving, and being together. Was that too much to ask? "Take as long as you want. We're not going anywhere," I called after her.

CHAPTER EIGHTEEN

When she came out of the shower, we were shy at first. Pepito and I were already in bed, and I had thrown one corner of the covers back. Ryan got in without hesitation. I wasn't so bold about holding her, but five minutes later when I put my hand on her waist, she instantly moved into the curve of my body. I wrapped my arms around her and closed my eyes.

At my request, she had set her cell phone to wake me up no later than five thirty. I wasn't asleep when the alarm sounded, but Ryan must have been exhausted because she didn't move when I had to reach across her to disable it. Pepito grumbled from the foot of the bed and opened one eye to glare at me.

She was lying on her side. The black band that usually held her hair back had come off while she slept, and I picked it up off the pillow and tossed it onto her nightstand. With trembling fingers I moved her hair back from her face. Her mouth was open slightly and her face was relaxed in sleep. Her skin was so fair that her eyelids were pink from crying. Something warm and painful settled in my chest. And when I went downstairs to work out, it was more to escape what I felt happening to me than to see the screen say three miles again.

Ryan was still sleeping when I left the house, so I left her a note about calling to check on her and shut the door quietly. I spent most of the ride to work thinking about the things Ryan had told me the night before, and I closed my eyes, trying to imagine the pain and sadness she must carry around with her. Her father had scarred her in more ways than the obvious, and her family seemed to want her to pay for it for the rest of her life.

❖

Ryan looked wonderful in her button-down shirt and blue jeans. There was something about the way she was sitting, her eyes focused, her back straight, her hands ten and two on the steering wheel, confirming how nervous she was. I felt very protective.

"Relax, they won't bite," I said, but I was lying and I think Ryan knew it.

"I don't want to make a bad impression."

"I don't care about their impression of you. I just don't want them to make you feel uncomfortable."

"You don't like them much, do you?"

Startled, I said, "Of course I do. They're my family."

Ryan said nothing and I settled back in my seat. I was in a mood. I would clobber another bird and split my pants in public all over again if it meant another reprieve from this particular Sunday brunch.

We pulled into the driveway and I was relieved that Hector wasn't there to give me a message from his daughter. Ryan was quiet when we approached the house.

"You doing okay?" I was stalling, and not very well.

"I'm fine. Should we ring the doorbell?"

"No, haven't you heard? The door to hell is always wide open," I said as I walked in.

I could clearly hear whatever sports game my dad was watching as it traveled down the hall. I sniffed and grimaced. Déjà vu. Dad and Ned were sitting in their La-Z-Boys, black-stocking feet raised, staring intently at a soccer game. Ned was wearing a black patch over his eye.

"Hey," I said. If I had been speaking to people with pulses, I might have worried that my voice revealed how much I dreaded having to be there.

"Your mother and Christina are in the kitchen," my father said in lieu of a greeting.

"Yeah, I figured. Dad…Ned…this is Ryan."

"Whoooaa, did you see that?" my father yelled and Ned grinned. His teeth were as abnormally white as Selena's had been. I steeled myself for the chest ogling, but he barely even acknowledged me before turning back to the TV screen. *Hmm, maybe the humiliation of having popped a button was worth it.*

"How's your eye?" I asked out of guilt. "Christina said you only had to wear the patch for a few weeks." I left out the fact that I was surprised that he would wear it long after he had to, but I'm sure he got my implication.

"Doctor just wants to make sure my cornea's healed." His tone was defensive as he turned in our direction and seemed to notice Ryan for the first time.

My mother came bursting through the door from the kitchen, saving me from having to respond. "Mia, good, you're here, and Christina said you were bringing a little friend."

"Yeah, Mom, this is Ryan." I glanced sideways at Ryan, who although slender-looking on first examination could only be described as "little" by my mother. "Ryan, this is my mother, Ardis Sanchez."

"It's nice meeting you, Mrs. Sanchez," Ryan said.

My mother took in Ryan's jeans and shirt. Ryan wouldn't know it, but she had already been categorized. No one had ever worn jeans to Sunday brunch. My face felt like a block of ice. This woman had birthed me, raised me. I knew what she would do. *What the hell was I thinking bringing Ryan here?*

"Mia, you look a little gaunt. Have you been sick?"

"No, not really." I hoped Ryan remembered my warning about not mentioning the bike incident. My mother would go off on a tangent about the dangers of bikes.

"Why don't you girls come into the kitchen with us? We're just about ready to serve," my mother said with that little thrill of excitement in her voice that should have disappeared over the five years we had been having Sunday brunch, but hadn't.

My father and Ned did what they always did when told that food was about to be served; they ignored whoever was speaking.

Ryan and I followed my mother into the kitchen, and much to my surprise Christina came around the center island and gave Ryan a hug. "Hey, I'm glad you could make it."

Ryan looked surprised and I raised an eyebrow, not knowing what the hell the hug was about but somewhat glad for it. If my mother thought that Christina was also Ryan's friend, she might lay off. *Who am I kidding?*

"So, Ryan," Mom said in that voice she only used for company, the one that had no trace of an accent and was as nondescript as a prerecorded telephone message, "what do you do for a living?"

"Ryan's in construction," I said before Ryan could answer.

"Ah, I see. One of Mia's cousins owns a construction company. Trino Sanchez?"

"Mia told me she had a cousin in construction, but I didn't realize it was Trino Sanchez. He's doing all the new construction down by the waterfront, isn't he?"

Ryan must have gotten a brownie point for knowing about Trino, because my mother looked pleased. "Yes, all those beautiful new condos. Trino is going to take my sister and me through them when they're done. I keep telling Mia's father that we should sell this big house now that the kids are gone and move into one of his condos."

I raised an eyebrow at Christina, but she refused to play and continued her chopping.

"So, Ryan, do you cook?" my mother asked.

"Not very well, I'm afraid."

I reached out and touched Ryan's wrist. "Not true, you're a great cook."

Ryan smiled and looked shy. My mother frowned at me and I was tempted to drop my hand, but I didn't until she looked away.

"You must be doing something right, because Mia doesn't look like she's gained any weight since I saw her last." *Just take that as a backhanded compliment and let it go.* "So what kind of things do you cook?"

Now, you'd have to know my mother to realize that this is one of those conversations I didn't want Ryan to have. She would find fault with anything Ryan said.

"I cook pretty much anything. Chicken, some fish, though I don't like it much. Beef." Ryan looked confused, so I jumped in.

"Mother, Ryan didn't come over here to talk about her culinary skills."

My mother finally looked Ryan up and down and said, "I bet your family eats a lot of red meat, huh?"

"Yeah, yes. Some."

"Where are you from? Christina didn't say."

I looked from my mother to Christina and back again. Why would Christina say where Ryan was from? I don't even remember it coming up in the card game. The only reason my mother would make such a comment was if they had been discussing Ryan.

"I'm from Texas," Ryan said.

"Oh, I believe we have some relatives still in Texas." My mother said it as if Texas was the homeland and those relatives, and therefore Ryan, were backward and not something one talked about often. "We don't really have much contact with them, though. They're just distant relatives."

Ryan watched my mother struggle with a jar of olives and held out her hand. "Can I help you with that?"

My mother hesitated and gave the jar to Ryan. Normally she would have taken it out to my father, who would have opened it without tearing his eyes away from his TV set. My mother's thank-you sounded almost annoyed when Ryan handed the open jar back a second later.

"I'm done, Mother," Christina said.

"Good. Mia, why don't you go out and tell Ned and your father that brunch is ready. Ryan, you can help me set the table."

I met Ryan's eyes to see if she had a problem with being forced into this role, but she seemed willing enough, and as I walked out the kitchen door she was gathering up the napkins and silverware.

Ned and my father dutifully moved toward the dining room though it was clear that the game wasn't over. One thing about both of them was that they reacted well when being herded toward a meal, as was evident by the full girdle paunch my father wore and Ned's smaller, but catching up fast, one.

"So, where is it you said you worked, Ryan?" my mother asked as she dished salad onto her plate.

"Ryan is self-employed," I said before Ryan could answer. This time I could see the question in Ryan's eyes as she looked at me, but I looked down at my own plate instead. I was just trying to make life easier on her. I would explain later.

The table was silent for a while as everyone ate their salad, and I hoped dinner would pass as uneventfully as possible. "So does Brenda know you're living in her house?"

I almost choked on a piece of romaine at the question. "It's not her house, Mother."

"Her name is still on it. Isn't it?"

"She isn't here. She's not paying the mortgage."

"Doesn't mean it isn't still partly her house."

"I don't know if Mia's talked to…Brenda, Mrs. Sanchez," Ryan quietly but firmly interrupted.

"If you must know, Ryan is staying with me while she finishes some work on the house." I glared at Christina, who promptly looked down at her plate. *Thanks a lot for inviting Ryan and not helping me defend her. I owe you one, Christina.*

My father and Christina were concentrating on their food. Ned was studying the side of Ryan's face with interest. It took me a moment to remember that he was probably looking at her scar. I hit the side of my plate with my knife loud enough to get his attention and casually rubbed my thumb over my left eyebrow, the one that corresponded to his good eye. I glared at him until I was sure he understood. *You want to keep the other eye healthy, you leave her alone.*

I didn't resume eating until he did. My stomach was in knots. I supposed it could be worse.

"Where'd she say she was from again?" My father leaned toward my mother as if Ryan wasn't sitting a few feet away from him.

"She said she's from Texas, Emanuel."

"Ah, I was stationed in Texas."

Of course you were stationed in Texas.

"They had a lot of pretty girls in Texas. I'm surprised they let one of you go."

Ryan flushed at the sexist comment and I looked gratefully at my father. He wasn't a bad man, he knew a pretty girl when he saw one. He just liked to make up stories. We all have our foibles, right?

"They still got that grassy knoll in Texas?" he asked Ryan.

"Yes, I believe they do," Ryan said quite seriously.

"You know, a friend of mine wanted to ride up there on PTO to see the president, but we didn't make it. It would have been something to be able to say I had been there when the president was shot."

This time next year you'll have yourself sitting atop the grassy knoll with a picnic lunch when the gunfire starts, I thought unkindly. I looked to my mother for help, but she seemed to think the conversation was entirely appropriate and was moving on to her main course. I had just decided to relax and enjoy my meal when my mother paused, her serving spoon in midair as she studied Ryan's face intently.

"With your coloring, Ryan, you should think about putting highlights in your hair. I bet Regis down at the salon would be happy to take a look at you."

Regis was my sister's hairdresser up until my mother went to him; now she had taken him over.

"Ryan doesn't need highlights, Mom."

"Ryan can speak for herself, Mia."

I looked at Ryan, who had been diligently eating her food. She looked pained. "I suppose there's no harm in getting a consultation."

My mother looked like she was about to stick her fingers in her ears and yell neener-neener, but that would be too damn undignified for her.

"Good, it's settled. You can come with me next weekend and we'll see if he can squeeze you in. While we're there, we can swing by Macy's. They should be having their twice-yearly sale. Christina, you should come too. We can make it a girls' makeover day."

I could see Ryan's hand moving out of the side of my eye. I only had to turn my head slightly to get a better look at her face. She was barely chewing, looking down at her plate as if it were hypnotizing her. The first bright licks of anger had flickered the moment my mother felt it was her duty to point out that Brenda's name was on the house. Her insistence that Ryan needed highlights fanned my anger into a full blown inferno.

"That sounds like fun," Christina said dully.

I said, "Ryan doesn't need highlights." The whole table grew so quiet that you could hear a pin drop. Or a button fly off a dress.

"Maybe she would like highlights," my mother said tightly.

"If she wanted highlights, she would have them by now. And she certainly doesn't want some sixty-year-old drag queen making her look like...like you."

The insult hit home and my mother inhaled too fast and something went down the wrong way. The table erupted with the sounds of coughing and my father slapping at my mother's back. My sister was holding a glass of water and Ryan had placed her fork neatly on her plate. Ned was the only one who seemed oblivious and kept eating.

"Mia, that was uncalled for," Christina said sternly.

"I don't think it was. Mother already has you to play dress-up with. She doesn't need Ryan."

"If Ryan wants to go shopping with us, she can."

My mother tried to speak but dissolved into more coughing. Ryan was staying quiet, and rightly so. This really had nothing to do with her, and everyone at the table knew it.

"She has a way of convincing you that what she wants is what you want, doesn't she, Christina?"

"I don't know what you're talking about. Mom just invited Ryan to come with us. If you don't want her to go…"

"Ryan, unlike you, can do whatever she wants. But I will not have her bullied." Silence resulting from my words was as loud as a clap of thunder. "I'm sorry," I said under my breath, too afraid to look at Ryan.

I was sure she would be angry and embarrassed—hell, maybe even fearful based on the choking raspy quality my mother's coughing fit had taken on. I felt Ryan lean toward me and I did the same without removing my gaze from my mother.

"Does Regis do bikini waxes?" she asked under her breath.

I whipped my head around so quickly that a sharp twinge of pain shot up the side of my neck. I was horrified. The idea of Regis anywhere near her bikini area just made me want to projectile vomit. Ryan was steadfastly refusing to look at me even though I was boring holes into her quivering jawline.

"Can I get you something, Mrs. Sanchez?" Ryan asked sweetly and I reached under the table to pinch her thigh. She grabbed my hand and held it there. I flushed, my appetite for conflict receding. Ryan loosened her grip on my hand, but I left it there and soon her fingers were separating mine, her palm resting on the back of my hand.

"I'm fine," my mother croaked.

"Mia, is there something you want to say?" Ned asked in a tone of voice I had heard him use on my nephew.

All the warm fuzzies crept out of my body and I turned toward my sister's one-eyed husband.

"Yes, Ned. I'm gay," I said with false geniality.

He flushed. "We all know you're gay, unless Brenda *really was* just your roommate all these years."

It was as if the warmth was ripped from my body. I could have scripted Ryan's hand slowly easing away from mine. The chuckle from my sister put the icing on the cake. "Actually, Ned, I should thank you for the opening. I do have something to say."

"I think you've said enough already," my mother wheezed.

"No, Mother, not nearly enough, and that's why I'm so angry. I spent four years of my life with a woman who never once told me that

I was attractive. What's sad is, I didn't know it was wrong. I thought I was lucky to have her because you seemed to believe that."

"Mia, maybe this isn't the time," Christina interjected.

"Christina, I know you don't care to hear this, but I have to say it. Brenda left me. I didn't ask her to go, I didn't tell her it was over, I didn't tell her I was unhappy because I didn't know I was. But she chose to leave, and you know what? I don't hate her for it."

"Are you finished?" If I hadn't seen Christina's mouth move, I would have sworn the question had come from my mother.

I took a deep breath. "No, I'm not." I turned to my mother first. "Your highlights are really bad. You look like a drag queen who's trying too hard." I turned to Christina. "Your husband stares at my breasts every time I see him." Someone gasped, but I didn't see who it was. "I never said anything because I didn't want to hurt you. I think you knew, though, didn't you? I used to think that you helped me find less revealing clothes because you cared about me, but now I think you did it because you wanted to keep your husband from staring at me."

"Mia, maybe we should go." Ryan's hand was back on mine.

"Just a second, Ryan. I need to finish this because next month it will be as if it never happened." Christina might not have been looking at me, but she couldn't tune out my voice. "Why did you marry him? What happened to the little girl who wanted to marry a rich Prince Charming? Mother convinced you that marrying a dentist was the best you could do, right?" I let my dislike of Ned show. "It's not like he's good-looking or even particularly rich."

"That's enough," he bellowed.

"This is not your house and this is not your table!" I bellowed back.

"But it is mine," my father said quietly. "And I would ask that you kindly take yourself away from it until you find your manners."

"I'll leave, but I have one last thing to say, because I'll be damned if I subject myself to one more 'family brunch.'" My mother had picked up her fork and was stabbing at her salad as if she was going to ignore me. Anger was rolling off of her like steam, and deep down, I shriveled, appalled at what I was saying. "You won't have my weight problem to concern you anymore. So maybe you can pay some attention to your other daughter's weight problem."

My mother laughed, but there was no humor in it. "Your *sister* doesn't have a weight problem."

"No? Try figuring out why she never puts any of that food in her mouth." Christina's fork dropped into her plate with a loud clank. "While you're spending so much time worrying about every pound I gain, you should be noticing that Christina is going the opposite direction. The only time you compliment either of us is when we look like we've lost weight. But even you must not think she looks good, because I haven't heard you compliment her in a few months."

"Stop talking about me like I'm not here," Christina said, but there was no anger in her voice.

"Sucks, don't it? Get used to it, because once I'm not around you'll get all her attention. And by the way…you look like a coat rack, Christina. Eat something." The look on Christina's face caused me to temper my anger. "You're my little sister. I love you. If you need me, I'll be there. But I'm not going to let you pull me into the body-image issues that you inherited from Mother anymore. Figure out what's causing you unhappiness and get it out of your life before you turn into someone you don't want to be."

I stood up and Ryan did too. I looked pointedly from my mother to Ned before turning and walking out of the room. I could hear Ryan murmuring something that sounded like "thank you for the wonderful meal," but I had already slammed out of the house before she had finished. I had the engine running by the time she came jogging out and hopped in the car. The squeal the tires made as I peeled out of my parents' driveway was unintentional, but no less gratifying.

"We get to do that every month?" Ryan sounded like a kid who had just stepped off the newest roller coaster. She was grinning so wide that I felt an answering one pull at the side of my own mouth before reality stopped it cold.

"Nah, I doubt I'll get an invite for at least two months, and then they'll act like none of this happened. Damn it. I am so angry I could punch something." I realized too late that I might be scaring Ryan because of her background, but she was looking at me with half-lidded eyes and a wide, sensual smile.

"I know exactly what you need to get rid of some of that aggression."

CHAPTER NINETEEN

I know exactly what you need to get rid of some of that aggression. Now I ask you, who wouldn't think they were about to get some sex? I thought, *Finally, she's come to her senses.* By the time we reached the house I was so ready for it I could have done a few jumping jacks as a warm-up. Hell, when she told me to get dressed in my workout clothes, I was good with that too. I figured she was just freaky. I could do freaky. I would love to do freaky. Besides, sex was a workout, wasn't it? But she meant a real workout—cardio, to be exact. "How's it going down there?"

If the question hadn't sounded so amused, if sweat wasn't pooling into all the right places, I might have been able to answer her in a civil manner. All I managed was two gasps and a grunt, though. I refused to let her know how pissed I was. Actually, "pissed" was probably not the right word; disillusioned, annoyed, agitated, and horny were more accurate.

The treadmill beeped three times. I slowed my pace and allowed myself to roll off the back. I stood there glaring at the blinking monitor nestled between the headrests. "Three miles? What the hell?" I wiped the sweat from my eyes and looked at the readout again "Did I really just run three miles?"

"Yup, unless all that cursing and grunting was a recording."

I jumped. "I didn't hear you come down."

"Sorry, I wanted to bring you this."

In a perfect world, I would have grabbed the towel she held out to me and coolly walked up the stairs while dabbing delicately at my moist brow. In order to do that, I would need to calm my breathing enough that my breasts didn't look like they were about to heave right out of my sports bra.

It wouldn't have been so bad if she hadn't looked like she'd just had a shower.

"You probably shouldn't have pushed it so hard," she said. "You had that bad spill last week."

"I'm fine." I brushed past her to go up the stairs and into the kitchen. The fact that she was behind me was the only reason I made it to the top at all. I had overdone it; she was right, which pissed me off even more.

My intention was to head upstairs to hop into a shower where I could stew in peace. On a whim, I stopped at one of the drawers and began rooting through it for a corkscrew. An acquaintance of Brenda's had given her an expensive bottle of red wine that she was quite proud of. It had been gathering dust for over a year.

I took great pleasure in opening it and pouring myself a glass while Ryan watched.

"Mia?"

"I'm going to go take a shower." Glass in hand, I brushed past her. I would probably regret how I was treating her tomorrow, but for now I just wanted to be by myself.

I walked up the stairs and into my bedroom, trying to figure out why I was so angry and who I was angry with. My mother was, well, my mother. I usually got over my anger at her pretty fast. Was I mad at Christina for taking Ned's side of things or for letting herself be pushed into some obviously unhealthy behavior? Or was it Ryan?

It couldn't be Ryan. She hadn't done anything. Well, she had done something: she had been able to stick to her guns about not sleeping with me. Why couldn't I just let it go? It was obvious that she didn't want me as much as I wanted her or she wouldn't be able to keep me at arm's length. I slid the shower door open and turned on the water. I was acting like a spoiled brat. I knew it, and now so did Ryan, which only made me feel worse.

Embarrassment chased away my anger and I found myself wanting my anger back. I let the water sluice over my head until it became tepid. It was too early for me to turn in and not have Ryan become suspicious. I would have to see her, apologize for my behavior, maybe make up something about being on my period. When I reached out to turn off the water I noticed that not only were my fingers wrinkled, but the veins on the backs of my hands were standing out like a topological map.

"Lovely, no wonder she has no problem keeping her hands to herself," I said as I wrapped a towel around my body and went in search of underwear.

I was rooting around in my drawers when I came across the black bra and panty set that I had purchased on my last shopping trip with Christina. I figured if Ryan and I ever slept together, I would need something to lounge around in like those women on TV who never managed to take their bra off before sex.

"I might as well get some use out of them," I said. The bra was the only front-clasping one that I owned. It lifted my heavy breasts up, giving them an illusion of perkiness I hadn't seen since I was thirteen. My mood lightened and I pulled on the matching panties. "Hmph, I don't think I look half bad."

Who was I kidding? Between the veins on the backs of my hands, the messed-up attitude, and this huge inch I could pinch… It was a moment, more like a split second before I realized the significance of my thought. I pinched the skin at my side, then pinched it again. An inch, maybe a little more, but I'd been pinching at least four or five for the last year.

"Holy shit." I took another long draught of my wine and looked at the backs of my hands.

I still thought they were ugly, but surely it wasn't just pure dehydration? Maybe it was because my hands had less fat on them. Did hands get fat? I stepped away from the mirror above my dresser and turned to the closet mirrors. I hated the mirrored closet doors in my room. They had been Brenda's idea and I had always thought they were tacky. The idea of standing in front of my closet and gazing at myself in bra and panties was, well, embarrassing. I went looking for my robe instead.

I stood in my closet, not seeing anything, because I felt befuddled. When had this happened? I thought maybe my clothes were fitting a little better, but they certainly weren't falling off me, and shouldn't people be complimenting me if I had lost weight?

When my mother asked me if I had been sick I had immediately assumed that she had used her mother ESP to pick up on the fact that I had fallen from my bike. Both Goody and Ryan had complimented me in the last couple of weeks—had that been because of weight loss?

I had trashed my old scale out of frustration and now I was actually contemplating running over to Mr. Gentry's house to ask him if I could hop on his. I laughed. He'd get a kick out of me in my new lingerie, asking to use his bathroom scale.

So would Ryan. I sobered up at that thought.

I wasn't fooling anyone. I could parade around up here all I wanted, but I would never be bold enough to show my body to anyone, least of all Ryan. I wrapped the robe tightly around myself and I was going to belt it, but I caught a flash of movement in the mirror as I walked by. I hadn't had time to get any sun this year so my skin was embarrassingly pale, but the mirror tugged at me and I found myself standing in front of it.

I slowly opened one side of the robe and then the other. I was looking at myself in a pair of black panties and matching bra that would have been sexy on anyone else. I had just begun to feel stupid when I focused on my breasts. They were somewhat hard to miss. In fact, they had always been one of the first things people, men especially, noticed about me. So I'd learned to confine them. Christina would call me up telling me about this new reducing bra or this suit that would minimize my chest.

I stepped closer to the mirror, letting the robe fall around my shoulders. If I saw a woman with breasts like those, would I look? I grinned. I'm not a breast girl, but mine aren't bad. In fact, they looked damn good in the black bra, and it did nothing to minimize. I put my hands up and shivered as the warmth traveled through the fabric and warmed my nipples.

I turned to the side so that I could see my profile. I still thought my hips and ass were too big, but there was a curve to my waist that I hadn't noticed before. I turned to look at myself straight on. My stomach was flat. I had no six-pack and I doubted I ever would, but there was no bulge or cute little pooch. I placed my hands on my sides, trying to encircle my own waist. Ryan had held me there and all I had been able to do was worry that she was feeling my fat rolls.

I tried to see in myself what Ryan might have seen. I tried to remember what she looked like when we had kissed those few times, the way she looked at me when she thought I wasn't looking. I thought about what Goody said about how aroused Ryan looked after girls' poker night.

I was not a skinny girl—I had never been—but I was not

unattractive. At one point in my life I had known that but had become clouded by self-doubt as a result of the words of people who professed to love me.

But, Mia, you have such a pretty face. As if cued, my mother's words came screaming back to me.

No wonder I hate being told I'm attractive. My mother had used it as a put-down for as long as I can remember. Realization unfurled in my mind, along with all the old pains: my mother's constant badgering about my weight, Christina's insistence that I hide my body, the schoolyard bullies who had managed to squat on a spot in my memory long after they should have been forgotten.

Why did I allow myself to be treated like that?

I wrapped the robe around myself and sat down on my bed. I heard music turn on downstairs. Ryan was probably painting. I pictured her down there in her uniform of choice, jeans and T-shirt, and I had to push the thought away when I realized how uncomfortable I was making myself. It wasn't so much that I was aroused—not true; the very thought of her did arouse me—but I had this certainty that she and I were meant to be together, that every moment we spent circling each other was just wasted time.

The red wine was giving me strength I wouldn't have had any other time. It made me feel like I was floating outside my body, watching myself turn the knob and calmly walk down the stairs to the living room. Either Ryan would reject me or we would make love. Either way, this uncertainty was going to end tonight.

❖

You know that saying, "You shouldn't play with fire"? I always thought that was one of those "no kidding" kind of things. But there I sat, in my robe and black silk panties and bra, watching her work.

Her first reaction didn't disappoint. Her smile froze and her eyes widened and she turned away from me too quickly. Unfortunately, that initial reaction was what gave me the courage to sit down, wineglass in hand. She had made it quite clear that she didn't want to sleep with me. Hell, I wasn't exactly sure I knew what to do if she changed her mind. Yet I was sitting there, sipping my wine and staring at her like she was a piece of meat.

She was doing her damnedest to ignore me, but I could see her looking out of the corner of her eye. She would have to redo the wall she was working on because she had been painting the same spot for several minutes. The truth of the matter was, I was having fun. I was taking my frustration out on her, and it was mean, and I loved it. I hoped like hell she slept like shit, and I didn't give a good goddamn if she was pissed at me for it. If I was going to be uncomfortable, everyone should be. Selfish? Absolutely. But I hated the fact that she seemed to have no trouble forgetting some of our heated moments together.

"Excuse me?" Ryan mumbled.

"Uh-huh," I said around my wineglass and lifted my legs up so that my robe fell to the side and my thigh—not a bad-looking thigh, actually—was exposed.

I saw her arm bulge when she gripped her towel. She picked up her shirt and began to walk away. Shit, she was leaving.

"Hot in here, isn't it," I said loudly. "You mind if I take off my robe?"

I expected her to tell me to do whatever the hell I wanted to do before stalking out of the room. When she instead turned around and gave me the same piercing glare that she had given Brad Jackson when we were arguing, I knew I had gone too far.

"No, I don't mind, go ahead and take it off," she said.

If my glass wasn't already propping up my bottom lip I'm sure my mouth would have fallen open. I had expected her to ignore me, walk out of the room, hell, even laugh at me, but not this. She dropped the shirt she had been holding and stood with her hands on her hips.

"What?" I said, too wine-stupid to lower my glass.

"I said go ahead and take the damn robe off." Her mouth was tense and I could see the anger in her very stance.

Okay, Mia, this is where you apologize and slink off into some corner of the house.

"Oh wait, let me guess. That was a tease too, huh? You just wanted to see what I would say?" Ryan said.

Now I was angry. Good. Anger was way better than embarrassment. My hands went to my robe and I stood up. Why had I even started playing this game? There was no way I could win, and what if I did win? What then? She admitted that she was still attracted to me and then what? There was still the fact that she didn't want a relationship with me.

"You want me to take it off?" I asked as if it were a threat.

"You're the one who asked if you could. What are you waiting for?"

"Fine." I was angry that she had called me on my bluff and angry that she didn't seem to give a shit either way. If she didn't give a shit, why did I? "I'll take the damn robe off."

I let it drop to the floor and stood there in my Vicky Secrets, glowering at her.

That only lasted about two seconds, though, because she was staring at me as if I had lost my mind. When it dawned on me that I was actually standing there in my underwear and she was fully dressed, I felt like crying. I couldn't bend down to pick up the robe and I didn't want to run out of the room, because my panties were already riding up a lot higher then they should have.

"What are you doing?" Her voice was so soft that I almost didn't hear her.

"I'm acting real stupid," I said, and I realized that I was about two seconds from crying.

"Why?"

"Because I *am* real stupid."

"Uh-huh. Come here," she said.

Pepito came trotting into the room and stopped. He looked at me and then looked at Ryan before ambling over to my robe and lying on it. Now I would not only have to bend down to pick up the robe, I would have to knock him off it. I felt trapped.

"Come here," she said again.

"No." I bit my bottom lip hard.

I watched Ryan wipe her hands roughly on the towel she was holding before dropping it onto the newly polished floor. She was frowning and I was about to cry, and Pepito had front-row seats. He whined.

"Go get in your bed, Pepito," Ryan said softly to him, but her eyes never left mine.

I couldn't look away from her, but I saw a flash of movement and the clicking of Pepito's nails as he left the room. Pepito, unlike me, was no damn fool. I felt my chin wobble even more as Ryan moved closer. In my fantasy, she always smiled when she threw me down and made love to me. She wasn't smiling now, and if I were smarter and not so afraid that I had developed a major wedgie, I'd turn around and get the hell out of there.

"What exactly are you trying to do?"

"I don't—" I broke off because I had been about to tell the truth. I didn't know what the hell I was trying to do, but I certainly hadn't planned on standing there in my underwear. New or not, it was embarrassing as hell.

The scent of the citrus lotion I had rubbed into to my skin seemed overpowering. Had I put it on because I thought she liked it? Of course I had, dumbass that I was.

It seemed like an eternity before she was standing within touching distance of me. I don't know what I expected, but it wasn't to have her warm forehead pressed against mine. I was trembling with embarrassment.

"Why are you so damn beautiful?" she asked in a low whisper, and I burst into tears.

CHAPTER TWENTY

At some point she must have realized her gentle shushing was getting nowhere, so she kissed me. It wasn't the passionate kiss we had shared at the front door or in the kitchen, but it was warm and soft and somehow communicated how she felt about me more than either of those passionate moments.

"I'm sorry. I don't know why I'm acting like this," I mumbled against her lips.

"You're just frustrated. I am too. I'm trying to do the right thing, but you're making it so hard."

I felt like a complete brat when she held the sides of my face and kissed both of my eyelids. My eyes swollen, my nose red, and my lips puffy, all wrapped in black silk underwear. Goody would have said I looked a hot mess. Ryan didn't look much better. I reached up to hold her face as she was holding mine. Although I didn't think she had been crying, her nose and eyes looked as red as mine.

"I hate when people cry. Especially you," she said, answering my question before I could voice it.

"I don't mean to," I said. "I just feel like Brenda has me over a barrel. I would have never guessed that I would feel this way about anyone, let alone so soon, but—I didn't ask for this, Ryan. You didn't either, and I'm scared you might…"

"Scared I might what?"

"Change your mind about waiting for me. I don't want to lose this before I find out what it is."

"You don't know?" She worded the question so cautiously that I hesitated to answer.

"I don't remember ever feeling this way about anyone. How can I feel so good and be so angry at the same time?"

"At me?" she asked.

"No, of course not." I leaned away from her. "I feel good when I'm with you. I'm angry at Brenda. I feel like she's managing to keep us apart even though she isn't here."

Ryan smiled sadly. "If she was here, I probably wouldn't be."

Ryan was right; if Brenda had stayed, if she had done as I wanted and communicated with me, I wouldn't be holding Ryan now. I might have never come full circle with my family and my body-image issues. The thought was so horrifying that I was struck speechless.

Ryan was watching me closely. "You win," she said in a toneless, almost stunned voice. "I can't pretend anymore. If you really want this I won't deny that I want it too."

"Really?"

"Really."

"Why now? Was it the snot or the swollen red eyes that won you over?"

Ryan chuckled and I couldn't help but notice that she sounded really sad when she did. "You had me from the first kiss."

"Then why did you tell me we could only be friends?"

"Because I don't want to be hurt, Mia."

How in the hell could I hurt her? The pulse at the hollow of her neck was beating so hard I could see it. As far as I knew she hadn't cried this time, but she had been close to it. She was holding me loosely around the waist, periodically wiping at any stray tear that escaped my eyelids. I had never thought Ryan particularly sensitive, but she was telling me that she could be hurt easily. The thought made me feel protective until I realized that I would have to protect her from myself.

"I should have never moved in here. I told myself that it was convenient, but I was fooling myself. I moved in here because I wanted to be closer to you."

"May I ask you a question?" Ryan stiffened and I winced. "Sorry."

"S'okay, just ask."

I took a deep breath. "What do we do now?"

"Now we do this." She pulled me forward until I felt her warmth against my stomach. Her lips were a lot gentler than I expected, but

I was still grateful for her strong hands on my hips, both holding me close and steadying me. One or both of us sighed, and I felt a ripple of power travel through her body.

"Did you buy these to seduce me?" Her eyes hummed with electricity.

"Yes, I did," I said with an honesty born from knowing that I was wanted.

"Nice choice. You should take them off if you intend to ever wear them again."

"What, you mean right here?" I asked.

Apparently, she missed the newsletter explaining how she was supposed to do all the work because I was shy. Of course, standing there in my "come fuck me" lingerie made it hard to make that point without sounding like I was trying to be coy.

Her chest rose and fell. I was trying her patience, and this time I wasn't even trying to. "Mia?"

"Hmm?"

"Are you sure? We can back off if you want."

"No, we can't, Ryan. I'm tired of—"

She cut me off with a kiss. "Then let's go upstairs."

She bent down and picked up my robe. I'm sure she didn't mean to, but the silk brushed against my leg as she rose to hand it to me. I put it on, grateful that I wouldn't have to walk around with only the underwear on. I had turned a corner, a huge one, by standing practically naked in front of Ryan, but I drew the line at parading around the house like that.

I was halfway up the stairs when I realized I was headed to my bedroom to have sex. As if she had read my thoughts, she said, "Mine, not yours."

"Oh." I meant to say okay but it never quite got out. This is what I wanted and now I had it.

I stopped at Ryan's room, formerly my guest room, and all kinds of weird thoughts came to mind. Like the fact that her bed belonged to my grandparents and that I'd hardly ever gone into this room until Ryan moved in. She reached around me and pushed the door open. Once inside, I turned to find her standing a long distance away from me, her arms folded.

"Hey? Why are you way over there?"

She smiled and came closer. She tucked her hands neatly into the curve of my waist. "The walk gave me too much time to think, I guess." Her voice trembled and I leaned away from her.

"You need another look at the panties?" I was trying to make her smile, and I got five times better.

She threw her head back and laughed, one of those full-bodied things that were equal parts relief and amusement. I leaned forward and kissed her neck. When she shuddered this time, I knew it wasn't from nervousness. My skin was so sensitive that I felt the heat of her fingers against the robe as she untied my belt. She let go of me long enough to raise her arms so I could pull her tank top over her head.

My fingers were drawn to her stomach. "I had such a hard time not getting caught ogling you when we worked out. I love the way you look in a sports bra."

Ryan smiled. "Why do you think I always wore just a sports bra? I froze my butt off down there."

"Ah, so I wasn't the only one playing games?"

"Maybe not." She ran the back of her fingers along the outside of my bra. I knew without looking down that my nipples would be straining against the fabric. "But you stopped playing fair when you purchased special props."

I might be shy, but my fingers weren't. The whole time Ryan was speaking they had been working on the fastener of her pants. I told myself that I would just stop there, that we would slow things down, but my hand was dipping beneath her waistband and she was closing her eyes. She rocked forward as I came in contact with heat and moisture.

"We'd better sit down before I fall down," she said.

"Should we shut the light off first?" I asked.

Her face became serious "We can if you want, but I've been thinking about being with you from the first day I met you. I'd like to see you. What if we left it on for now? If you change your mind, I'll cut it off, I promise."

I nodded and we were falling and the bed was beneath my back and Ryan was on top of me. Her denim-clad legs rubbed against my freshly shaved ones. Without breaking our kiss she used one hand to unfasten the front clasp of my bra. I was only allowed to feel nervous for an instant because she was sucking the overly sensitive nipple of my right breast while her other hand was gently stroking my left one. She moaned almost as if she felt the surge of heat in my underwear.

Abruptly, she sat up and a little involuntary moan of protest left my lips.

"I need to get these off," she said desperately. She stood up and unzipped her jeans. I got a brief glance of cotton briefs before they were pushed down unceremoniously. Then I saw her flattened triangle of hair, neatly cropped and as blond as the hair on her head. I couldn't help myself; I scooted forward until I was sitting at the edge of the bed. My movements must have stopped her because she met my eyes then.

"Let me help you," I whispered and reached up to take off her bra.

She had to stand so close to me that my nose was pressed against her sternum as I unclasped her bra. She shivered again.

"Cold?" I asked.

"Not at all."

I could feel her breathing on the top of my head. I pulled the bra from her and let it drop to the floor. She stepped out of her shoes and jeans and stood naked before me. She had the most exquisite breasts I had ever seen. Mine had always been too large and cumbersome. Hers were perfect for her frame. Her torso was long; there was not an ounce of fat on her anywhere. I had seen her legs before, but now that I was seeing the rest of her body, I realized how perfectly they complemented her. Long, lean, and powerful looking.

I had gone from the top of her head to her toes and back again before I realized she was getting nervous. "I can't believe you made me wait this long to see you," I said.

She smiled, her look of relief so apparent that I felt another rush of something warm that had nothing to do with the silky feeling between my legs. I wrapped her in my arms and pulled her close. I pressed my face into her stomach and tried to catch my breath. Her hands were in my hair, releasing it from its knot.

"I love your hair," she said.

I kissed her stomach. She shivered and I kissed her again, this time close to her navel. I used her hips to keep her still as I kissed lower and I used my foot to ask her wordlessly to open her legs. I hesitantly kissed the line of hair. It tickled my lips and she inhaled. Her fingers stroked my scalp, telling me that she liked what I was doing. So I continued to kiss the neat patch of hair until her hips urged me to quicken my pace. I looked up at her to make sure she was okay and I had to bite my lip to keep from saying something crazy like "I could look at you like this forever." Her hands were still in my hair but her eyes were closed, her lips parted, and her hair hung forward, almost obscuring her face.

"I want to taste you."

She looked startled. "I should shower first."

"You want me to stop so you can go take a shower?"

"No," she said immediately.

I sat down on the bed and scooted back, pulling her with me, then kissed away whatever words she was about to say. She pulled me on top of her, and this time I felt the smoothness of her legs against mine. And where her jeans had chafed, a spark of electricity went through me. I moaned and leaned back so that I could kiss the pulse at her neck. I worked my way down to her stomach where, now that I was lying between her legs, I could smell how aroused she was.

Her hands were in my hair again, stroking, rubbing, hinting, and when my tongue dipped into her navel she arched her pelvis, bringing her heat against my breasts so that my nipples grazed her hair. We both moaned, and this time when I kissed her, I was close to the lips of her vagina. She arched her pelvis again and I opened my eyes to see that her clitoris was pushing between her labia, calling to me. I kissed the top of the opening and she moaned again. Her hips were moving now, and almost against my will, my tongue crept out and slid between her hot folds.

"Mia," she whispered. Her legs tensed, telling me that she had raised herself to look at me.

For once I didn't care about being looked at. I didn't care if she saw the way I was shaking. I steadied her hips into a rocking motion that suited me. I was finding it hard to keep my pace slow. Her breathing deepened and her head was turned to the side. Although one of her hands still dug deep into my scalp, the other clenched her pillow. I licked her clitoris from top to bottom and finally let my tongue slip deep within her opening. She let out a long, loud moan that no doubt carried to the other side of the house and released my head. She used both hands to clench her pillows now, and I quickened my pace. I reached beneath her body to hold her ass to steady her movements and to lift her closer to me.

My shoulders kept her open for my exploration. A rush of moisture met my lips and I buried my face even deeper. She moaned again, this time more high pitched, more out of control. The muscles of her legs stiffened again and she tried to close her legs, but I hung on because I wasn't quite through yet.

"Oh my…" she called out and then she began to shake, grinding herself against my open mouth.

I held her tightly against my mouth, forcing her to experience every wave of pleasure. She was sobbing now, but her hips were moving in unison with my tongue. I moved deep within her as she gave one lazy rock of her hips and I surged deep with her trembling walls. I heard my name bounce off the walls of the room.

When she stopped shaking, her hands were back in my hair, soothing me as I soothed her. I didn't want to stop for fear of what I would see in her face. But finally she did stop me by gently holding my shoulders and drawing me up.

Her eyes were gentle and warm. She looked relaxed, unstressed. No frown creased her brow. I reached up to touch her face; the small line of her scar felt soft beneath my fingertips. I wanted to learn every part of this woman's body.

She leaned in for a kiss. My panties were already soaked, but when she pulled away and kissed me again, her tongue toying with mine as she tasted herself, it caused my hips to jerk. Her hand went to my panties and she eased them down. I lifted my hips to help her. One-handed, she reached between my legs, her fingers grazing my crotch, and she pulled from the middle. I jumped.

"Please, Ryan," burst from my lips. "Please."

"What?" she asked only raising her mouth from mine enough to allow herself to speak.

"Don't tease me," I said. "Not this time."

She sat up enough to help me take off my panties. "You have no idea how beautiful you are, do you?"

Mirrors to the soul. Isn't that the saying? Ryan's eyes looked both earnest and aroused, and within their depths, I saw something that made my heart beat even harder. "I know now," I said. When she finally rested her body on top of mine, my hips surged instantly to meet her. With three thrusts of my hips I was well on my way to an orgasm.

"I want to feel you," Ryan said and I cried out when she moved to the side. She was breathing as hard as I was.

I reached for her shoulder just as her fingers gently parted the lips of my vagina and her fingertips touched me for the first time. "Oh,"

I breathed and closed my eyes to escape the heat of hers. Her fingers were so gentle it was excruciating.

"Do you know how long I've wanted to see you like this? Aroused while I touched you? From the very first moment I saw you I knew we would be together like this. I knew even when I was fighting it. I knew the moment I agreed to move in here with you." Her voice had deepened and I could hear that she herself was getting aroused again. She captured my mouth with hers and I raised my head to try to continue the contact. "Do you like this?"

Her fingers dipped into me and I tensed, but then raised my hips to give her better access. "Yes," I whispered.

I expected her to sink into me then but she didn't; she continued her strokes, occasionally dipping into me and bringing the wetness out to lubricate my clitoris. My hips rocked beneath her hand until finally I was meeting her finger each time she dipped into my opening, teasing me until finally I forced her into me.

A moan ripped from my throat as she anticipated the move and sank two fingers deep inside me. I held on to her wrist even though I was trembling. She pulled almost completely out of me and the only protest I was able to form was to continue to hold her wrist. She didn't pause; she sank deeply into me again and I fought the orgasm I felt mounting. I didn't want it to end.

She slowly pulled out of me and, for some reason, the only words I could voice were, "Don't leave me."

When she answered, her voice was near my ear. "I'm not going anywhere, sweetheart. It's okay."

I opened my eyes and instantly was engulfed by her blue ones. She sank deeply into me and I felt the orgasm as it passed the point of being put off again. One more thrust of her fingers, this one not as gentle as the others, and my orgasm crested and was upon me. Almost as if she read my mind, she thrust hard into me. I could feel the muscles in her arms bulge as my lower body almost lifted from the bed. I cried out, begging her to keep going as I closed my eyes against the love in hers. Ryan's final four thrusts lifted me off the bed and were so powerful that I was left speechless.

She stopped the minute the last wave of my orgasm ended. "Mia, was it too hard, baby?"

I opened my eyes. She was hovering over me. The worried look on her face was not what I expected to see after lovemaking.

"No, it was perfect." I swept her hair back and held it between my fists. My arm trembled as if I had just done ten sets with twenty-pound weights.

"Are you sure? I didn't mean for it to end up being like that."

"It was perfect. You stopped exactly at the right time." I felt embarrassed. How could I tell her that I liked a little roughness when I was that aroused? How could I tell her that I liked how gentle she was before that?

"Good. Because I liked it that way too."

The few moments of clarity had already faded, and again I was finding it hard to concentrate.

"Is it all right if I…?" With a mischievous smile she gestured downward.

"You might have to give me an hour or so before I can have another one."

"I just want to taste you."

"Really?"

"Yeah."

"If you don't mind that I'm—" My words were cut off because Ryan's mouth was devouring me.

I was wrong; it didn't take me anywhere near as long as an hour.

CHAPTER TWENTY-ONE

Half-dreams. I love waking to those. They're probably not really dreams, more like waking thoughts or in my case, a memory. I was conscious enough to recognize the scent of our lovemaking in the covers. I relived each touch, each gasp. The way her mouth had felt so gentle that it had been torturous. The way she had refused to move any faster than her own slow, attentive pace.

She was apologizing for the abandon that she had taken me with on our first time. I had grabbed her hand, but my throat seemed incapable of doing anything resembling dialogue. She had captured my clit between her teeth and was stroking it slowly with her tongue. Each languorous swipe of her tongue caused a pleasure so painful that by the time she took me fully, I was begging.

I'm not sure what drove me to full wakefulness—my arousal, my hand reaching for Ryan, or the realization that she wasn't lying next to me.

"Ryan?" I called to her, but even as her name came from my taxed vocal cords, I knew she wasn't in the room.

I pushed the covers back and sat up. My muscles immediately reminded me of the requests I had eagerly complied with the night before. *Can you open wider for me? May I touch you here? May I taste you there?*

Her voice had been so soft, her eyes gentle with a small touch of fear that I would refuse her. I didn't, not once, and not once did she do anything that didn't bring me to a full-fledged orgasm. So why had she left me lying there alone? Was she regretting her decision to be with me? Even now, with insecurity taunting my every move, I didn't regret anything we did for one moment. I forced myself up and out of bed.

My toes curled against the chill of the hardwood floors. I passed Ryan's dresser and stopped to look at myself in the attached mirror, another antique formerly owned by my grandparents and grudgingly bequeathed to me by my mother. I finger-combed my hair into a semblance of order. My lips had always been one of my best features, full and perfectly proportioned. They looked pouty now, as if they had been thoroughly kissed. And they had. God, could that woman kiss. I touched my neck and shoulder where she had nuzzled me when I had briefly lain on top of her, our hips rocking against each other in our desperate race toward orgasm. How many times had I reached for her last night? I frowned. More times than was decent, I'm sure.

My robe had been draped across a chair in the corner of Ryan's room. I found my bra and panties folded neatly beneath it when I picked it up. I pictured Ryan quietly folding them as I slept in her bed. I left them sitting in the chair and pulled the robe around myself.

When I stepped out into the darkened hall and passed my room, I immediately noticed Pepito curled in the center of my bed, and the fact that my bathroom door had been left open. I was certain I hadn't left it that way; I always had the niggling feeling that Pepito jumped onto the bathroom counter to lick my toothbrush when I wasn't around. I walked downstairs and toward the kitchen, but my heart had sunk to my toes before I even breached the threshold. If Ryan were in the kitchen, Pepito would be there too; he would never miss an opportunity to net himself a dropped morsel or a handout.

The last place I expected to find her was the basement. Most of my muscles already ached, but the light was on when I opened the door, and as much as I was sure that I hadn't left it that way last night, I still found myself silently praying that I would find her there.

She was sitting on the weight bench, her hands hanging loosely between her legs. She looked sad, defeated. My heart sank further.

"Ryan?"

"You're awake," she said and my tension receded as she stood up, walked toward me, and wrapped her arms around my waist. I was standing on the last step so I had to lean into her.

"I thought you'd left the house," I said against her neck.

"No, I had a message from my mother so I came down to call her back. I thought I would work out since I was already up. I didn't want to wake you."

I glanced at the clock. 5:00 a.m. wasn't exactly early for Ryan, but I knew for a fact that she had been busy torturing me not three hours before. "So how long have you been up?"

"A little over an hour."

"Why didn't you wake me?" Ryan dipped her head and said something under her breath. "What was that?" I lifted her chin and smiled at her. My earlier insecurities had faded into the back of my memory like my waking dream. This was rcal, Ryan was real and she was here and I could feel her breath quicken as I leaned into her body.

"I got scared that watching you sleep wouldn't be enough. I thought we might have overdone it last night."

"See, that's where we're different. I think we did it just right last night. But let me see if I understood you correctly. You can work me until I'm about to fall over down here, but in bed I get a reprieve? I think you've got your priorities out of whack, Ryan." She laughed and any evidence of sadness disappeared.

"Wait, did you just say you watched me sleep? I hope I didn't drool."

"Yeah, you did. You snore too."

"Wow. Thanks, sweetheart. I had no idea how sexy I was." I laughed, but I was more than a little embarrassed.

Ryan's face became serious. "I was kidding. You looked very sexy and so beautiful I had to make myself get out of bed so I wouldn't wake you up to make love again."

We shared a kiss that sent a sharp shock to my crotch. I'm sure my toes would have curled if I wasn't already using them to grip the edge of the step for balance. Ryan drew away first; apparently I have no willpower where chocolate *and* sex were concerned. Who knew?

"Go get dressed and join me for a workout before we kill each other." She was laughing, but her tone was serious, worried.

"Something's wrong, isn't it?" I asked and mentally steeled myself against her answer.

"Everything's perfect," she said and the look she gave me almost convinced me that it was.

Almost.

❖

Perfect lasted three days. That's how long it took me to find out what was troubling Ryan.

"Hey, anyone here?" I could clearly hear the faucet running in the kitchen and the sound of Pepito's nails on the floor. I secretly enjoyed the way Ryan and Pepito came to greet me when I came home in the evening. Idiotic, I know, but it made me feel loved and cherished. I sniffed the air appreciatively.

"You don't need to keep cooking for us," I said when Ryan appeared in the kitchen doorway.

"You keep saying that."

"Because you keep doing it." I kissed her hard and wiped the lipstick from her bottom lip. I lifted a pot and leaned in for a sniff. "God, I'm starving. I seem to be eating more, not less, now that I'm working out."

"Here, let me take your bag." She grasped the handle, but instead of releasing it I used it to bring her in for a kiss. Her lips were soft beneath mine; they trembled slightly before they opened.

"You said you were hungry?" she said as she took the bag from my hand. That heavy, scared feeling I had experienced when I woke up alone three days ago returned full force. It was obvious she needed to tell me something but didn't know where to start.

"Ryan? I know you told me everything was fine, and I don't want to harp on it, but I feel like you have something on your mind."

Ryan hesitated, then said. "Yeah, I guess I do." I hadn't noticed her accent for some time. Either it had thickened or I was being overly sensitive.

"Would you mind if we went out front? I...I have a phobia about important conversations in kitchens." I didn't wait for her answer. I just turned away and trusted that she would follow me.

My heart thrummed with every step I took. Part of me wanted to rush into the family room and the other part of me wanted to drag my feet to hold off the inevitable. I sat down and patted the couch next to me. Ryan seemed reluctant to sit down. I took her hand to reassure us both. "Tell me. Please."

"I don't know where to start."

"Start from the beginning. Is it bad news?"

"No, at least I don't think so. My mother seemed to think it was." Ryan shrugged. "She called me the other day. You know, when you found me in the basement. She had called to ask me to give Brady money to get back home. Can you believe that? I told her he stole from you and she still wants me to give him money."

"She's his mother. She probably doesn't want to believe he's as bad as you're saying."

"She'll have to believe it now. I bought him a bus ticket back home. Hopefully he won't sell it."

"I would think your mother would be happy about that?"

"She is, but she expected me to come back with him. I told her I would be staying here."

I grinned at her. "I'm still waiting for the bad news, because so far you're batting a thousand by my book."

Ryan didn't return my smile and I placed my hand on her leg when I realized that she was still very distressed. "You know I finished the work at Mrs. Margolis's, right?"

"Yes, I talked to her the other day. She's still raving about the work you did."

Ryan smiled. "Apparently she's been doing a lot of that. I got a phone call from Decker Kenly."

"Decker Kenly? His company makes my cousin Trino's outfit look minuscule. Does he want you to work for him?"

"No, for his mother."

"His mother?"

"Yeah, she and Mrs. M are friends. Mrs. Kenly went out and bought a fixer-upper without talking to her son first. A real dive of a place, but it's in a great area. East Fifty-sixth. Anyway, he needs someone to rehab it so he can flip it and get her some of the money back. It's too small a job for any of his contractors and he doesn't want to put much money into it. His mother saw the work I did at Mrs. M's and they gave me a call the other day."

"Oh, Ryan, that's fantastic!" I reached out to hug her. She hugged me back and I could feel her mouth stretch into a smile against my shoulder, but the tension was still there.

"They've had problem with kids breaking in and vandalizing it. He wants someone to stay in the house."

I leaned back so I could see her face. "Is that normal? I mean, why can't he hire a security guard?"

Ryan shrugged. "Mrs. M told him that I was staying here with you, so he came up with the idea of offering me the job and no living expenses for the time it'll take me to rehab the house. Probably two or three months."

"Two to three months?" I wanted to tell her she couldn't do that. I wanted to tell her that what we had was too new, but how could I? Ryan and I had no commitment. Hell, by most people's standards we had done things backward anyway. "When?"

"As soon as possible. I thought maybe this weekend."

"You're moving out this weekend?" I blinked, too stunned to even think about crying. This was all wrong. "But what about us?"

Ryan looked sad. "I'd hoped you might still want to see me."

"Of course I do, but…" I couldn't really say what I was thinking, could I? That I didn't want to sleep without her. That a week wasn't nearly long enough. "Do you really have to live in the house?"

"If something happened and I didn't, I would feel bad. Besides, this could be huge."

I did understand what she was saying; this could be the break she was looking for. Unfortunately, my heart only understood one kind of break. *Stop it, Mia. She isn't leaving you, she's just…*

"I need to." She seemed to struggle for her words. "Have you talked to Brenda?"

"Brenda? Is that what this is about?"

"No. I'll admit that the thought of her is always there, but no. The reason I'm taking this job is because it pays well and it could give me a step in the right direction. Mia, how do you feel about me?" I was too shocked to answer right away, and she went on in a manner that told me she had thought carefully about this. "I know you care about me. I know you like being with me as much as I like being with you. I can see it in your face. I just need you to have true closure with Brenda before I feel comfortable moving to the next step."

"Why is everyone so damn sure there hasn't been closure? She left me, remember?" As far as I was concerned, it was over when she walked out that door.

"She'll be back."

"Not for another three months."

"Okay, she comes back in three months and then what? I skulk out the back door as she comes through the front? I'm sorry, Mia, I can't do that."

"Ryan, you know I would never ask you to do that."

She went on as if trying to convince herself as well as me. "I have to start living for me. Doing what's right for me."

I understood what Ryan was saying. She couldn't put her dreams on hold while I got closure with Brenda. But I needed to end things with Brenda the right way, in person and not over the phone.

I wanted to explain to Ryan, to tell her what I was feeling, but I wasn't sure I understood it fully myself.

How *do* you end four years of a relationship with thousands of miles between you? If you just ended it over the phone, wouldn't that mean that the relationship wasn't very important to begin with? And if it wasn't important, did that mean that you'd wasted four years of your life?

Was my heart really worth so little? And if it was, how could I ever offer it to Ryan?

"Mia, don't look so sad. It's not the end of us. We're just going to start where most people begin."

Ryan led me toward the kitchen and the dinner she had made. I sat down and feigned enthusiasm as I listened to her tell me how she had finished the last few projects in the house. I even managed a question or two. But I wasn't enthusiastic, I was scared. How could I let her know that I was ready to move on with her when Brenda and I still had so many loose ends to tie up? I couldn't exactly ask her to wait in the wings until I was done cleaning up my life, could I? What if I did tell her how I felt and she decided she didn't want to deal with all the complications?

The last thought was the glue that sealed my lips. The mess with Brenda was my problem, not Ryan's. She already had too many things to worry about. The best thing I could do was wait for Brenda to come back so she and I could deal with our situation ourselves.

❖

Ryan had promised to wait until I was done with my shower before she started the dishwasher. She would have to wait a long time, because the idea of making love with her tonight filled me with fear. It would feel too much like good-bye sex. Coming home to her had been wonderful. Making love with her for the last few days had been amazing, and now she was telling me she was going to move out?

I had to have the worst luck in the world. My chest felt sore and stuffed full of hurt. I was too scared to cry and too sad to get out of the shower and go to Ryan. I had been too hasty, too willing to believe in happily-ever-after despite the failure of my relationship with Brenda. Maybe I had been too quick to enter into another relationship. Maybe I should give Selena a call; were friends with benefits so bad? I thought of Selena and her nails and I laughed, a choking sound that sounded like a cough, or maybe it was a gag. I could never do that. It wasn't my style, and if it was so great, why did Goody spend most of his non-working moments looking for Mr. Right?

A change in the air pressure and a slight breeze of cool air alerted me before I saw the shadow of Ryan's figure entering the bathroom. "Mia, it's me. Can I come in, please?"

"You're already in, aren't you?" I tried to sound lighthearted, but I doubt she was convinced.

She opened the glass door and my nervous system went haywire. She had taken off her clothes. "I meant, can I come inside?"

I stepped back so that she could get in. She cupped her hands beneath the showerhead and pushed water through her hair until it darkened three shades and hung down her back. She opened her eyes and caught me watching her.

"There's no more hot water," I said.

"That's okay. We'll make our own."

I looked down and forbade myself from reaching out and pulling her hips toward me. She touched my arm and I fell into her, letting her kiss away some of the hurt.

"You were hiding from me," she said when the kiss ended.

"No, I was taking a shower." I managed to keep defensiveness out of my voice.

"Okay, you were hiding from me while taking a shower."

"I'll let you finish yours," I said, reaching for the door handle.

Her palm on the back of my hand stopped me before I could open the door. "I could have taken a shower in my own room."

I allowed myself to be pulled back until her breasts were pressed into my back. I shivered with both want and fear.

"Tell me," she said into my ear.

"I don't want you to move out." I had to raise my voice to be heard over the water.

She tightened her embrace as if she feared I was going to try to break free and run away from her. "You knew I would have to eventually."

"You're right. I did. Sorry I'm being so irrational." I hadn't meant to sound so sarcastic, but Ryan must have heard it the same way I did, because when I leaned back to look at her I realized that my words had hurt her. This was as hard for her as it was for me, and I was treating her like shit because she was trying to make her own way.

"I'm sorry." I reached up and cupped the right side of her face. And I thought she was going to cry. "I'm sorry," I said again.

We held each other for one long moment. "I'm not leaving you, Mia. There are things I want to do. I just want you to be as proud of me as I am of you."

"I am proud of you." I reached down and grabbed her hands. "I love what you do with these." Ryan's lips quirked into a smile and I slapped at her shoulder lightly. "You know what I mean."

"Yes, I do," she said.

This time when we kissed a fire was lit in my lower belly. I backed her up against the shower wall and she jumped when the chill hit her back. I pressed my body against hers and her fingers sank into my wet hair. Our first night together had been explosive. We couldn't get enough of each other. Now I felt like I needed to imprint her on my memory, savor everything about her.

I was standing between her legs, pressing into her with my hips. When I stepped away, she tried to pull me back to her but I slipped a hand between us and touched her with my fingertips. I loved the way she felt, so delicate and so small, yet strong. Capable of handling anything I could dish out and then some. I took her slowly because I wanted it to last.

A small amount of pressure with my thumb to the right of her clitoris, and her hips would increase their slow, rotating grind and start speeding toward orgasm. Slow or not, though, there came a moment when her hips missed a beat and she quickened her pace. The shower all but drowned out the sound of her breathing and I pressed the back of her neck so that her head was resting on my shoulder.

I watched as pleasure infused her face. She threw back her head and closed her eyes. The running water, her cry of release, and her gasps afterward drowned out my voice as I told her what I had no right to.

"I love you," I whispered. "I love you and I don't want you to go."

CHAPTER TWENTY-TWO

Ryan kept her word. She called me at least once a day at work, and if we didn't see each other after work, she called me before I went to bed. Still, in the two weeks since she had moved out, I missed her terribly.

Not half as much as Pepito, though. He moped around so much that I had to borrow one of Ryan's T-shirts so that he could sleep with it. I snagged one for myself as well. Ryan had been very adamant about not sleeping at the house because she felt it would be too easy for us to fall back on old habits. Last night had been one of the few occasions I was able to change her mind.

I was walking home from the bus stop, daydreaming about our lovemaking, when a familiar figure standing in front of my house brought me up short.

After four years of living with someone, you'd think you would cease to notice new things about them. I studied Brenda's profile as she accepted her bags from the cab driver. I had never thought her beautiful, but she had a magnetism that attracted people of all kinds to her. Brenda would never be lonely, nor would she ever really miss anyone. There would always be someone to hold her attention if she wanted.

Her brown-black hair had grown out and the sun or the same person who had dyed her graying temples had given her highlights where there used to be none. Her long-sleeved shirt was tucked neatly into her jeans and belted, making her look smart if not exactly comfortable. My thoughts turned to Ryan and how comfortable she always looked.

She stood with her hands on her hips and her legs splayed, much as she had when we had first viewed the house together. I watched her step over to the lawn and then look up toward the awnings and trellis that Ryan had painted an almost eye-aching white. Brenda looked as if she was trying to find fault in something.

As I approached I noticed that the door was ajar, indicating she had already been inside. The idea that Brenda had a key to the door disconcerted me. The fact that she had always had one didn't matter; after so many months it felt like an invasion. *I should feel something. After four years I should feel something, shouldn't I?*

Brenda had walked back into the house and was turning to close the door when she spotted me. "There you are." She said it as casually as someone who had been gone for twenty-four hours instead of two and a half months.

"I wasn't expecting you today," I said dully.

Brenda had a rakish grin that I had always believed attractive. Now it felt crass and out of place, like a precursor to something painful. "I decided to come home early. So you better tell that live-in girlfriend of yours to hightail it out the back door because your wife is home now."

The words were so close to those Ryan had uttered that a sob wrenched from my throat. Brenda looked shocked and pulled me into a hug. I let her because I needed to lean on something.

"I'm home now. You don't need to cry."

I let out a choking laugh and she patted my back as if to say, "let it out." The laugh had a strangely calming effect. The last of the sobs had stopped when I realized that the whole time I had been clinging to her, what I had taken for comforting back rubs was actually Brenda feeling my body.

"You've lost weight!" Her fingers were on my sides now and then went to my arms. "You've lost a lot of weight. How much have you lost?"

I sniffed and wiped at my eyes. "I don't know. I bought a scale about a week ago, but I haven't been on it yet."

Brenda's eyes grew wide. "Where is it?"

"In my bathroom."

"Let's go see." She grabbed my hand and dragged me down the hall and up the stairs. I vaguely wondered where Pepito was and I got my answer when I saw a flash of brown, gray, and white shoot beneath the bed. I also spotted several pieces of Brenda's luggage in the middle of the floor next to the bed, the bed she obviously assumed we would still be sharing. I felt exhausted when I stepped on the scale.

"Here, step off." She stepped on the scale, smiled at the number she saw there, stepped off, and pushed me forward again. "Step on again." She glared down at the scale and back up at me. "Do you know how much you weighed before I left?"

I told her because I didn't care if she knew. I wasn't ashamed of my weight anymore.

"That means you've lost twenty-two pounds." Her voice was full of awe, and I finally looked down at the scale myself.

"That can't be right. I would know if I had lost that much."

"Well, you have. I'm very proud of you, hon. Have you told your mother?"

"I haven't spoken with my mother in weeks. Even if I had, I doubt I would have told her about this."

"Really?" Brenda seemed surprised. "I would think you would be crowing about it from the rooftops."

"Actually, what I'd be crowing about is the fact that I'm working out for an hour, six days a week. I'd probably tell her that I don't feel as hungry as I used to and I don't feel like my clothes are as tight. I might even tell her I love feeling strong."

"That's great, sweetie. But you know your mom better than anyone. She won't care how you did it, just that you did." Brenda wrapped her arms around my waist and pulled me close. "We should go celebrate. We could go to that Italian place you used to love eating at."

"Mia? Did you know the front door was…?" Ryan stopped in the doorway as if a pane of glass had been erected in front of her.

Completely still, she looked from the luggage to Brenda's arms wrapped around my waist. Pepito scrambled from under the bed. He ran at Ryan and rebounded off the tops of her thighs. I had seen him do this to her before and she would always respond by dropping to her knees and playing with him, but this time she barely looked down at him. Her hair was pulled back in its usual ponytail and she looked freshly showered. Is it possible for someone to become more beautiful in twelve hours?

I wanted to go to her, but something held me back. I looked down and found that Brenda was still holding me around the waist. "Ryan, this is…" I reached down to push Brenda's hands away.

"Brenda," Ryan said without removing her eyes from us.

"I'm sorry, have we met?" Brenda released me and held her hand out.

"No." Ryan's voice was stiff, unemotional, and polite. "I'm just the person who did the work on the house."

Brenda dropped her hand to her side after it became obvious that Ryan had no intention of shaking it. "Oh, has there been some work? I didn't get a chance to look around the house. Mia and I ran right up to the bedroom as soon as I walked in the door."

Ryan's eyes went to mine. The pain on her face was enough for me to wish the mask back in place. "It's not what it looks like." I immediately realized how guilty I sounded.

Ryan turned and walked away. I could hear the sound of her footsteps and as she took the stairs three at a time. Pepito ran after her.

"Ryan, wait a minute." I started after her, but Brenda grabbed my hand.

"Where are you going? I just got back."

"Damn it, Brenda, let me go." I wrenched my hand away from her and rushed after Ryan. Pepito was sitting forlornly at the front door. Ryan was in her car and had already turned on the engine. I don't know what possessed me, but I ran down the walkway and jumped in front of her car just as she pressed on her gas pedal. She lurched to a stop and I slapped the hood with both hands.

"You promised you wouldn't ever leave without talking to me," I screamed.

She stared at me through her windshield. She looked as if she were about to say something, but she bit her bottom lip so hard I wouldn't have been surprised if she drew blood.

I walked around the side of the car. "Roll down your window," I pleaded. She hesitated so long that I thought she would refuse before finally cranking the windows down. "Look at me, please?"

She continued to stare out her front windshield even though I was no longer in front of her. "What you saw in there was Brenda pulling me into the bathroom to see how much weight I'd lost. I haven't seen her in months, and that's the first thing she said to me. Ryan. Ryan, please look at me. You and I were just together last night. I could never sleep with her after being with you. Please tell me you believe me. Whatever else you might think, you have to know that I'm not that kind of person."

She swallowed and took a deep breath. I took that to mean that she did believe me.

"Will you come back inside and talk to me? Please?"

She finally looked at me. "I don't think I can right now. Besides, she's in there, waiting for you." Her voice sounded bitter, defeated, and it was my fault.

"Ryan, please don't go off angry."

"I'll call you." She rolled up her window and I was forced to step away from her car.

I had no choice but to watch her drive away.

❖

"I don't know, Goody. It must be me. I must have something wrong with me that makes women think I'm leaveable." I had asked Goody to meet me for coffee because there was only so much working out a person could do.

"You must not be that leaveable. Brenda's back, isn't she?"

"I can't even look at her without feeling resentful."

"Then why don't you ask her to move out?" Goody sipped on his hot chocolate, frowning a little because, as its name implied, it was hot.

"Because it's her house too."

"So, you're going to end up like a het couple with kids, forever linked because of a house. Do you even like that house?"

I was about to say of course I did, but I couldn't. When we bought the house I thought it would be the perfect home, now it was just somewhere to sleep. "I miss Ryan," I blurted. "I miss her so much."

I picked up my glass of water and brought it to my lips in the hopes that Goody would think some condensation from my glass had somehow leapt into my eye. Goody set his hot chocolate down and his eyes zeroed in on the tears. I wiped at my cheek with a napkin. I laughed in order to keep from turning into a sobbing mess at the table.

"Oh, sweetie." Goody put his hand over mine. "You're as dumb as a sack of hammers, aren't you?" The cutting words did not match the compassion in his eyes.

"Thanks, Goody. I knew I could count on you in my time of need."

"You know I'm usually behind you, but I'm sorry, you need to handle your business a little bit better." I wanted Goody to just stop talking. I already felt frustrated and trod upon.

"Let's recap here. You asked Ryan to move in with you. You ask her to fix up a house that you purchased with your lover. You ask her to help you get into shape. And then, after Ryan does a smash-bang job of all of that, you repay her by letting your ex move back into the house. About the only thing you didn't do was have sex with her." Goody's eyes grew wide. "You didn't have sex with her, did you?" He stared at me for a moment. "You had sex with her, didn't you, bitch?" His finger came up. "We'll talk about the fact that you didn't tell me any of this later. But you had sex with her, took her to your family function, and then you let your ex-girlfriend move back in with you? Girl, if I didn't now you better, I'd think you had grown balls overnight, because that's truly some fucked-up dip you're passing out."

"What are you talking about? I didn't do—" I stopped, because on the surface I'd done all those things and more. *I am a passer-out of fucked-up dip*. "Shit," I mumbled.

Goody rolled his eyes and picked up his cocoa. "What are you going to do about it?"

"I could go see her. Beg her to let me have another chance. Not that we really had a relationship or anything."

"Oh, don't let yourself off the hook that easy. I think you did have one. Right up until you let the skank move back in your house. Did you try calling her?"

"I've left so many messages on her cell it's embarrassing."

"I can't say I would be particularly eager to talk to you either."

"Don't be like this. I made a mistake. Please, just help me figure out what I should do." I was shocked to see my own hand as I reached for his half-eaten bran muffin. I paused and drew my hand back and placed it around my water instead.

"I can't help you with this one, *chica.* I'm usually the one in Ryan's shoes. I do know you need to clean up your mess and I would suggest you do it quick, because a catch like Ryan ain't going to wait for you like you waited for that skank all these years. Most of us ain't so desperate."

"Thanks a lot. If I had had a friend like you when I was younger I'd have been a hundred pounds heavier." My heart sank as hurt flashed across Goody's face. "You know I didn't mean anything by that."

He stood up. "I need to get going. I'll see you tomorrow."

I watched Goody walk out of the coffee house. I drained the rest of my water, looked longingly at the muffin, and dropped a few dollars as a tip on the table and left. Life was beginning to feel like two fifty-pound weights sitting squarely on my shoulders.

❖

In the real world, storybook endings are few and far between. I knew that, but I couldn't understand how things could go so wrong in the span of a few days. Nor could I have known how much my heart would ache every time the phone rang and it wasn't Ryan.

Brenda moved back into the room that we used to share, while Pepito and I—he was even less forgiving than I was—slept in Ryan's room. I was still thinking of it that way—as Ryan's room.

Brenda was back, and all I could think of was Ryan. My only relief, the only way I slept, was to work out for an hour every night before I showered and went to bed. But even then, the moment I closed my eyes, I thought about her, about what she was doing and how she was feeling and if she missed me as much as I missed her.

I was on the bus on my way home when I came up with a new question to torment myself with. *What if she finds someone else?*

The invisible dagger that cleaved open my chest stayed with me for the entire bus ride home. Even a four-mile run on the treadmill didn't help to alleviate the pain.

Brenda was sitting at the table when I came upstairs from my workout. She pointed to the bottled water sitting at the table across from her. "You got a minute?" she asked.

"Yeah, can I get a shower first?"

"I have a flight to Paris in a few hours. Don't worry about driving me, I'll park at the airport, and I'd rather this not wait until I get back."

I resisted the urge to sigh, sat down, and twisted the top off my bottled water.

"You're really getting yourself into great shape. I'm proud of you."

I took a drink and stared at her. She had one of those looks on her face that I hated. The "see, I told you and I'm always right" look. She was actually taking credit for the fact that I was working out.

"Ryan taught me how fun it could be."

"About Ryan." I stiffened at her dismissive tone. "She called while you were downstairs."

I wanted to scream and ask her why she hadn't come to get me, but I stayed calm. "What did she say?"

"Just that she got your messages, but she has been really busy. She said she would call you back when she could."

"Oh." The dagger was back and twisting its way south.

If I were alone, I'd probably jump up and call her and ask her not to do this, not to separate from me, from us, but I wasn't alone and Brenda was staring at me, studying my reaction.

"That what you wanted to tell me?" I asked gruffly.

"No, I wanted to tell you that I think we should seek counseling when I get back."

Now she had my full attention. "For what?"

"Our relationship."

She has got to be kidding.

"Just hear me out, okay? I know you were with this Ryan character. You and she probably had a lot of fun together. But we have much more than that. We have this house. We have a life together. I'm not sure what happened, maybe it was early midlife crisis, I don't know." Brenda shrugged. "I do know I still love you. I don't care what you did while I was gone. I don't care about anything that's happened over the last few months. I shouldn't have left. I shouldn't have done a lot of things, but I can't take those things back. I just want you to think about what we still have. I want our life back, Mia. And I think you do too."

She stood up. I had to lean my head back to look up at her. She bent down and kissed me. I was so shocked that I froze. Her hand was on my neck for support. Her lips were seeking, questioning. Her tongue probed my mouth, coaxing my tongue to respond. When I didn't, she pulled away. I could tell by the look on her face that she was confused.

"I need to get going. Can we finish this conversation when I get home next week?"

I'm sure I only blinked, but something in the motion must have relieved Brenda because she smiled and patted my check. "Everything's going to be great." She squatted on the side of the table until I could only see the top of her head. "Pepito, take care of Mia."

Pepito growled at her and she stood up quickly.

"He's still pissed at me for leaving. Good Lord, that dog can hold a grudge longer than most humans. See ya later, hon."

She swooped down, gave me another impersonal little kiss, and swept out of the kitchen, leaving me and Pepito staring at each other. Pepito broke the trance first with a little sneeze of disgust. He turned around and walked away. I heard him a few seconds latter as he bunny-hopped up the stairs, probably going to lie in his box-bed to comfort himself with the scent of Ryan's T-shirt.

Everything felt so wrong. What the hell was I doing? Why was Brenda kissing me? Why was I letting her think there might be a chance for us? Whether Ryan wanted to be with me or not, there was no chance for Brenda and me. And I had just let her skip out of here believing everything was back to normal. I leapt up and made a mad dash for the door. I threw it open and ran outside just as Brenda slammed her trunk and walked around to the side of her car and sat down in the driver's seat. Her mouth was pursed in a whistle. *She's whistling, for God's sake.*

"Brenda, wait," I called out and jogged up to her car before she could close the door.

Mr. Gentry stopped raking his lawn and shaded his eyes to watch me though the sky was overcast. Anger kept me from being cold though it couldn't have been more than forty-five degrees.

"What is it, Mia?" Brenda had a slightly annoyed look on her face. "I have to get going."

"This won't take long. I just wanted you to know there won't be any counseling. We'll talk when you get back, but the conversation will be around how we dissolve our shared assets amicably."

The stunned look on her face gave me no pleasure. I bent down and leaned on her car door so that Mr. Gentry wouldn't hear us. "Have you ever looked at someone and instantly realized that you could spend the rest of your life with them? Did the person who made you think I wasn't enough for you make your heart leap into your throat when you saw her? When you heard her voice? Did you ache for her at inopportune moments?"

Brenda laughed. "No, of course not."

"Then I feel sorry for you, Brenda." I was tired and I was sad and I was hurt, but I really did feel sorry for Brenda because she did have the right idea. All of us deserve to feel something special in a relationship. She just went about it the wrong way, and she still didn't know what she was missing. But I did. *Maybe I should be feeling sorry for myself.*

"So what are you saying? You aren't in love with her, are you? I saw the way that she looked at you, but I thought you were with her to get even with me."

"You saw the way she looked at me and you still don't get it? Why were we even together if you never felt that way about me?"

"We made a damn good couple," she said. "You can't just throw everything we had out the window because you think you've found someone else."

"I didn't. You did. And now I'm telling you I want more. I want someone who loves me as much as I love them. Who enjoys my company, who listens when I talk."

The sadness had lifted. I was talking to Brenda, but I knew I was the only one listening. She would always assume that this had happened because I believed she'd cheated on me. I was beyond caring if she had.

"I'll let you get going." It wasn't lost on me that Brenda had been leaving the entire four years we were together. The only difference was me. I wouldn't be counting the minutes until she returned.

"I guess there's no point in me calling you tomorrow, is there?"

"No, no point at all. Have a safe trip." I shut the door.

Brenda put the car in reverse, and rolled her window down. "Did you ever feel those things for me? Did your heart leap into your throat when you saw me? Did you ache for me at inopportune moments?"

I hesitated.

"I didn't think so. You don't miss what you never had, Mia," she said and backed out the driveway.

I watched Brenda's car round the corner and started back toward the house. Mr. Gentry was still standing with his chin resting on the back of his hands. He had to have seen and heard at least some of what had just happened.

"I take it you're gonna be selling soon?" he asked.

I looked back at the house and after Brenda's retreating car. "As soon as I possibly can."

"Pity, you're a nice neighbor. Got to say though, I like your blond handyman girlfriend much better than that one."

He went back to raking his lawn and I stood there for a moment before the chilly air and Pepito's shrill barking reminded me that I needed to get inside.

Chapter Twenty-Three

I know it's not very big, but it's in a great neighborhood and I can walk to pretty much anywhere. It has this great attic space upstairs that would be perfect for an office, except it gets pretty hot up there so I'll have to install an air-conditioner of some sort."

She's babbling. She doesn't babble. Her back was to me and she was struggling with something. I had given up trying to get her to answer her cell phone and had come over to the small house on East Fifty-sixth in the hopes that Ryan would let me in so that I could talk to her. She had let me in, but I had been unable to get her to sit still or be quiet long enough to get a word in. "Ryan, what are you doing?"

"Trying to get this damn lid off."

"Here, let me." I squatted next to her and took the small metal pry from her hand and worked it around the edge of the paint can. "Are you still angry with me?"

"No."

"Then why are you avoiding me?"

"I'm not. I left a message that I would be busy."

I reached out and brushed her hair away from her moist forehead. She went statue still. "You *are* avoiding me and it hurts. You've been avoiding me since Brenda came back. What you saw looked bad, I understand that, but you should have let me explain. If you had stayed, I would have made her tell you nothing was going on between us."

She stood up and so did I, but she picked up the can and moved toward the back of the house. I sidestepped a broom, a dust pan, and a box in order to follow her. I could see every muscle in her back and in her triceps bulging as she walked. "Ryan, would you please stand still long enough for me to talk to you?"

"I need to finish this tonight. The HVAC contractor isn't coming in for a couple weeks and it's supposed to get cold soon."

I took a deep breath. "Okay, I guess I'll have to talk while you work."

She didn't answer me, and if I didn't already regret coming there before, I was regretting it then. She had stopped in a small room off the main hallway and was studying the walls as if she had never seen them before. If I wanted to talk to her, I would have to talk to her back.

"I see you're busy, so I'll make it quick. I think you're doing exactly what you said you wouldn't do."

"I'm not running away. I'm just busy."

She squatted again and this time my eyes lingered over her back and ass. I took a deep breath, remembering how she felt and how her eyes had pleaded with me to help her that first time, how when she finally had reached orgasm they had welled up.

"Is that why you're here?" She stood up and took an almost angry swipe at one of the corners of the wall. "Because I didn't call you back?"

There were so many answers I could have given her, wanted to give her, but I chose the ones that would get me to point B the fastest. "I'm here because every time I walk through my own front door, I look for you. I'm here because every time I go to the grocery store I see you turning corners, then I run like hell to catch up only to startle some woman who looks nothing like you. I'm here because I miss having you lying next to me. I'm here because there's a little dog that hates my guts because he thinks I did something to drive you away. I'm here because I think he's right."

She had stopped painting, her head tilted to the side as she listened. When she finally faced me, her eyes were gauges of pain. It hurt knowing that I was the cause of it. "Where's Brenda?"

"She's in Paris."

"Ah, so is that why you're here? Because you got lonely again?"

"What a shitty thing to say." I was so stunned that I couldn't muster any anger, just shock.

She stooped and lay the paint brush across the top of the can. "All my life…" She paused, as if thinking about her words, then continued.

"All my life I've done what's best for other people. For my mother, for Brady, for anyone that I cared about. I gave and I gave until there was nothing left for me."

"I know and I'm—"

"Let me finish."

My face heated at being spoken to so sharply. She was having no problems looking at me now.

"When I moved in with you, I told myself I was just taking advantage of a good opportunity. You needed work done on your house, you had the extra room. You had workout equipment and you weren't charging me for rent. I figured it was a mutually beneficial situation. I was lying to myself and I knew it from day one."

I dropped my eyes to the floor and opened my mouth to force air down my throat. Ryan must have misinterpreted the action as me preparing to interrupt, because she said, "Let me finish," again, but this time, gently, "I should have never been in your house. I should have never slept with you."

I turned away from her and started for the door. *I will not cry here. I will not.* I had heard enough. *She should have never slept with me? Was that all it was for her?* I was halfway across the room when she stopped me with an awkward one-armed embrace from behind.

"Stop it," I said, but I didn't move and she didn't take her arm from around my waist.

"You've had your say, now let me have mine. I was half in love with you before I even moved into your house. By the time we made love, I was doing everything I could to keep you from finding out."

Her words were like a shock to my system. I turned around so that I could see her face. "Why wouldn't you tell me?"

"What should I have said? That I thought you should leave Brenda to be with me? That you should throw away four years of your life to be with someone who had been leeching off you, who was unemployed until recently and could offer you nothing?" She crossed her arms in front of herself, and I could see the whites of her knuckles as she held herself tightly. "I wanted to," she said softly. "But then I walked in and saw you two in your bedroom."

"I explained that."

"Her luggage was in your bedroom."

"She sleeps in there. Pepito and I sleep in your room." I didn't realize I was as angry as I was until I heard the sound of my own voice. "So you thought you'd help things along by storming off?"

I was so angry that I could have reached out and shaken her. After I kissed her, after I held her tight against me, after I told her I loved her, I would shake the shit out of her for being so goddamn stubborn.

"She wanted you back, and I could see you struggling with what you were going to do about it."

"I wasn't thinking about it the way you thought I was. I was trying to figure out how I was going to end it without hurting her. I didn't want to damage her dignity like she had damaged mine. I was already thinking about selling the house."

She looked surprised. "Why would you sell the house? You love that house."

"It's a house. It doesn't take care of me when I'm hurt. It doesn't cry just because I'm crying. I don't love that house. I love you."

She took a step back and looked at me, horrified.

"Your reaction is not what I envisioned," I said dryly.

"Are you sure?"

"Let's see. I can't sleep. I've lost so much weight that my clothes fit like shit, and you're the only thing I seem to think about clearly. And right now I feel like I'm about to die because I just professed my love for you and you're backing away from me." I laughed but there was no humor in it. I felt as horrified as she looked.

"And you're sure about this?"

I gritted my teeth. "I already told you, I'm positive."

This is where I would like to say that she took me into her arms, but I can't. She turned away from me, picked up her brush, and began to paint again. I watched her for a few minutes before I took off my sweatshirt, picked up a roller, and began to paint too.

We worked long into the night, barely speaking to each other, barely looking at each other until the whole house was finished. She thanked me as if I were a complete stranger, her hand held out and open as if for a shake. I told myself that strangers didn't avoid eye contact and strangers didn't tremble when the offered handshake turned into a hug. I contented myself with turning my lips into her neck. I let her go and left quickly, telling myself that I would come back and I would continue to do so until she told me to stop.

❖

The house I co-owned with Brenda sold fast. The only bump in our separation process was in regard to who would keep Pepito. Things smoothed out considerably when Brenda realized that Pepito's aversion to her was getting worse, not better. He and I moved into a cute little apartment with mirrored closets that we both loved looking into. I haven't seen or heard from Brenda since we signed the last of the paperwork on the house.

Pepito and I spent our evenings and weekends working for Ryan, painting, cleaning, whatever she needed. I should say I painted; Pepito lounged in the bed that Ryan had bought for him. I won't lie and say I didn't long to do more than the heated kisses and looks that we shared, but I was happy that she was willing to let me back into her life again. I was determined to wait as long as she needed me to.

You would have to ask her what finally made her decide that she was ready to let go of whatever fears she was harboring about entering into a relationship with me. It had been a normal Saturday. We had worked until sundown and then had dinner on a blanket in the middle of the floor. The kiss good night had been long and lingering, but they all had been that way of late. I was carrying a limp and sleepy Pepito to the car when I heard the front door open. I turned around expecting to see her jog down the walkway carrying one of Pepito's toys or one of my jackets. But she just stood there, the right side of her face in shadow.

"We forget something?" I walked back slowly until I could see the distressed look on her face. I took the final four steps to the front door.

"Will you stay here tonight?" she asked.

Finally! I forced myself to stay calm. I had waited this long; I could wait a few more seconds. "I'd like to stay, but I want to make sure we want the same thing. I didn't handle the problem with Brenda well and I ended up hurting you, but I always had the best intentions where you were concerned. I don't just want tonight. I want forever after with you. Is that what you want?"

"It's what I've always wanted," she said and stepped to the side.

Pepito sighed in his sleep and gave my ribs two kicks as if to say, "it's about damn time." Ryan closed the door behind us.

❖

I was less than twenty feet from the finish line, and I was a mess. Ryan had convinced me to try a 5K rather than the PDX Challenge after I admitted that I had not learned how to ride a bike as a child. I had made the mistake of telling people at Goldsmith that I was running, so I had spotted familiar faces dotted throughout the crowd. Sweat poured off my forehead and I could feel every ounce of the ten pounds I still wanted to lose. My eyes stung as I forced myself to keep putting one foot in front of the other. I was exhausted, but it never crossed my mind to stop. I heard Ryan's voice urging me on as I jogged, limped, sort of fell across the finish line, and then someone was holding me and screaming in my ear and I lifted my arm like I had just won the Olympics.

This was it. What I had been working toward for the last six months. This was the very moment. I wasn't first—hell, I probably wasn't even one hundred and first—but I had finished, and that was a first for me.

I wiped sweat out of my eyes to see Amy holding Pepito up in the air. I snatched Pepito from her and kissed his little head, narrowly avoiding being kissed back.

"Where's Ryan?" I had to yell because there were so many people celebrating around me.

"I'm right here."

I turned around and fell into her eyes. She was looking at me with so much pride and adoration that I had to blink tears of joy.

She kissed me hard. "We were on the other side. I told Dominique it wasn't a good idea to have the baby stroller in your way when you crossed the finish line. I got a great picture of you too. Do you know what you came in at?"

"No, I don't." The event volunteers hustled us off to the side of the finish line. I was grateful that Ryan held me against her side because the idea of walking even those few steps seemed daunting now that I had stopped. I looked around for Christina, my official timekeeper.

"Ninety-second," she said from somewhere behind me. I turned to find her with a sticky-faced Justin in one hand and a stopwatch in the other. "Right smack-dab in the middle."

We grinned at each other and I felt something warm and fuzzy bloom inside. Things were still strained between me and my mother, but Christina was seeing someone for her eating disorder and she was separated from Ned, so I refused to regret anything I'd said at Sunday brunch.

Someone handed me a T-shirt and I held it up in front of me. It was two sizes too big and it looked as if it had been made in a speed-sewing contest. It was probably the tackiest but most prized garment I would ever own. I reveled in the energy of the crowd, reliving the rush of triumph as another runner crossed the finish line.

"Wow, that has got to be the most amazing experience ever. One of the most amazing experiences, I should say." I smiled suggestively at Ryan and she flushed.

Goody laughed. "You two should be way over that stage now. Hey, Steve should be off work soon. Maybe we could all go get something to eat to celebrate?"

"Eh, I don't think I can eat anything right now. A hot bath sounds great, though." I caught Ryan's eyes on me again. Her shy look hadn't faded. "Something on your mind, sweetheart?"

"I have something for you. Sort of a celebration gift…you like the cottage, right?"

It wasn't like her to be so tongue-tied these days. Puzzled, I said, "I love the cottage."

"I went to go see Decker Kenly while you were getting registered. He's putting it up for sale."

"Oh." I liked my apartment, but some of the most wonderful nights and mornings had been spent making love with Ryan in the cottage, and Pepito loved peeing on the flowers she had planted out back. We would miss staying there. "Where are you going to stay? Hey, why don't you stay with us? Pepito and I would love it."

Someone bumped into me, pushing me closer to Ryan. She wrapped her arms around me and said, "That's not what I had in mind."

She pulled something out of her pocket and put it around my neck. I held it up. A key tied to the end of a blue silk ribbon. She pulled another ribbon out, this one shorter, and instead of a key dangling from the end, there was a small metal bone. I read Pepito's name along with the address for the cottage.

"He said it was mine if I wanted it. I've been saving all my money so I have the down payment, but I told him I would talk to you first."

"Down payment?" I glanced from the key to Ryan. "You're going to buy it?" Tears pricked the corners of my eyes. "The cottage is yours?"

"Ours." Her voice was hoarse. "I want to be able to make love with you without wondering if you're going to leave me the next morning."

She didn't have to convince me of anything. I poured all of my love and my answer into a kiss, crowd be damned.

When we finally parted I saw the joy and the love I felt for her mirrored in her eyes. I saw myself as she saw me. Exhausted. Lank, sweat-drenched hair. Ten pounds overweight, and without a dab of makeup on my face.

I felt beautiful.

About the Author

Gabrielle Goldsby grew up in Oakland, California, where at the age of nine, a childhood illness left her confined to bed for weeks. It was then, thanks to her mother's efforts to save her own sanity, that she discovered a love of reading. After receiving a bachelor's degree in criminal justice administration, she spent time as a gang and drugs prevention counselor, a flooring specialist for a large home-improvement store, a facilities manager inside some of San Francisco's largest law firms, and an administrative assistant in the semiconductor industry. These varied occupations have become the basis for many past and future writing projects.

She resides in Portland, Oregon, with her partner of eight years.

Books Available From Bold Strokes Books

Such a Pretty Face by Gabrielle Goldsby. A sexy, sometimes humorous, sometimes biting contemporary romance that gently exposes the damage to heart and soul when we fail to look beneath the surface for what truly matters. (978-1-933110-84-4)

Second Season by Ali Vali. A romance set in New Orleans amidst betrayal, Hurricane Katrina, and the new beginnings hardship and heartbreak sometimes make possible. (978-1-933110-83-7)

Hearts Aflame by Ronica Black. A poignant, erotic romance between a hard-driving businesswoman and a solitary vet. Packed with adventure and set in the harsh beauty of the Arizona countryside. (978-1-933110-82-0)

Red Light by JD Glass. Tori forges her path as an EMT in the New York City 911 system while discovering what matters most to herself and the woman she loves. (978-1-933110-81-3)

Honor Under Siege by Radclyffe. Secret Service agent Cameron Roberts struggles to protect her lover while searching for a traitor who just may be another woman with a claim on her heart. (978-1-933110-80-6)

Dark Valentine by Jennifer Fulton. Danger and desire fuel a high-stakes cat-and-mouse game when an attorney and an endangered witness team up to thwart a killer. (978-1-933110-79-0)

Sequestered Hearts by Erin Dutton. A popular artist suddenly goes into seclusion, a reluctant reporter wants to know why, and a heart locked away yearns to be set free. (978-1-933110-78-3)

Erotic Interludes 5: Road Games, ed. by Radclyffe and Stacia Seaman. Adventure, "sport," and sex on the road—hot stories of travel adventures and games of seduction. (978-1-933110-77-6)

The Spanish Pearl by Catherine Friend. On a trip to Spain, Kate Vincent is accidentally transported back in time—an epic saga spiced with humor, lust, and danger. (978-1-933110-76-9)

Lady Knight by L-J Baker. Loyalty and honor clash with love and ambition in a medieval world of magic when female knight Riannon meets Lady Eleanor. (978-1-933110-75-2)

Dark Dreamer by Jennifer Fulton. Best-selling horror author Rowe Devlin falls under the spell of psychic Phoebe Temple. A Dark Vista romance. (978-1-933110-74-5)

Come and Get Me by Julie Cannon. Elliott Foster isn't used to pursuing women, but alluring attorney Lauren Collier makes her change her mind. (978-1-933110-73-8)

Blind Curves by Diane and Jacob Anderson-Minshall. Private eye Yoshi Yakamota comes to the aid of her ex-lover Velvet Erickson in the first Blind Eye mystery. (978-1-933110-72-1)

Dynasty of Rogues by Jane Fletcher. It's hate at first sight for Ranger Riki Sadiq and her new patrol corporal, Tanya Coppelli—except for their undeniable attraction. (978-1-933110-71-4)

Running With the Wind by Nell Stark. Sailing instructor Corrie Marsten has signed off on love until she meets Quinn Davies—one woman she can't ignore. (978-1-933110-70-7)

More Than Paradise by Jennifer Fulton. Two women battle danger, risk all, and find in each other an unexpected ally and an unforgettable love. (978-1-933110-69-1)

Flight Risk by Kim Baldwin. For Blayne Keller, being in the wrong place at the wrong time just might turn out to be the best thing that ever happened to her. (978-1-933110-68-4)

Rebel's Quest: Supreme Constellations Book Two by Gun Brooke. On a world torn by war, two women discover a love that defies all boundaries. (978-1-933110-67-7)

Punk and Zen by JD Glass. Angst, sex, love, rock. Trace, Candace, Francesca…Samantha. Losing control—and finding the truth within. BSB Victory Editions. (1-933110-66-X)

The Devil Unleashed by Ali Vali. As the heat of violence rises, so does the passion. A Casey Clan crime saga. (1-933110-61-9)

When Dreams Tremble by Radclyffe. Two women whose lives turned out far differently than they'd once imagined discover that sometimes the shape of the future can only be found in the past. (1-933110-64-3)

Stellium in Scorpio by Andrews & Austin. The passionate reunion of two powerful women on the glitzy Las Vegas Strip, where everything is an illusion and love is a gamble. (1-933110-65-1)

Burning Dreams by Susan Smith. The chronicle of the challenges faced by a young drag king and an older woman who share a love "outside the bounds." (1-933110-62-7)

Fresh Tracks by Georgia Beers. Seven women, seven days. A lot can happen when old friends, lovers, and a new girl in town get together in the mountains. (1-933110-63-5)

The Empress and the Acolyte by Jane Fletcher. Jemeryl and Tevi fight to protect the very fabric of their world…time. Lyremouth Chronicles Book Three. (1-933110-60-0)

First Instinct by JLee Meyer. When high-stakes security fraud leads to murder, one woman flees for her life while another risks her heart to protect her. (1-933110-59-7)

Erotic Interludes 4: Extreme Passions, ed. by Radclyffe and Stacia Seaman. Thirty of today's hottest erotica writers set the pages aflame with love, lust, and steamy liaisons. (1-933110-58-9)

Unexpected Ties by Gina L. Dartt. With death before dessert, Kate Shannon and Nikki Harris are swept up in another tale of danger and romance. (1-933110-56-2)

Broken Wings by L-J Baker. When Rye Woods, a fairy, meets the beautiful dryad Flora Withe, her libido, as squashed and hidden as her wings, reawakens along with her heart. (1-933110-55-4)

Combust the Sun by Andrews & Austin. A Richfield and Rivers mystery set in L.A. Murder among the stars. (1-933110-52-X)

Tristaine Rises by Cate Culpepper. Brenna, Jesstin, and the Amazons of Tristaine face their greatest challenge for survival. (1-933110-50-3)

Passion's Bright Fury by Radclyffe. When a trauma surgeon and a filmmaker become reluctant allies on the battleground between life and death, passion strikes without warning. (1-933110-54-6)

Sleep of Reason by Rose Beecham. Nothing is as it seems when Detective Jude Devine finds herself caught up in a small-town soap opera. And her rocky relationship with forensic pathologist Dr. Mercy Westmoreland just got a lot harder. (1-933110-53-8)

Grave Silence by Rose Beecham. Detective Jude Devine's investigation of a series of ritual murders is complicated by her torrid affair with the golden girl of Southwestern forensic pathology, Dr. Mercy Westmoreland. (1-933110-25-2)

Too Close to Touch by Georgia Beers. Kylie O'Brien believes in true love and is willing to wait for it. It doesn't matter one damn bit that Gretchen, her new and off-limits boss, has a voice as rich and smooth as melted chocolate. It absolutely doesn't… (1-933110-47-3)

Carly's Sound by Ali Vali. Poppy Valente and Julia Johnson form a bond of friendship that lays the foundation for something more, until Poppy's past comes back to haunt her—literally. A poignant romance about love and renewal. (1-933110-45-7)

Of Drag Kings and the Wheel of Fate by Susan Smith. A blind date in a drag club leads to an unlikely romance. (1-933110-51-1)

100th Generation by Justine Saracen. Ancient curses, modern-day villains, and a most intriguing woman who keeps appearing when least expected lead archeologist Valerie Foret on the adventure of her life. (1-933110-48-1)

The Traitor and the Chalice by Jane Fletcher. Tevi and Jemeryl risk all in the race to uncover a traitor. The Lyremouth Chronicles Book Two. (1-933110-43-0)

Whitewater Rendezvous by Kim Baldwin. Two women on a wilderness kayak adventure—Chaz Herrick, a laid-back outdoorswoman, and Megan Maxwell, a workaholic news executive—discover that true love may be nothing at all like they imagined. (1-933110-38-4)

Erotic Interludes 3: Lessons in Love, ed. by Radclyffe and Stacia Seaman. Sign on for a class in love…the best lesbian erotica writers take us to "school." (1-9331100-39-2)

Punk Like Me by JD Glass. Twenty-one-year-old Nina writes lyrics and plays guitar in the rock band Adam's Rib, and she doesn't always play by the rules. And oh yeah—she has a way with the girls. (1-933110-40-6)

Forever Found by JLee Meyer. Can time, tragedy, and shattered trust destroy a love that seemed destined? When chance reunites two childhood friends separated by tragedy, the past resurfaces to determine the shape of their future. (1-933110-37-6)

Sword of the Guardian by Merry Shannon. Princess Shasta's bold new bodyguard has a secret that could change both of their lives. *He* is actually a *she*. A passionate romance filled with courtly intrigue, chivalry, and devotion. (1-933110-36-8)

Sweet Creek by Lee Lynch. A celebration of the enduring nature of love, friendship, and community in the quirky, heart-warming lesbian community of Waterfall Falls. (1-933110-29-5)

Wild Abandon by Ronica Black. From their first tumultuous meeting, Dr. Chandler Brogan and Officer Sarah Monroe are drawn together by their common obsessions—sex, speed, and danger. (1-933110-35-X)

The Devil Inside by Ali Vali. Derby Cain Casey, head of a New Orleans crime organization, runs the family business with guts and grit, and no one crosses her. No one, that is, until Emma Verde claims her heart and turns her world upside down. (1-933110-30-9)

Chance by Grace Lennox. At twenty-six, Chance Delaney decides her life isn't working, so she swaps it for a different one. What follows is the sexy, funny, touching story of two women who, in finding themselves, also find one another. (1-933110-31-7)

Erotic Interludes 2: Stolen Moments, ed. by Stacia Seaman and Radclyffe. Love on the run, in the office, in the shadows…Fast, furious, and almost too hot to handle. (1-933110-16-3)

Turn Back Time by Radclyffe. Pearce Rifkin and Wynter Thompson have nothing in common but a shared passion for surgery. They clash at every opportunity, especially when matters of the heart are suddenly at stake. (1-933110-34-1)

Promising Hearts by Radclyffe. Dr. Vance Phelps lost everything in the War Between the States and arrives in New Hope, Montana, with no hope of happiness and no desire for anything except forgetting—until she meets Mae, a frontier madam. (1-933110-44-9)

Innocent Hearts by Radclyffe. In a wild and unforgiving land, two women learn about love, passion, and the wonders of the heart. (1-933110-21-X)

Protector of the Realm: Supreme Constellations Book One by Gun Brooke. A space adventure filled with suspense and a daring intergalactic romance featuring Commodore Rae Jacelon and a stunning, but decidedly lethal Kellen O'Dal. (1-933110-26-0)

Course of Action by Gun Brooke. Actress Carolyn Black desperately wants the starring role in an upcoming film produced by Annelie Peterson. Just how far will she go for the dream part of a lifetime? (1-933110-22-8)

Coffee Sonata by Gun Brooke. Four women whose lives unexpectedly intersect in a small town by the sea have one thing in common—they all have secrets. (1-933110-41-4)

The Temple at Landfall by Jane Fletcher. An imprinter, one of Celaeno's most revered servants of the Goddess, is also a prisoner to the faith—until a Ranger frees her by claiming her heart. (1-933110-27-9)

Rangers at Roadsend by Jane Fletcher. Sergeant Chip Coppelli has learned to spot trouble coming, and that is exactly what she sees in her new recruit, Katryn Nagata. The Celaeno series. (1-933110-28-7)

The Walls of Westernfort by Jane Fletcher. All Temple Guard Natasha Ionadis wants is to serve the Goddess—until she falls in love with one of the rebels she is sworn to destroy. The Celaeno series. (1-933110-24-4)

The Exile and the Sorcerer by Jane Fletcher. First in the Lyremouth Chronicles. Tevi and a shy young sorcerer face monsters, magic, and the challenge of loving. (1-933110-32-5)

Force of Nature by Kim Baldwin. From tornados to forest fires, the forces of nature conspire to bring Gable McCoy and Erin Richards close to danger, and closer to each other. (1-933110-23-6)

In Too Deep by Ronica Black. Undercover homicide cop Erin McKenzie tracks a femme fatale who just might be a real killer…with love and danger hot on her heels. (1-933110-17-1)

Hunter's Pursuit by Kim Baldwin. A raging blizzard, a mountain hideaway, and a killer-for-hire set a scene for disaster—or desire—when Katarzyna Demetrious rescues a beautiful stranger. (1-933110-09-0)

Erotic Interludes: Change of Pace by Radclyffe. Twenty-five hot-wired encounters guaranteed to spark more than just your imagination. Erotica as you've always dreamed of it. (1-933110-07-4)

Justice Served by Radclyffe. Lieutenant Rebecca Frye and her lover, Dr. Catherine Rawlings, embark on a deadly game of hide-and-seek with an underworld kingpin who traffics in human souls. (1-933110-15-5)

Justice in the Shadows by Radclyffe. In a shadow world of secrets and lies, Detective Sergeant Rebecca Frye and her lover, Dr. Catherine Rawlings, join forces in the elusive search for justice. (1-933110-03-1)

A Matter of Trust by Radclyffe. JT Sloan is a cybersleuth who doesn't like attachments. Michael Lassiter is leaving her husband, and she needs Sloan's expertise to safeguard her company. It should just be business—but it turns into much more. (1-933110-33-3)

Fated Love by Radclyffe. Amidst the chaos and drama of a busy emergency room, two women must contend not only with the fragile nature of life, but also with the irresistible forces of fate. (1-933110-05-8)

Storms of Change by Radclyffe. In the continuing saga of the Provincetown Tales, duty and love are at odds as Reese and Tory face their greatest challenge. (1-933110-57-0)

Distant Shores, Silent Thunder by Radclyffe. Dr. Tory King—along with the women who love her—is forced to examine the boundaries of love, friendship, and the ties that transcend time. (1-933110-08-2)

Beyond the Breakwater by Radclyffe. One Provincetown summer, three women learn the true meaning of love, friendship, and family. (1-933110-06-6)

Safe Harbor by Radclyffe. A mysterious newcomer, a reclusive doctor, and a troubled gay teenager learn about love, friendship, and trust during one tumultuous summer in Provincetown. (1-933110-13-9)

shadowland by Radclyffe. In a world on the far edge of desire, two women are drawn together by power, passion, and dark pleasures. An erotic romance. (1-933110-11-2)

Love's Masquerade by Radclyffe. Plunged into the indistinguishable realms of fiction, fantasy, and hidden desires, Auden Frost is forced to question all she believes about the nature of love. (1-933110-14-7)

Honor Reclaimed by Radclyffe. In the aftermath of 9/11, Secret Service Agent Cameron Roberts and Blair Powell close ranks with a trusted few to find the would-be assassins who nearly claimed Blair's life. (1-933110-18-X)

Honor Guards by Radclyffe. In a wild flight for their lives, the president's daughter and those who are sworn to protect her wage a desperate struggle for survival. (1-933110-01-5)

Love & Honor by Radclyffe. The president's daughter and her lover are faced with difficult choices as they battle a tangled web of Washington intrigue for…love and honor. (1-933110-10-4)

Honor Bound by Radclyffe. Secret Service Agent Cameron Roberts and Blair Powell face political intrigue, a clandestine threat to Blair's safety, and the seemingly irreconcilable personal differences that force them ever farther apart. (1-933110-20-1)

Above All, Honor by Radclyffe. Secret Service Agent Cameron Roberts fights her desire for the one woman she can't have—Blair Powell, the daughter of the president of the United States. (1-933110-04-X)

BOLD STROKES BOOKS